Umbrellas
up the
Mountain

and other stories

by

Niko Zinovii

Zinovii Art Studio

Santa Monica, California

chrysos
argyros
chalkos

Published by: Zinovii Art Studio
Santa Monica, California
www.zinoviiartstudio.com

ISBN: 978-0-9860685-3-9   (trade paperback)
ISBN: 978-0-9860685-4-6   (ebook: ePub)
ISBN: 978-0-9860685-5-3   (ebook: mobi)
LCCN: 2017904935

First Edition, 2017
Printed in the United States of America

Umbrellas up the Mountain

and other stories

Dedication

To those who imagine

Contents

Stories

Opening Note from the Author

Contained in this book are eight tales of speculative fiction that this author wrote from February 2016 to March 2017. They are presented chronologically in the order in which they were written. They can be read in any order.

The title of this book, *Umbrellas up the Mountain*, is the title of one of the stories contained within.

Niko Zinovii
Santa Monica, CA
17 March 2017

Niko Zinovii

The Last Frog

The sound of thunder rumbled gently overhead as Wilhelm Fiedler, silent, alone and aloof, stepped out upon the gray sea of cobblestones that paved St. Peter's Square. The dark stones were still shiny and wet from the light rain that had fallen earlier that morning, and Wilhelm's dampened footsteps echoed softly across the nearly empty piazza as he leisurely walked away from Vatican City.

His tousled, dark golden-blonde hair, handsome face, solemn features and quietly intelligent blue eyes all combined to cast quite an intriguing appearance. At moments, he almost appeared crestfallen, but then the thoughtful remoteness within his soulful eyes would gain sway...

Glancing upward, Wilhelm eyed the puffy gray and white clouds rolling in from the east. They appeared rather majestic against the day's emerging blue sky, almost as dramatic as the colossal Tuscan colonnades that now surrounded him, encircling the square with their magnificence.

Wilhelm slowed as he noticed a lone seagull standing atop the older fountain of the piazza.

"Now how did you get here?" Wilhelm asked aloud, smiling curiously. His smile was so genuine, so much that of an innocent, curious boy, that it changed his countenance almost entirely, lighting up his eyes with a palpable sense of wonder and a deep appreciation of life and its mysteries.

Since childhood he had always found himself charmed by the natural world, by the unexpected sights it offered. Perhaps this was why he had become a scientist, a biologist?

As Wilhelm wondered if the bird had arrived by following the Tiber inland from the sea, it began to rain, a sudden sun shower, and he opened his umbrella. A man did the same nearby. Wilhelm watched as a young woman, a tourist, was invited beneath the stranger's umbrella.

In his mind, Wilhelm found himself, at that moment, inspired to compose a little poem:

A sudden shower.

Two strangers

share an umbrella.

A large raindrop smacked down hard upon the back of Wilhelm's hand, where his flesh was red and swollen. The pain yanked Wilhelm back to his visit with Cardinal Giancomo De Sica, whose garden he had just left. In his mind's eye, he relived the end of his visit as it had taken place:

"You've been stung by one of my bees?" Cardinal De Sica asked, running a heavy hand through his unruly hair. Hirsute and rotund, the cardinal's appearance reflected more a state of moral and cultural decline than the piety expected of a member of the Roman Catholic clergy.

"Yes," Wilhelm responded, "but I forgive your bee. He's paid for this with his life. It seems unfair that he should have had to. But the natural world is often unjust."

Wilhelm looked up at his host, who stood there bathed in an aura of epicurean sensibilities, more resembling an ancient Roman decadent than a priest. At once Wilhelm realized the gulf between them, for they lived in very differently perceived worlds.

"Forgive me," Wilhelm added. "Life always gives me, in the end, the impression of cruelty."

De Sica stared at Wilhelm, needing more.

"I'm basically an unhappy man," Wilhelm added cryptically.

The cardinal paced about Wilhelm. "In your presentation to the Council, you claimed that there is nothing more alone in our universe than man."

Wilhelm nodded in acknowledgement. He had just given a talk to the Pope's Council of Cardinal Advisors advocating that human beings of Earth were the only intelligent life in the universe. An opinion shared by a number of notable biologists: Life on Earth was a fluke, unlikely to have been repeated anywhere else in the universe. Life had arisen by the accumulation of numerous chemical accidents in one place. Man was the product of a cosmic accident. Man was unique in the cosmos.

"Well, let me tell you," De Sica continued, softening, eyeing his guest with genuine priestly concern, "there is nothing worse for a man than being truly alone."

"A naturalist…" Wilhelm defended himself slowly, "spends much of his time alone. I'm accepting of this. Only in moments alone, with nature… does a man briefly escape his solitary destiny."

De Sica did not fully understand, but realized that the sentiment likely tied into Wilhelm's earlier presentation.

The rain stopped, and Wilhelm's mind returned fully to the present. As he lowered his umbrella, he heard something hauntingly forlorn, otherworldly. It sounded like the distant wailing of an ancient horn, on the bare edge of audibility. But the sound came from above…

The seagull flew off.

Wilhelm looked up, straight up, stone faced.

As the odd, lonely sound grew louder, its source, a flying saucer, peacefully dropped out of the clouds, descending vertically, slowly, silently, like something out of a dream. It landed softly, between the Maderno fountain and the Egyptian obelisk that marked the center of the square. The paving stones surrounding the saucer frosted over, their wetness turning to ice...

Wilhelm stared at the saucer absolutely dumbfounded.

Then he smiled. He could not help doing so, for he had been wrong, completely and utterly wrong. Man was not alone in the cosmos. Yet Wilhelm had believed so certainly that sentient, technological man was a solitary anomaly... Through his mind flashed auditory segments of the presentation that he had so confidently given to the Council of Cardinal Advisors earlier that day:

—"SETI's radio antennas have been pointing up into the heavens for over half a century now, listening, searching the sky, scanning the darkness for a signal that might suggest an intelligent, extraterrestrial sender. So far nothing. Only an eerie silence; a Great Silence. I believe it's because no one is out there. We are alone."

—"This unusual silence implies that one or more of the steps necessary to birth life and give rise to tool-using, intelligent animals are staggeringly improbable. I believe it implies the presence of a 'Great Filter,' one that exists somewhere between lifelessness and sentient beings expanding through the cosmos."

—"Has Earth successfully passed through this Great Filter somewhere in the past? Was it the origin of life? Was it reproductivity? Single-cell life? Complex single-sell life? Sexual reproduction? Multi-cell life? The rise of tool-using animals with big brains? Society? Language? Colonization? We don't know for sure... But I suspect, I hope—no, I believe—it was the genesis of life, which we still struggle to understand. I believe this was the Great Filter. The birth of life, it must have been the result of a succession of flukes, each one far more unlikely than its predecessor, which all together could only occur once in a trillion trillion rolls of the dice. It wouldn't matter if the Milky Way contained fifty billion planets capable of sustaining life. Only one planet would. Only one planet does: Earth."

—"But the bleak and haunting thought is... what if this Great Filter is not in Earth's past? What if life on our planet has not already passed through it? This Great Filter must then lie somewhere in our future. Something... unknown... awaiting us. Something that will... stop us... from leaving Earth, colonizing the stars, spreading through the cosmos. As it may have stopped others. If it does lie in our future, it's certainly something to fear. For it will certainly cause our end. As it may have for others... leaving nothing but the eerie silence we observe."

And Wilhelm's thoughts jolted and his focus returned fully to the present. Summing up his courage, he walked toward the saucer resting before him. For his life was dedicated to science, and he believed with all his heart that the ultimate aim of science was to clarify man's relationship to the universe. He saw this as his great chance.

The frost surrounding the saucer was already melting in the early afternoon sunlight. Wilhelm's feet splashed in the wetness before he came to a stop, standing there silently before the strange, featureless alien craft. It was much smaller than Wilhelm would have guessed an interstellar craft would need to be in order to successfully cross the immense gulf of empty light-years lying between distant stars... It did not look large enough to carry more than a single occupant.

A single occupant? Wilhelm wondered. *An emissary from an alien world?*

And Wilhelm wondered from how far off this saucer had come. How many light years had it traversed? So very far it must have traveled... Had it flown close to the speed of light? Did it shrink time? Was its pilot a near immortal in this sense, compared to the transient lives of the untold number of humans who must have lived and died since the launch of this alien craft?

As a number of the Vatican's Pontifical Swiss Guardsmen, dressed in their flamboyant blue, red, orange and yellow Renaissance uniforms, rushed up behind Wilhelm, the bulbous center of the saucer sank in, rather ominously, and opened like a great eye. Within that eye, in a fetal position, rested the likeness of a living creature...

For an eternity of seconds there was only silence; men stood motionless, their thoughts held frozen.

"Wilhelm," Cardinal De Sica's voice broke the spell, "what is it?"

Wilhelm motioned for the cardinal and the guardsmen to remain where they were. He then slowly walked forward a dozen careful steps and knelt upon the wet paving stones in order to look directly in at the craft's motionless single occupant.

The creature was clearly not of this Earth—although its resemblance to a man-size, swollen-headed frog was uncanny: large protruding eyes, a stout body, four muscular limbs folding underneath... dappled green skin splotched by black... no tail.

The frog's two bulbous eyes were closed, but Wilhelm immediately identified them as the eyes of a predator—for they were on the front of the face, the stereo eyes of a hunter. Like man.

Wilhelm looked for its hands. *Does it have an opposable thumb?* There, folded beneath it, a protruding hand. It was large, with multiple opposable digits and fingertips that expanded into flat, adhesive discs. The digits were fully webbed. There were also loose flaps of skin on the lateral margins of its limbs—all signs of an amphibious existence.

It appeared to be in a state of hibernation, perhaps suspended in some type of low-temperature cryonic freeze. And it seemed to be... thawing...

Is it benevolent? Did it come here for reconnaissance? Or merely out of curiosity? Wilhelm wondered as he stared at it, marveling at the power of convergent evolution that must have come into play to shape this visitor into such a familiar earthly form. Wilhelm saw in this frog a hundred million years of evolution. He saw its distant ancestors swimming, roaming, and hopping through a wet, green world of beauty and danger. He saw in this alien the accumulated wisdom of untold generations of living things that had survived by successfully coping with life's challenges of environment—and perhaps even with threatening, bellowing monsters. Its ancestors had succeeded in passing all of life's tests, meeting life's purpose of survival and replication. And now it was here... on Earth.

The frog—remaining motionless, its limbs still awkwardly folded, stiff—opened its eyes.

Wilhelm felt the frog's bright, intelligent eyes regarding him carefully. And more, Wilhelm felt himself held absolutely captive by the will of those eyes. There was a world of expression in those searching, unblinking eyes. And questions: *What is man? What are his strivings? What does he want? What is it that gives him contentment and purpose? Where does man fit into the scheme of the cosmos?*

It began to shower again.

As the raindrops splashed down, the frog jerked itself free and dropped down upon the cobblestones of St. Peter's Square. Glancing up at the rain clouds, it puffed its belly out and began to hop, bounding up and down as if it were celebrating a hundred springtimes, as if in utter ecstasy it wanted to leap up into the very sky.

So intense was the frog's hopping dance that Wilhelm felt himself completely captured by it, part of it. Although standing motionless, he felt his mind blindly hopping along with the frog. Feeling the rain, the wet pavement, the moisture in the air. Living it. The hopping, the dance. Wilhelm looked up and in place of the raindrops, in his mind's eye he saw a sky filled with swimming tadpoles—an imagined reflection of this frog's alien, watery world.

The frog splashed down into the Maderno fountain, and Wilhelm felt himself jarred back to this world, reeling in amazement, disorientated, as if he were a bird that had suddenly crashed into an *invisible* window.

As the frog crouched there in the fountain, drawing comfort from the pool of water, Wilhelm approached it, kneeling beside it, outside the fountain.

Once again, Wilhelm looked into those magnificent alien eyes. The frog struggled to clear its throat. Wilhelm wondered for a moment if it was preparing to speak. Would it try to speak to him in the Old Latin of the ancient Roman Republic? Was that why it had landed within Rome? Had its kind visited Earth before, millennia ago, when Rome had been the center of civilization?

No, it only croaked. As it croaked, it made gestures with its hands. Wilhelm remembered a colleague of his who contended that language had evolved from gestures...

The frog suddenly grasped Wilhelm about the wrist. Wilhelm felt the formidable strength in its four-digit opposable grip. But he felt no threat from the alien, for there was a reassuring comfort within the frog's bright eyes.

The frog then rose upright, tall, standing bipedal like a man, lifting Wilhelm off his knees. With its other hand, the alien removed a shiny object from a pouch about its waist. It was a thin, transparent rod with a syringe-like point. The frog used this device to inject something into the radial artery of Wilhelm's wrist. It was painless.

The frog then squatted back down into the fountain and waited. Wilhelm looked behind himself at Cardinal De Sica, at the Pontifical Swiss Guardsmen and at the gathering crowd, and suddenly, feeling unusually relaxed, he smiled and knelt back down beside the frog. And he waited too.

It took some time. But then he felt the emotions of the frog. And more, he saw visual images in his mind. And he heard the frog's mind speaking to him. Wilhelm struggled to understand how this miracle was achieved. What had been in that syringe? Had nanomachines been inserted into his bloodstream? Nanobots that had made their way to his brain, dispersing into his left temporal lobe, into his thalamus, into his visual cortex, into his amygdala and limbic system? Nanobots that were now wirelessly receiving signals from a similar web of nanobots deep within the mind of this alien visitor. Making telepathy possible?

As Wilhelm and the frog communicated wordlessly, mind to mind, Wilhelm gained an immediate insight into the alienness of this visitor from another sun. The frog was slightly less intelligent than Wilhelm himself, for the frog only needed to be intelligent enough to serve the hive. His amphibian kind reproduced by generating an immense number of eggs; individuality meant little. It was the survival of the species that was paramount. He was a worker bee, satisfied to serve the hive. This was why he was willing to fling himself across the light-years, alone, to visit Earth. He was a honeybee, out performing his duty. As long as the hive existed, and he served it, he was content. This was what the frog strove for, what gave him purpose.

Wilhelm curiously asked the frog why his kind had sent him to Earth. The answer amazed Wilhelm. It was to gift the technological secret of near-limitless free power to man. The frog would share this secret now, speaking through Wilhelm to the human race.

All the citizens of Vatican City gathered inside St. Peter's Basilica, the world's largest church, the center of Christianity. Also present were statesmen and dignitaries of Rome, diplomats from nearby embassies, and members of both the local and international media. Wilhelm found himself standing at the high altar of the basilica, alongside this bipedal frog from a distant world.

The frog, speaking through Wilhelm, expressed how he had ventured to far-off, tiny, isolated Earth because his kind felt bound to man of Earth, due to the unitive power of the apparent rarity of sentient life in the galaxy. For the frogs had thus far found no evidence of any other race of intelligent beings in the cosmos...

The frogs thus considered developing man of Earth to be an extension of themselves. The spiritual and moral and technological needs of man were their concern. Their aspirations were to commune harmoniously and munificently with man.

The gift that the frogs wished to bestow upon mankind was the technology necessary to construct a "swarm," which would consist of a large number of independent constructs orbiting in dense formation around Earth's sun, to capture nearly all of the star's immeasurable energy output. Wireless transfer would then direct this energy to Earth, providing mankind with near-limitless power.

This technology of the frogs was still far in man's future. Man of Earth would inevitably attain this technology, it was a natural technological progression, but the frogs wished to bestow it upon man now, for the present benefit of mankind, in order to commune with man of Earth.

The frogs did not fully understand man's nature of individualism; it remained elusively enigmatic to them. So different was their evolved perception. But they believed that superabundant power would start great waves of change in humanity, assisting mankind to summon up what was most exalted in man in order to develop the intellectual and spiritual will for genuine communion, and the wisdom to recognize the potentiality that man and frog together might attain.

—Wilhelm suddenly heard, in his mind, the abrasive interruption of the alien saucer communicating directly with the frog, telepathically. Wilhelm felt the resulting distress in the frog, but he could not completely understand the content of the message, it being so utterly alien—a product of artificial intelligence? But Wilhelm intuitively felt compelled to immediately rush outside, out into St. Peter's Square, to look up into the sky…

In a state of panic, Wilhelm found himself leaping from the altar and running after the frog, who was already madly bounding toward the great open doors of the basilica.

Outside, there was a brilliant reddish-white star in the sky, shining like the planet Venus but magnitudes brighter, eerily visible in the daylight—as bright as a full moon.

A supernova… Wilhelm concluded. *A stellar explosion…*

And the frog collapsed, racked with pain, its legs folding, its chest convulsing, hauntingly mournful, anguished croaks issuing forth from its alien throat.

The gathering crowd did not understand. But Wilhelm did. The supernova was the frog's star. The frog's sun. The frog's planet was no more. Its race was no more... No more hive to serve. No purpose to live for...

As Wilhelm stood there, watching the frog, he realized what the Great Filter of his talk was. It was sun exploitation, the audacious attempt to tame and imprison a star... The frogs had not passed through the Great Filter. The frogs were no more. All but one, the one weeping at Wilhelm's feet: the last frog.

"You've given us the most precious gift..." Wilhelm whispered reverently to the frog, who was now lying there like the dead honeybee in Cardinal De Sica's garden. "You've given us tomorrow."

Cardinal De Sica stepped up beside Wilhelm, trying to understand. Wilhelm made no attempt to explain. The world would soon enough learn of the warning delivered this day. Of what the Great Filter was. How to avoid it. There was now hope in the natural world for lonely man...

"Everything that was," Wilhelm commented, "has vanished from his heart, leaving not a trace..."

Sighs murmured through the crowd, sounds driven by purely instinctive feelings. A little girl nearby cried. An infant wailed. An old woman's eyes swelled with compassion, sympathy and helplessness.

Wilhelm heard in his mind his own voice from his earlier conversation with Cardinal De Sica: "... Life always gives me, in the end, the impression of cruelty."

And Wilhelm stood there in silence, with the frog. Slowly the empathy, the sadness in the crowd, dissolved and the people began to talk and disperse, falling back into routine, stepping back into their lives.

Columns of sunbeams gently flowed down from a high, ethereal cloud. In a nearby pillar of light, Wilhelm noticed a butterfly, and he found himself, at that moment, in sadness but in hope, inspired to compose a little poem:

In a sunbeam,
a butterfly
dances...

Recommendations

- "The Great Filter—Are We Almost Past It?" A paper by economist Robin Hanson, published September 15, 1998.

Acknowledgements and Identifying Notations

• The idea of an extraterrestrial having evolved to be akin to a worker bee, whose purpose is to serve the hive, was a possibility suggested by theoretical physicist Michio Kaku in his book titled *The Future of the Mind: The Scientific Quest to Understand, Enhance, and Empower the Mind*, specifically in chapter 14, "The Alien Mind."

• The idea of telepathy via nanoprobes in the brain likewise was presented by Michio Kaku in his book titled *The Future of the Mind: The Scientific Quest to Understand, Enhance, and Empower the Mind*, specifically in chapter 3, "Telepathy: A Penny for Your Thoughts."

• The interesting speculation of the possibility of a Great Filter was presented by economist Robin Hanson, in his September 15, 1998 paper titled "The Great Filter—Are We Almost Past It?"

• The protagonist in this story, Wilhelm Fiedler, being stung by a bee and his reaction to it was inspired by a lovely short story titled "Daydream," written by the actor Basil Rathbone—known for his inimitable portrayal of the fictional detective Sherlock Holmes—and published by *Esquire* magazine in 1956. This story is also presented in Basil Rathbone's autobiography, pages 184 to 188.

• Near the end of this story, when the protagonist states, "Everything that was has vanished from his heart, leaving not a trace," his remark pays homage to a haiku poem by Japanese poet Iio Sōgi (1421—1502):

Everything that was
Has vanished from my aged heart
Leaving not a trace

A Note from the Author

This author hopes the reader enjoyed this modest tale of extraterrestrial visitation and found the implications that it raises thought provoking.

This story was partially inspired by the following haiku poem by Chiyo-ni (Kaga no Chiyo) (1703-1775), considered one of the foremost women haiku poets.

Rain clouds—
the frog
puffs his belly out!

The "swarm" in the story is a version of a Dyson sphere, a hypothetical megastructure that completely encompasses a star in order to capture most or all of its power output.

Most of the story was written one rainy day in Santa Monica, California, while this author, drinking Persian tea, glass after glass, was listening to traditional music performed by Mohammad-Reza Shajarian—an internationally and critically acclaimed Persian classical singer and one of this author's favorite vocal performers.

The two poems in this story are this author's first attempt at poetry.

Niko Zinovii
Santa Monica, California
2 February 2016

The Last Frog

Niko Zinovii

As Old as Stars

As Natrum, a slim, young Indian man, a Hindu, walked along the shoreside wharf of Ischia's picturesque harbor, passing the bobbing and gently swaying fishing boats moored alongside, he noticed a number of white pelicans noiselessly gliding out over the Tyrrhenian Sea, gracefully slipping off across the Bay of Naples. For a moment, he imagined the great birds as a line of snow painted across the horizon…

There was a distant, bright flash, somewhere inland. *Lightning*, Natrum thought, *yesterday in the east, today in the west.* He then glanced over the charming little seaside village that he now called home, and an unexpected depth swelled up in his dark eyes, mirroring the extraordinary sensitivity of his heart. This island of Ischia, almost entirely mountainous, was no more than a small, craggy volcanic outcrop rising up out of the sea, caressed endlessly by the Mediterranean's gentle and timeless waves, and yet it was now the center of his world.

The wistful, squawking cry of a seagull suddenly made him think of how he had recently abandoned his education to come here, to Ischia. He was still young, a mere twenty-three years old; he could not help but feel troubled, wondering if he yet possessed the necessary wisdom to have made the right life choice. The way he had turned his back on his studies as he had, to do what he now did…

As he walked past mounds of individually piled fishing nets, red, blue, and brown, wet and smelling of salt and fish—the smell of the sea—he felt in his heart his love for the sea, and all it contained. And he momentarily longed for his forsaken study of the underwater realm.

Natrum nodded good morning as he passed fishermen slopping amorphous pink octopuses into wooden buckets, slapping down large, sturdy silvery fish upon tall crates of ice. The young Indian physically stood out in marked contrast to the stout, olive-skinned Italians about him, yet they all smiled back at him genuinely, greeting him warmly, as if he were one of their own.

Natrum's smile dropped, however, and his paced slowed as he approached rows of oxygen cylinders and rubber wetsuits, black and yellow, hanging upright outside an old stone building framed by archaic vaulted archways. Inside one of the passageways, Natrum found Vittorio, leaning over and studying an underwater chart of the surrounding Tyrrhenian Sea.

"Your underwater excavation…" Natrum complained with restraint, seriously expressing his concern yet remaining quite respectful. "The vacuum tubes you use to remove stone and debris, they're very loud."

"Loud?" Vittorio shrugged and ran a hand through his gray hair, looking at Natrum with a kindly expression. The middle-aged, semiretired Italian was the type of man who somehow made one feel completely at ease, someone whom anyone could easily befriend. There was a charm in his lighthearted manner, a debonair brightness in his easy smile.

"How so?" Vittorio asked, his hands moving with the subtle, poetic gestures typical of his lively and expressive culture.

"Under the water," Natrum responded, trying to remain firm but softening, "they're quite loud. Disturbing."

Vittorio placed a fatherly hand on Natrum's shoulder and guided the slim young man farther into the antique passageway. "We're uncovering valuable relics, Natrum," Vittorio offered. "Look at this."

The Italian waved a hand before a slab of stone, the encrusted marine life skillfully removed from part of its great length. On it were carvings of ancient Roman ships, dolphins, and mermaids.

"Amazing, isn't it?" Vittorio smiled proudly. "We found it farther out in the bay, at a depth of twelve meters. There's clear evidence of a catastrophic, sudden event, an abrupt end, like Pompeii but much earlier, possibly 100 BC. Probably an earthquake or a tsunami."

Natrum found himself entranced by the figures of the mermaids, so much so that he ran a hand, gently, over one of the engravings. The artistry of the mermaid was exquisite, and more, it captured something ineffable, the appearance of an otherworldly creature, something beyond myth, for there was something hauntingly... real... in its fishlike, chimerical appearance.

"Please," Vittorio pleaded politely, eyeing Natrum's probing hand.

"Sorry," Natrum apologized for his indiscretion.

Natrum then added, after he took one last long look at the artifact, "It's beautiful. Mysterious."

"The most beautiful thing we can experience," Vittorio mused, reflectively, "is the mysterious. It's the source of all true science."

"And art," Natrum added, his inner spirit coming to life.

"What are you going to paint today?" Vittorio asked as he walked Natrum out to the dock.

"If I knew," Natrum answered, with a rising smile, "I wouldn't paint it."

"Artists!" Vittorio flipped up a friendly hand for emphasis, winked, and then walked off. "*Ciao.*"

Stripping down to his bathing suit, Natrum slipped a single Aqua-Lung upon his back. He then picked up his canvas, paints, and palette knife and peacefully swam out into the splendidly deep bay lying before him, one of the most beautiful in the Mediterranean. For it was time for him to be alone with his own thoughts, under the sea.

~

At a depth of fifteen meters, Natrum floated in a seated position, peacefully, near the bottom, a lean, young aquanaut painting beneath the waves. For his oil paints were waterproof, his canvas impermeable to seawater.

After a long silence, he began to sing softly, plaintively, in his native language as he painted. Using his palette knife in place of a brush, he moved it in slow, passionate, artistic strokes. The result was a canvas showcasing a huge rock decorated by red sea fan, yellow gorgonian, and orange sponges, all set against a backdrop of vibrant blues—which breathtakingly evoked the natural beauty and mystery of the undersea world.

The sea is so old, Natrum's thoughts wandered, *almost beyond imaging.* And Natrum paused to listen to the strange grunts, croaks, and clicks in the by-no-means-silent depths. He smiled like a boy. *Only the sea retains its mystery. And its life, so extravagant... so beautiful... so wondrous... Some of the loveliest forms ever conjured up by nature. Flashes of silver, empowered by exquisite symmetry... rooted animals that bloom like flowers... Oh, how the vanished life must have looked in the oceans of the Devonian!*

Since Natrum had first learned to dive, several years ago—primarily to feel the exhilaration and fear of entering a familiar yet alien realm—whenever he saw photographs taken under the sea, he always felt in his heart that something was missing, that something vital was lacking. The images never fully captured the sea's true colors, or the sensation and the wonder of being underwater. In his paintings, he wanted one to feel what it was actually like to be beneath the waves, to be so intimately embraced by the oceanic abyss... to hear the sea calling to that small ancestral remnant within man that went all the way back to that dim dawn when sea life had audaciously invaded the land.

As he painted, as he sang, Natrum continued to ponder the immensity of the sea, marveling at its elusive secrets. It was then that he noticed the shadow of another diver, someone passing somewhere above him. But when he looked up, he only saw sparkling sunlight. He hoped that Vittorio's small army of volunteer archaeologists were not so soon invading his peace, disturbing his artistry. No—he caught in his peripheral vision the *swoosh* and disappearance of the tail of a large... fish?

~

That evening, as the sun set, casting colors of red, orange, and yellow, Natrum, barefoot, made his way out to his small storage shed, located on the outskirts of town. As he did so, he paused to smell and touch a bush of jasmine growing wild. Unable to resist its fragrant allure, he pulled off a small branch of the white, yellow, and pink flowers. Immediately he smiled as he felt himself regretting picking, and not picking more, jasmine.

As Natrum lifted a key to unlock the door to his shed, he noticed on the heavy lock, stopped from flight and sleeping, a small butterfly. Gently, he opened the lock without disturbing the petite specimen of art and beauty.

Stepping into the shed and seeing the baskets upon baskets of dull yellow sponges stacked within, he suddenly no longer felt full of artistic appreciation, or energy, or new ideas, as the full weight of his recent life choice settled heavily upon his weary and slender shoulders. In response, he felt himself only wishing to be home, in his tiny rented abode by the sea. He yearned to spend his night there in tranquility. But a wholesale buyer was scheduled to visit tomorrow, to bid on his sponges, and he needed to make sure his last count was correct.

Last year he had sold 30,000 of his sponge cuttings. But his harvests of late had not been as large... Had he not been as ambitious this past year? Still, the endeavor was supplying him with year-round income, sufficient at least to cover his meager expenses. Yes, he was poor, but not in spirit. And he dreamed well on an empty stomach. And sponge farming allowed him the time he needed to paint, the enterprise being but part time, requiring only three full work days per week. And the work was relatively easy, and it was done underwater, where he enjoyed spending his time. Only the first year of establishing the aquaculture farm had been laborious, setting up all those sponge-growing lines and supporting cables at a depth of ten meters.

A student of ichthyology turned artist slash sponge farmer... Natrum's thoughts tensed and turned inward as he began counting baskets, remembering cleaning each and every sponge, carefully spraying them with fresh seawater, using Vittorio's loud, high-powered water pump, graciously loaned to him.

And he began to question if he should continue his art, wondering if he was contributing anything of real value to the world, to the future of civilization... He remembered his big showing last year, in Naples. Everyone had seemed so interested in his underwater paintings, in the fact that he actually painted under the sea. They had asked so many questions. But no one had asked "How much?"

Natrum sat, rubbing a troubled hand over his troubled forehead. Since adolescence he had felt the inner need to contribute something to man's future, to make a mark. He only wanted to live a life with purpose, one of direction, in order to produce some meaningful contribution to humankind, to leave the world a little better off than when he had come into it.

He recalled the intellectual arousal that he had experienced when studying ichthyology. He remembered the excitement of new ideas, of pursuing undiscovered facts, of trying to remove truth's protective layers. But he had also felt the haunting need to contribute something different, something more personal… something more consequential. So he had abandoned science for his stronger passion of art. To paint under the sea… But where was this leading? Was it the right choice?

And so there he sat, in his tiny shed, beneath the same sky, passing through this world in self-exile on a tiny Italian isle that was of no more import than an unnamed pond. He suddenly felt quite alone, and lost. He felt himself akin to a small stone dropping down a deep well, destined to make but a small splash.

"Natrum?" Vittorio's thickly accented voice broke the moment.

Natrum turned to find Vittorio standing in the doorway.

"Is something wrong?" Natrum asked, noticing the uncharacteristically disturbed expression on the archeologist's face.

"Have you been out here long?" Vittorio questioned him.

"No. Why?"

"Did you see anything tonight?" Vittorio asked hesitantly. "Anything… unusual?"

"No," Natrum answered, rising, his interest aroused.

Vittorio nodded, the tension in his face increasing.

"What is it?" Natrum asked.

"I saw something," Vittorio admitted.

"What?"

"Lights."

"Lights?"

"Bright lights." Vittorio forced his speech, upset. "In the sky. Red. White. Blue. Moving along the coast."

"A plane?"

Vittorio shook his head.

"I don't understand," Natrum confessed.

"Neither do I," Vittorio remarked cryptically.

Natrum stepped outside and searched the darkening sky with his eyes. Clouds. Some stars appearing. "I don't see anything."

"The lights," Vittorio explained, "they, um… they dropped onto the sea, and sank…"

"Are you sure it wasn't a small plane?" Natrum asked respectfully, earnestly, trying to understand. "That crashed into the sea?"

"No." Vittorio soberly and firmly shook his head. "It came down… vertically… fully under control. It landed softly on the sea without a sound. And then… it submerged… I could see red lights, moving beneath the surface, as if it was searching for something. I watched it for a while. Until the lights dimmed, and disappeared…"

Natrum just looked at Vittorio. He had known Vittorio for two years now. Vittorio was the most grounded, levelheaded man he had ever met.

Vittorio shrugged and looked up at the emerging stars, as if struggling with the ramifications of his sighting. "I wonder, if people looked up at the stars more, if they really looked… I wonder if they might come to see reality differently…"

Natrum remained silent, at a loss for words.

"When one gazes up into the infinite," Vittorio continued, calming appreciably as he freely expressed thoughts that were deeper, philosophical, "it reduces one... does it not?"

"I don't know..." came Natrum's slow answer.

"I spent my day," Vittorio added, "painstakingly removing layers of encrustation from that slab I showed you. Trying to gain a glimpse into man's past... And now, it all seems so trivial... so meaningless."

Natrum looked up at the stars with Vittorio. And they both stood there in silence for a time.

"Natrum," Vittorio asked in a whisper, "do you believe we are of some importance?"

"... Do you?"

"Not anymore... Knowledge, it changes the knower. It squashes a man down to his true size. It's so damn humbling..."

And there was silence once again between the two men.

"Come on," Natrum finally said, compassionately taking Vittorio by the arm. "Let me walk you back."

~

Near midnight, Natrum found himself standing alone at the lonely end of the more isolated of Ischia's two jetties, his inquisitive eyes gazing up into the heavens. As the stars crept across the darkness, he turned his gaze to the glowing moon, the only other world within sight.

What did Vittorio see?

And Natrum's thoughts deepened: *We're like a small grain of sand, our world, our Earth, wandering aimlessly through space... And we are even less...*

Drifting clouds finally provided his questioning mind and tired eyes relief from his moon viewing. It was only then that his thoughts relaxed as his senses drifted aimlessly to the murmur of the endless waves below him.

He thought of how those waves crashed so tirelessly, over time eroding rock into pebble, and then into sand.

It was then that he noticed the lone, tired fisherman slowly rowing into the harbor. Trailing his small boat was the eerie glow of luminescence. The splashing oars likewise generated ripples of dancing light. *Dinoflagellates*, Natrum correctly identified the microscopic planet life, the living, wandering specks responsible for producing the glowing wake.

But what produced Vittorio's lights?

Shrugging, Natrum finally surrendered to the mystery and gave in to the overwhelming, ancient urge to simply shed his shoes, step into the sea, and walk barefoot up the shoreline.

~

It was far from town, where the beach finally turned stony, that Natrum saw her, lying there in the moonlight like something out of myth: a mermaid... Her beached form was so utterly strange, so uncanny, such an imaginative blend of fantasy and plausibility—a real-life incarnation of Vittorio's mysterious carvings.

Will you turn toward me? Natrum found himself wondering meekly as he stood there motionless, breathless, overcome by curiosity yet restrained by fear.

Slowly, he took a step toward her oddly still figure. A cloud passed before the moon and the night darkened. As it did so, lines and dots of bioluminescence decorating the mermaid's back and tail produced a dazzling display of flickering light. Natrum remembered from his studies how certain fish were endowed with light-emitting organs called photophores... but such a feature was common only of fish living in the deep.

Natrum smiled as he felt the luminous beauty gently washing away his fear. *Do you come from the blue depths,* he asked in his imagination, *from a drowned kingdom of coral and shell?*

Stepping forward, he carefully knelt beside her. Moonlight washed over the two of them, dimming her bioluminescence to near imperceptibility. Natrum could now see that her sleek body was scaleless and a beautiful, otherworldly silver in color, covered by dusky, irregularly shaped bluish and blackish dots and squiggles. A stunning deep red dorsal fin, undulating slightly, rhythmically, ran like a trailing crest from the top of her head down to the tip of her muscular tail.

Natrum found his mind's eye unconsciously conjuring up images of mermaids and mermen riding upon gigantic fanciful seahorses... And he suddenly felt the overwhelming need to touch her, to assure himself that she actually existed in reality. As his fingers made gentle contact, he received a powerful electric shock, which jolted him backward, knocking him down flat upon the sand.

As he leapt back to his feet, dancing about, physically and mentally shaking off the numbing pain, he remembered that mermaids of myth were not always benevolent. They also had a reputation for causing shipwrecks, even for dragging unsuspecting sailors down into the depths to meet their doom. He also recalled from his studies the electric eel and the electric ray, sea creatures endowed with specialized organs capable of generating strong electric currents.

It was then that the mermaid turned to him, displaying a face that showed so little expression that it looked as if God had not finished the artwork of his creation... Her rather large eyes opened slowly, weakly, and she looked at him as if he were the only one in all the world with enough wisdom and gentleness to understand that she needed help.

Something belted about her torso that resembled a small, spiny sea urchin moved and then unexpectedly spoke to him in Italian, in a watery voice. It said, *"Per favore..."* Please...

~

Natrum was rather surprised at how easily he carried the mermaid down the beach and to his small cottage by the sea. He never tired, not once. What surprised him even more was how he had found the courage to dare to touch her again. Fortunately, there had been no secondary defensive electrical discharge, only a limp, helpless embrace.

Kicking open the door to his humble abode, Natrum glanced momentarily at its bare walls, lined by his undersea paintings, and then he looked down at the fantastic creature he held in his slender arms. *In my hut this night,* he heard his inner thoughts rumbling, *there is nothing—there is everything!*

He slowly laid the mermaid down upon his couch, exercising great care. Retrieving a bucket of seawater from outside, he used one of his dull yellow sponges to gently and therapeutically wet her body and face. In doing so, he noticed what looked like a large bruise, a swelling on the side of her head.

Were you led by curiosity too close to the hull of a passing boat? And struck by its keel?

As he squeezed seawater over her strange form, he looked at her plain, silvery face. She looked peaceful, as if asleep. He wondered if she did sleep. He knew that many fish seemed to never sleep at all. Or age. How old might she be? Decades? Centuries? Millennia…?

Natrum found his eyes drawn to the curious thing on her belt. It was about three inches across, round and black and half covered by thick, blunted spines. It looked almost alive, only it appeared metallic… It seemed to be an artificial apparatus.

He looked back at her impassive countenance, at her closed eyes, and he suddenly realized that she had eyelids. And he remembered that fish did not. Fish never close their eyes. Or even blink. They have no eyelids.

Are you from our sea? … Or a far-off star? he wondered.

Her eyes fluttered and opened.

Like a curious observer, she lay there quietly, just looking him over for what seemed like an eternity. Slowly, she then struggled to sit up, and he helped her to do so. He watched her as her large eyes slowly swung about the inside of his small cottage.

"It's my little corner of the world," Natrum found himself saying, with unexpected ease. "A place far away, where I can be alone, and yet not feel lonely."

And Natrum paused, and then asked, "Where is your home?"

"Far away and long ago," her artificial sea urchin answered in its watery voice, this time in the language he was speaking, English.

She then noticed his many paintings, lined up side by side along the walls. She stared at each piece of artwork, deeply absorbing each one before visually moving to the next. About the room her eyes moved from painting to painting, until she finally returned to the first.

"I am in the sea," her voice box said rather softly. "I can hear the sea..."

And her eyes went around the room once again, in unusual appreciation. When her eyes returned to him:

"Art is a kind of cry..." the watery manifestation of her voice concluded. "Why do you sing when painting?"

"I don't know," Natrum replied, smiling, completely surprised. He had been observed? "I didn't know that I sang."

But she only looked at him, expecting more. Waiting for more.

"When I'm painting under the sea," he gave her the reason, "my entire soul is singing."

"Singing…" The odd voice repeated his last word, as if she were dwelling upon it.

She lifted the webbed digits of one of her red, finned hands and gently touched and felt his expressive face, marveling at his humanity.

"Why?" her voice box asked him.

Natrum did not understand.

"Why paint?" she made it clear. "Why art?"

"I feel the need to paint," he responded ingenuously.

"For what purpose?"

And Natrum thought. Finally he answered, realizing it for himself. "Art makes you think. It makes you feel. It makes you look more deeply. It says things that words can't… Art passes beyond human mortality. It can speak into the future. To other minds and hearts. It says… 'I was here, and here is something I want you to consider.'"

She looked deeply into his eyes and then pointed out his front door to the sea.

"You must go now?" he guessed.

"Yes," the watery voice confirmed. "Injured, ill… Friends will come now. To help."

"I think a friend of mine may have seen your friends earlier, searching for you."

She pointed again to the sea.

Lifting the mermaid gently, Natrum carefully carried her down to the sea and slowly walked into the waves with her.

"Upon your world," the mermaid's artificial voice rose over the sound of the sea, "life is still so young, not truly old, as stars are measured. You have begun the journey. But knowledge without greatness of spirit is not enough."

"Why are you telling me this?" Natrum asked, puzzled, still holding her, not really wanting to let her go.

"Inspire your kind to greatness through art," she explained. "We never had art. Perhaps it can save your kind from the terrible fate my world suffered…"

And Natrum now looked at her, expecting more. Waiting for more.

"We failed to rise above the jaws of nature," she went on, slowly. "Instead we swam toward the most base… And there was war and destruction… The loss of our entire ocean world… We few survivors, wounded by remorse and sorrow… we have since breathed out our diminished existence in seclusion, in your sea."

And behind the mermaid the water swirled and glowed red, and a great craft slowly rose up to rest upon the surface of the sea, its metallic hull bathed in red, blue, and white light.

With a splash, the mermaid disappeared beneath the waves, swimming toward and into the lights. Slowly, the lights sank back into the sea. The submerged object glowed red, and then the lights swooshed off toward the horizon, soon vanishing from sight.

As Natrum stood there in the caress of the waves, staring out into the ancient Bay of Naples, he heard in his memory the parting words of the mermaid:

"Inspire your kind to greatness through art."

And Natrum smiled. Reinvigorated, and at peace in his heart.

Looking up into the dark, starlit heavens, he wondered if, with art, mankind might endure its journey, and one day become as old as stars.

Recommendations

- *The Classic Tradition of Haiku, An Anthology*, edited by Faubion Bowers. Published by Dover Publications, Inc., in 1996.
- *Haiku, The Poetry of Nature*, edited by David Cobb. Published by Universe Publishing, in 2002.

Acknowledgements and Identifying Notations

• When Vittorio and Natrum speak of the beautiful and the mysterious, they are jointly paraphrasing Albert Einstein, who is quoted as having stated:

"The most beautiful thing we can experience is the mysterious. It is the source of all true art and science."

• It was the German philosopher Friedrich Nietzsche who once described art as a kind of "cry."

• In the following sentence taken from the narrative of this story:

He remembered the excitement of new ideas, of pursuing undiscovered facts, of trying to remove truth's protective layers.

The wording "to remove truth's protective layers" is based on a sentence from the speech astronaut Neil Armstrong made on July 20, 1994, at the White House in celebration of the twenty-fifth anniversary of the Apollo moon landing. The relevant excerpt from the ending of Armstrong's speech:

"We have only completed a beginning. We leave you much that is undone. There are great ideas undiscovered. Breakthroughs available to those who can remove one of truth's protective layers. There are places to go beyond belief. Those challenges are yours. In many fields, not the least of which is space, because there lies human destiny."

• The title of this short story was inspired by a single sentence from Loren Eiseley's 1972 book *The Unexpected Universe*. In chapter three, "The Hidden Teacher," Eiseley poetically wrote:

"Upon this world, life is still young, not truly old as stars are measured."

In tribute to Loren Eiseley, esteemed anthropologist, philosopher, and author, a version of this identifying sentence was woven into the mermaid's dialogue.

A Note from the Author

"As Old as Stars" is this author's second short story to date featuring mermaids, and also his second tale explaining the USO (unidentified submerged object) phenomenon as being crafts controlled by extraterrestrials.

The protagonist in this story painting under the sea pays tribute to the Cousteau aquanaut and cameraman André Laban, who was the founder of such underwater art.

This author hopes the reader appreciated the subtle notes of Haiku poetry that were woven into this purposely light and limited story. The Haiku poems that lent their influence are presented fully following this page.

Niko Zinovii
Santa Monica, California
3 April 2016

The original haiku poems and their authors

If only noiseless they would go,
The herons flying by
Were but a line of snow
Across the sky
Author— Yamazaki Sōkan (1464 – 1552)

The lightning…
Yesterday in the east
today in the west
Author—Tararai Kikaku (1661 – 1707)

I regret picking
and not picking
violets
Author—Anonymous

On the great temple bell
stopped from fight and sleeping
the small butterfly
Author—Yosa Buson (1716 – 1783)

Haiku should be just
small stones dropping down a well
with a small splash
Author—James Kirkup (1918 - 2009)

Clouds now and again
give a soul some respite from
moon-gazing—behold.
Author— Matsuo Bashō (1644 – 1694)

Clouds occasionally
make a fellow relax
moon-viewing
Author— Matsuo Bashō (1644 – 1694)

Will you turn toward me?
I am lonely too,
this autumn evening.
Author— Matsuo Bashō (1644 – 1694)

In my hut this spring,
There is nothing—
There is everything!
Author—Sodo Yamaguchi (1642 – 1716)

As Old as Stars

Niko Zinovii

Melody in a Bottle

Paul unconsciously shuddered as he opened the gondola's top hatch, bracing himself for the discomfort of the cold and tenuous air outside—for his balloon was adrift in the troposphere, 11,000 feet above the north Pacific.

"Nineteen degrees." Paul smiled enthusiastically as he read aloud the external thermometer, his voice rather charming, cultured, debonair. Pulling himself fully outside, he carefully and securely sat himself upon the gondola's rigid upper frame. He had just descended from a much higher altitude, a much colder altitude, so that he could depressurize the cabin in order to climb outside, check his craft's burners, take a breath of fresh air, and jettison unnecessary weight.

The six burners looked fine, the same for the heat shield and its tray. Before turning to the next task at hand, Paul found that he could not resist taking an upward glance at his balloon's swollen envelope, momentarily admiring its majesty. His craft was a top-of-the-line Rozière, a state-of-the-art hybrid balloon composed of internal helium cells resting atop a hot air cone, its Mylar envelope as tall as the Leaning Tower of Pisa.

Paul found himself silently wishing that his enclosed, pill-shaped gondola were proportionally as spacious as the sixty-foot-wide balloon looming above him—for his airtight cabin was little more than a long walk-in closet, housing a small navigation console, a narrow single bunk, a tiny electric stove, and a pressure-operated toilet. Fortunately, with huge portals forward, aft, port, and starboard, there was no immediate threat of claustrophobia, only of euphoria, as the most spectacular views were offered of Earth, her clouds, the sky, the moon, the stars.

Paul reached out to one of the thirty-nine remaining titanium cylinders used to store liquid propane fuel, all mounted and hung along both long sides of the gondola. Turning a lever, he released the single empty tank and watched it drop down toward the mighty Pacific, which rolled to every horizon, an endless expanse of calm blue lying over two miles below him.

It suddenly struck Paul how utterly silent it was at this dizzying height. There was no detectible sound of the sea. No rolling of waves. No cry of birds. Only the slightest sound of the wind, his constant companion on this venture.

It was then that Paul noticed that he was not alone. There was a small spider beside him, clinging to its elegant gossamer threads, which had become entangled about a protruding antenna.

"Ah," Paul commented to the spider poetically, his tone sensitive, elegant, an appealing aristocratic smile lifting on his face. "I see that your journey has been interrupted. Your parachute of silk no longer buoyed aloft, by the fickle whim of the air currents. I wonder where you were ballooning off to, my little ballooning spider. Did you launch yourself from Asia? To invade some isolated island? Or perhaps you planned to visit some far-off mountaintop?"

Paul's continental air and sophistication nicely complemented the unusual moment, bringing out the magic in it. Reclining and cradling an arm behind his head for a pillow, he appeared to really like himself—and to love life. He relaxed, totally, in no rush with living, exhibiting instead a polite, accepting embrace of life. He went on talking, speaking beautifully, gallantly, purely enjoying the moment, living in it, asking the tiny life form if he could perhaps be of some assistance.

But the spider was far from helpless. Spinning extremely fine silk, it constructed a new triangular-shaped parachute, remaining secured to it by long, sheer threads. Paul watched, marveling at the wonder of nature, as the spider allowed its new chute to catch the wind and whisk it off.

"Bon voyage, my little ballooning friend. Bon voyage."

Before climbing back down into the gondola, Paul paused to consider his journey so far—his effort to ride the winds around the world, to circumnavigate the planet, solo, nonstop. He recalled the impressiveness of northern Africa, which he had soared over at 142 miles per hour. He thought of Saudi Arabia, and then of India—where he had descended to a mere several hundred feet in altitude, just to listen to the everyday sounds of villagers talking, going about their mundane daily tasks. To smell the scent of curry and other spices wafted aloft. To intimately eavesdrop on the lives of those whom he would never meet.

With East Asia also now well behind him, he was facing six long days of ballooning across the Pacific. He would soon repressurize his cabin, to 3.5 psi, and ascend to 35,000 feet to catch the jet stream, which should carry him along at a respectable 105 miles per hour. The temperature would be approximately -67 °F. He would need to remain inside, breathing a nitrogen-oxygen mixture. Relying on the gondola's lithium hydroxide filters to remove carbon dioxide, keeping the air breathable. Relying on the craft's solar panels, suspended beneath the gondola, to recharge the on-board lead-acid batteries providing him with electrical power, light, and heat.

And he would sit there within the gondola, carried along by the wind, monitoring the weather, navigating by GPS, steering by ascending or descending in altitude to catch different winds for speed and direction.

Technically, he felt secure in his endeavor. But why had he become an aeronaut? A balloonist? At the age of forty. Why had he embarked on this grand venture? He, the Honourable Paul Heinrich Jörg von Eckener, scion of an aristocratic Austrian family, son of a Viennese baron. He, bachelor at large, and recent sole inheritor of his family's large fortune…

Was it because he had lived such a charmed childhood and young adulthood that now, suddenly minus all paternal accountability, he felt a yearning to temporarily turn his back on all present responsibilities? To momentarily live again so unbound? Paul suspected so…

From down within the gondola, interrupting Paul's introspection, the flutter of wings and the most beautiful song of impressive whistles, trills, and gurgles echoed forth.

"Fifi!" Paul responded with a special fondness, and he climbed down into the cabin.

Inside, Paul's little mechanical bird, Fifi, finished its song with a loud, whistling crescendo. The song was exquisitely magnificent, as lovely in sound as Fifi was in her appearance, her tinkling body being of burnished, lightly bronzed stainless steel, adorned with jewels.

Capable of limited flight, the mechanical nightingale flapped across the cabin to gently settle herself upon Paul's shoulder.

"Oh, Fifi," Paul admitted to his small robotic pet, with genuine loving affection, "if you ever break down, you'll leave me hopeless."

~

After sunset, adrift nearly seven miles high over the dark Pacific, Paul flicked on the Comstock autopilot, employing the computer to control the balloon's burners to maintain a constant altitude.

After adjusting the gondola's heater, he slipped out of his flame-resistant flight suit, uncorked a bottle of wine, poured a glass, and made himself comfortable.

"Fifi," he called out affectionately to his mechanical bird as he picked up his ten-string Davidic lyre, the ancient musical instrument of the Old Testament. The lyre was of concert quality, made of Israeli rosewood, deep in color and decorated handsomely by the unique patterns of its grain, dark wavering lines swirling majestically into natural logarithmic spirals.

Holding the small lyre in his lap, pressed close to his heart, he leaned his face on the side of its arm and began to play, masterfully, the rich, deep, and clear timbre of the instrument issuing forth echoes of the past.

Fifi hopped thrice to move closer to Paul. Perching near him, she blew soft melodious breaths, as if fluting through hollow wood, to complement his ancient notes. Slowly, a rhythm began to develop between the two of them, and the music became like a living thing. It was hypnotic and ever so beautiful, so moving. Paul played with the deepest passion, composing with intense feeling, reacting to Fifi's accompaniment with soulful eloquence, his music giving unbridled expression to the most human emotions of the heart and soul. The music became the very air he breathed.

By the second bottle of wine, Paul was lost in a meditative, musical trance, he and his mechanical bird—so much so that the frozen rain striking the Kevlar and carbon-fiber weave of the exterior of the gondola fell beneath his notice.

It was only when he heard the thunder that he came to his senses.

"Oh no," Paul mumbled, but his words were lost to the booming thunder that again rolled overhead, the untamed power of nature suddenly reverberating and echoing all about him. It sounded as if the heavens themselves were about to be torn asunder.

A brilliant white shock of lightning ripped across the darkness outside.

"No…" Paul disengaged the autopilot and fired all six of his craft's burners, attempting to rise above the storm. He was somewhere within a towering cumulonimbus cloud of severe atmospheric instability.

"Up, up damn you. Climb!" Paul cursed in desperation, wondering what the ceiling of the cloud might be: 40,000 feet? 50,000 feet? *What if it's 60,000 feet? Or higher?*

"Damn those weather forecasters!" Paul shouted—for he had been assured that he had a weather window. "This is a Rozière, not a superpressure balloon!" And he began to do calculation in his head. How high could his balloon climb? Could he climb into the stratosphere? How much of his precious fuel might he use up in doing so?

"It's too high… the cloud's too damn high…"

It was then that he noticed the ice and snow collecting on the portals as the banging of the hail grew louder.

The altimeter showed that the balloon, weighted by the snow, was dropping… But could he trust the device in this storm? After all, it measured atmospheric pressure. Altimeters were known to tell dangerous lies.

Paul shut off the burners, his mind racing. Could he perhaps descend instead and catch a lower air current? Avoid the updrafts. And drift laterally out of this monster cloud. Before the wind tore his balloon apart. Before snow or rain sank him into the sea. *My charts! Where are my charts?*

Paul stepped toward the navigation console, but he never made it. Turbulence sent his foot landing upon a rolling wine bottle and he stumbled. Hitting his head hard against the cabin's framing, he collapsed to the floor, unconscious.

Fifi fluttered down to Paul. Landing gently upon his chest, her metallic body jingling lightly, she cowered there in silence.

~

Paul awoke feeling stiff, achy, and incredibly thirsty. He noticed Fifi, lying inert upon him. The light in her robotic eyes was gone, her battery completely run down. Gently, he cradled her in one hand and rose to his feet, weak, unsteady.

The lights in the gondola were unusually dim. And it was cold. The craft was running on the backup batteries alone. How long had he been out? He looked to the chronometer.

"... Two days?" Paul found it difficult to believe.

There was daylight outside, but obscured by mist in every direction. He was within the calm fog of a cloud. *The clouds*, Paul thought. *The solar array can't see the sun.*

The altimeter read just 7,342 feet and showed that his balloon was slowly descending. Opening the propane valve, Paul fired flame into the envelope, to make his craft climb, up out of the cloud and into the sunlight. He needed electricity. And he needed to charge Fifi, even if it meant draining his batteries dry.

Drifting aimlessly for two days, he thought, realizing how terribly off course he likely was—how he was now lost somewhere over the vast Pacific...

~

Some hours later, Paul's balloon hung motionless above the clouds at 24,000 feet, in the sunlight, electricity restored, batteries charging.

Sponge bathed, nourished by freeze-dried food, hydrated, and refreshed, Paul sat at his navigation console, perplexed. He had a problem, a big one. His balloon had drifted into the Pacific's Intertropical Convergence Zone, a low-pressure area just north of the equator known as the Doldrums. Here, the sunlight beamed down so directly upon the planet that it caused the warmed air to rise vertically rather than blow horizontally, the result being either little to no navigable wind, like now, or tropical storms. The present lack of wind could last for weeks...

The nearest trade winds were quite a distance to the north, and the subtropical jet stream much farther still.

He had been unsuccessful in contacting anyone on his VHS aircraft radio. Same with the VHF/UHF band transceiver. And the marine band radio. And his emergency locator transmitter required another aircraft to be within range—and listening to 121.5 MHz to receive his signal, which apparently none were.

To make matters worse, he had no flight-tracking support team. Nor had he arranged for satellite-based tracking... He carried no emergency beacons to report to search-and-rescue satellites, to SARSAT. And he had opted not to bring along an Iridium satellite phone—for he had wished to be left alone, undisturbed...

Slowly, Paul came to the conclusion that under the circumstances he had no choice but to ascend higher into the troposphere, in an attempt to find some horizontal-blowing wind. Yet climbing too high... burning propane, venting gas... it would decrease the number of days his balloon could stay aloft. But what else could he do? A balloon navigates by either ascending or descending in altitude, to find different streams of wind to drift within.

With a nonchalant shrug and an attitude of equanimity, Paul fired flame into the balloon's envelope and began his ascent.

~

29,000 feet, the height of Mount Everest, and still there was no meaningful lateral-moving wind.

~

36,000 feet, the altitude frequented by commercial passenger jets, and still there was no horizontal wind. It was now -69.7 °F outside. It would remain this temperature throughout the rest of the troposphere.

~

42,000 feet: the upper limit of commercial passenger flights… and still nothing.

~

53,000 feet… Paul shivered emotionally as his balloon left the troposphere behind and entered the stratosphere. The temperature would now begin to get warmer, ozone heating this atmospheric layer as it absorbed energy from the ultraviolet radiation of the sun.

~

Five hours after beginning his ascent, at 70,000 feet, Paul stopped his climb, hovering slightly over thirteen miles above the central Pacific. There was still no horizontal wind. And he was now over a thousand feet higher than the world record of the highest altitude attained by a hot air balloon. Of course, manned and unmanned balloons using helium or hydrogen had ascended higher into the stratosphere… But there were dangers in doing so.

"Fifi," Paul called to his companion, to his muse, and she came to him, landing upon his shoulder, chirping softly, whispering melodiously into his ear. It calmed his concerned mind. But it did not alter their dire situation.

What to do? Perhaps wait… And think…

And so Paul prepared some tea on his twelve-volt water heater, sat back, and thought.

~

As the sun set, casting magnificent rays of waning light down upon the massing bluish-gray clouds below, Paul sat there, still thinking. His propane fuel still intermittently burning…

Slowly, the sun disappeared behind the curvature of the Earth, leaving behind a dimming ruby-red glow. The sky began to grow black, like the blackness of outer space, and Paul felt himself lured out of his troubled contemplation. For it was almost magical how the stars began to appear in the heavens, one, two, three, or more at a time, shining and twinkling resplendently.

Paul felt himself smile in appreciation as he witnessed a meteor flash down from achingly high above him. Then there were other shooting stars, amazing streaks of light, meteors burning up in the mesosphere as they plunged down through Earth's upper atmosphere.

And as the clouds far below him darkened still and began to thunder and storm, Paul found himself treated even further, now to a menagerie of spirit halos, red spirits, blue jets, tendrils, trolls, and elves, all fleeting, luminous optical phenomena of the stratosphere and mesosphere, associated with thunderstorms of the troposphere.

"Fifi…" Paul whispered in awe, needing to share the sight with someone, even a mechanical simulacrum of life.

Witnessing a disk-shaped elve rapidly expand to 300 miles across before vanishing in an instant, Paul rose to his feet and stepped up close to the huge portal before him. The weak luminosity of wispy red spirits resembling huge jellyfish, lasting but a few milliseconds, appeared and disappeared outside, dripping effervescent blue, tendril-like filaments of light beneath them.

Optical eruptions of blue jets, lasting a tenth of a second, reached up toward his balloon from the electrically active core of the thunderstorm below.

It all evoked a startling sense of the ephemeral...

It made Paul think of life, and of his late father... And he found himself, in response, reciting aloud an eleventh- or twelfth-century poem that had been haunting his psyche since he had read it just one month ago. His voice carried with it his characteristic charm and genteel elegance but also a palpable disquietness:

"O heart! Imagine owning everything in this world,

Imagine your pleasure garden luxuriant,

Then imagine your being there like dew,

Appearing at night and disappearing at sunrise."

Paul paced over to the starboard portal, which offered a better view. He felt it strange that it was of little consolation to him that he had made the right choice of ascending, given the thunderstorm below. But he did find himself grateful to have witnessed this atmospheric display, to have seen first hand these transient luminous events, even though they contributed to the unease in his heart.

It was then that Paul noticed something far off, perhaps twenty-five miles distant. It looked similar to a star, but brighter, and much larger. And it was oddly flashing intensely colored lights: red, green, orange, blue.

Paul rubbed his eyes, picked up his binoculars, and looked again, focusing with extreme concentration. The pulsating lights seemed to form a diamond shape. It was clearly not an atmospheric phenomenon. Was it some type of aircraft?

Hovering up in the stratosphere? He squinted, but the lights were so bright that he could not determine if there was any solid structure between them... And the object, its shape, oddly seemed to be changing. It now looked like a starfish with drooping arms—no, it was horseshoe in shape... He lost it.

Lowering the binoculars, he noticed it now positioned ten degrees to starboard. No, it disappeared again... only to reappear ten degrees farther off, as if it had... jumped... in an instant from one location to the other. Not in a second, but in an *instant.* Paul ran some mathematical calculations in his head. The ten degrees perhaps represented seventeen miles. *Seventeen miles in an instant?*

It jumped again, disappearing and reappearing back in its original position, traversing the thirty-four miles instantaneously...

What on Earth is this?

Paul could not resist the impulse to pick up a flashlight and signal to it, flashing his light off and on and then off again.

He suddenly wished he had not done so as a much smaller round object emerged from the bottom of the strange apparition and flew straight toward him at an incredible rate of speed. *A missile?* Overcome by fear, Paul dropped his flashlight.

When he looked back up, the small object was no longer there... No, it was still there, only now it was at seven o'clock. It hovered motionless for a second or two, and then it began to circle him in a wide, elliptical orbit, moving at a fantastic speed. Once, twice around him it went, and then it stopped dead, just hovering again, off in the distance.

Paul retrieved his binoculars, his hands trembling. He focused upon the object. It was bright... oval shaped. It had no wings... no tail... only a fuselage... no visible propulsion system...

What is this thing? Is it...? Can it be...? Interplanetary?

Paul opened the parachute valve at the top of his balloon's envelope. Gas escaped, and he began to descend.

At 55,000 feet, he hit the burners to stop, for he had that storm beneath him.

He quickly scanned the sky. There it was again... it had followed him down... Slowly it turned, and then it came straight at him on a collision course. Paul instinctively closed his eyes and threw his arms up in front of his face.

But there was no impact. The object simply stopped right in font of the portal, mere feet away, illuminating the cabin, emitting heat that Paul could feel on his face, on his arms, on his chest. It oscillated, wavered, before stabilizing and becoming still. It was a metallic ovoid about eight feet across, with two halves, a top and a bottom, divided by a band that ran horizontally around its center. Its top was an odd metallic aluminum in color, very shiny, brilliantly aglow, its bottom a vivid, unearthly red. It made a low whistling sound...

Slowly, ever so slowly, Paul dropped his arms, allowing them to just hang there limp at his sides. He felt his psyche reeling. Before him was something so unexpected, a technological object of utter mystery... A nonhuman craft, an alien craft that assaulted his perception of man of Earth as being alone, secure, in control.

"Fifi..." Paul mumbled. He heard the flutter of metallic wings and felt the lightness of his robotic bird settling upon his shoulder. But she made not a sound.

It was as Paul stood there in silence, staring at the ovoid in bewildered awe, that the brilliant white superbolt struck both it and the gondola, having flashed upward from the positively charged top of the storm clouds thousands of feet below.

The explosion of light lasted for a full two to three endless seconds, without flickering—this extraordinary upward lightning being one hundred times more powerful than a normal bolt. In those few seconds, one hundred billion volts of electricity tore through Paul's gondola, jetting straight up the length of his 180-foot-tall Rozière balloon.

This same remarkable electrical power simultaneously rifled into the ovoid...

The metal cage built into Paul's gondola provided sufficient capacity to save Paul from shock, the metal conducting the electricity. But the superbolt had punched sizeable holes into the cabin, causing an explosive decompression of the gondola.

Paul found himself knocked to the floor by the rush of noise, cold air, and mist. He knew that at this altitude he could expect to remain conscious without oxygen for perhaps five seconds. He also knew that for any chance of survival he needed to initiate an emergency descent to 8,000 feet.

Paul groped about, found and slipped on one of the cabin's emergency oxygen masks. But he was hyperventilating. If he did not slow down his breathing, it would lead to hypoxia and unconsciousness.

He noticed Fifi on the floor before him, staring at him. The sight of her serene, glowing eyes calmed him somewhat.

He reached up for the parachute valve but stopped. For he could feel that his craft was already dropping. *How? The lightning—it must have pierced the envelope of the balloon!*

There had been no explosion, of course, helium being an inert gas, but the rent in the envelope, torn by the superbolt, had quickly enlarged, sending the balloon into its rapid descent.

Paul collapsed back to the floor, clutching himself, shaking with bone-chilling cold. The cabin temperature must have dropped from 65 °F to -60 °F! Hypothermia would be setting in soon, and he would begin to freeze to death.

He looked at the altimeter, but his vision blurred before his eyes.

Rising, trembling, he opened the parachute valve fully and then collapsed into semiconsciousness. He sat there lightheaded, somewhat confused, disorientated, but oddly mildly euphoric. And strangely dissociated from himself and the danger.

Can I reach Earth safely? Falling through this storm? Land upon the sea, in an uncontrolled descent? At what speed?

Have to slow down…

Paul heard, above the rush of the wind, his Fifi begin to whistle, to trill. He drew strength from the beauty of her music. Struggling to his knees, he opened the propane valve and fired flame into the torn envelope.

He then stopped and waited, contenting himself to listen in appreciation to the melody whistled forth by Fifi, until he felt the sensation of downward speed, when he again fired flame, holding it until instinct told him to stop. He repeated this again and again.

When the altimeter read 8,000 feet, Paul left the full flame on. But the balloon kept dropping.

He heard himself call out weakly for his mechanical nightingale. He sighed as he felt her tinkling body perch upon his shoulder.

"Oh, Fifi…"

He held the burn, kneeling there for the longest time, until the gondola hit the sea.

~

Paul regained consciousness to the stinging of salt water spraying his face.

Must have blacked out...

Outside he saw waves washing over the portals, and a terrific rainstorm. His balloon had survived crash landing upon the sea. The gondola was designed to float—its twin keels would flood with seawater to maintain an upright position—but water was entering at an alarming rate through the holes punctured by the lightning.

"Fifi!"

She fluttered to him.

Paul yanked open the survival locker, pulling out an immersion suit, a life vest, and an inflatable raft.

He had to stop to read the emergency instructions on the hull beside the starboard portal. To blow it open, twist, and push. He did so. The suction pulled him forward, and he found himself splashing into and floundering about in the sea.

He yanked the inflation cord and the raft expanded with an explosive rush of air, unfolding and jerking into shape.

He flopped into the raft, rolling onto his back. Before he could call for Fifi she was there, landing upon his forearm.

Paul felt the sight before him to be utterly surreal as he witnessed, in the downpour, his craft's upper helium cell break free from the balloon's torn envelope and ascend straight up into the storm, a white bubble lifting off into the blackness, while the craft's huge primary helium cell, partially deflated and deformed, went bouncing and wobbling off across the waves, unable to get airborne.

And the torn envelope that remained, lying there heaped upon the sea... something within it began to glow... to move...

Paul sat up. *No, it can't be...*

But it was. The alien ovoid, engulfed and entrapped within the balloon's envelope, had been pulled down from the stratosphere...

Rising and writhing, the ovoid was oddly unable to free itself from the twisted fabric. As the ovoid rotated, Paul caught a glimpse of one side of it. It was badly damaged, its hull completely torn open...

Collapsing to the sea, the ovoid, still entangled within the balloon's envelope, bounced straight up and down once, twice, and then weakly skipped off over the ocean, heading toward the unseen horizon, dragging the envelope and its gondola away with it.

Paul sat there in silence for a long moment. He then put on his life jacket, took a compass reading, and began to paddle after his disappearing gondola.

~

It was well after midnight when Paul stopped paddling, quite tired. The ocean was flat and calm—the rain had stopped, the clouds had dissipated, leaving a dark, starry sky. Paul dropped a weary hand into the sea, feeling the current. He was still moving with it, and at a good rate. Heading east, although 6° south. He surmised that he was adrift somewhere in the Pacific's North Equatorial Countercurrent.

He sat there quietly for a moment, just listening to the soft sound of the huge Pacific slowly rising and sinking around him, darkly, rolling ever so leisurely.

He involuntarily yanked his hand out of the ocean when he noticed the odd phosphorescence in the black water about him, so vividly did the glowing resemble hot coals. But curiosity overcame him and he carefully scooped up a handful of the twinkling seawater. The glow was due to tiny, brightly shining shrimp.

He then caught sight of faint illuminations deep beneath him, coming from larger, ghostly creatures of indistinct, wavering shapes—round, oval, even triangular, often splitting into two or more parts which then swam away from each other. Paul wondered if they might be giant jellyfish, or perhaps some wonderful Jules Verne-esque species, phantoms unknown to science, denizens of the deep that might only be encountered by a small, silent craft helplessly adrift upon the open ocean...

"It's all rather beautiful," Paul commented softly, his cultured voice calm and untroubled, "isn't it, Fifi? I know that I should be upset, but that's not how I feel. I only feel grateful to be alive."

Paul noticed a torn piece of his balloon's envelope floating on the surface. He started rowing again.

"And so curious..."

~

Paul awoke at dawn, fatigued and blurry eyed, to the sound of the underside of his raft being torn open by the submerged reef, just covered by the waves, that he had run aground on.

He looked for Fifi and found her sitting there upon his chest, looking at him with her bright, lovely eyes.

"Fifi," he called to her, and she flapped a few times, alighting on his shoulder as he rolled out of the raft and into the sea.

Struggling over the sharp coral and through the shallow surf, Paul dragged the rapidly deflating raft up the sloping beach that rose directly before him, where he collapsed into the coarse sand.

Catching his breath, he slowly rose to his knees, and then to his feet. He took a dozen or so unsteady steps.

He had landed upon a low-lying coral island, a mere half a mile wide, maybe three times that in length. A flat, bulldozed plain of coral sand, scarred by a central basin, a barren land without a single tree. Uninhabited. Isolated, desolate. The few scattered clumps of grass and prostrate vines looked more dead than alive...

As the sun continued to rise, its early-morning rays brightening the surroundings, Paul noticed a single structure several dozen yards inland. It was shaped like a short lighthouse and built of white sandstone. He felt himself drawn to it, as if under a spell. Stepping over coral rubble and sandstone slabs, he slowly made his way up to where it stood, about eighteen feet above sea level, the island's highest point. When he reached it, he just stood there, his arms hanging lifelessly at his sides.

"No... Oh no..."

There amongst a few hermit crabs and nestling sea birds, erected before the basin of the isle's long-ago-dried-up central lagoon, stood the Amelia Earhart Day Beacon. The navigational landmark was crumbling, its bands of black paint almost completely eroded away.

And Paul knew exactly where he was. He was on Howland Island, just north of the equator. This was the remote island that Amelia Earhart, in 1937, on her round-the-world flight, had been hopelessly searching for before her plane disappeared, lost forever without a trace...

It was then that Paul noticed his gondola and the ravaged, heaped envelope of his deflated balloon, both lying perhaps a quarter-mile to the north.

"We did it, Fifi," he exclaimed, and he broke into a run. In his gondola there was food and water. It meant survival. And his radio meant the hope of rescue.

~

Paul slowed to a creep as he neared the wreckage that was his balloon, his eyes searching for the alien ovoid. It did not appear to be present...

"The solar array..." he whispered to himself. *It's missing.* He reasoned that it was likely crushed and lost upon his crash landing on the sea.

The gondola, dragged inland as it had been, was a wreck. He entered it through the blown-out portal. At once he checked the lead-acid batteries but found them to be severely damaged and:

"Completely dead..." he grumbled.

The VHS aircraft radio was useless. As was the VHF/UHF band receiver and the marine band radio...

There was dried food, water. Even wine. As he quenched his thirst and chewed on a handful of dried vegetables, he thought he heard something. And Fifi, on his shoulder, began to whistle.

"Quiet, Fifi!"

Paul cautiously climbed out of the gondola. Warm air, rising, flopped the envelope of his balloon over, turning it toward the sea, revealing the wreckage of the alien ovoid, lying there in the depression of the evaporated lagoon.

Paul dropped his vegetables and stood there for the longest time, thinking, summoning up his courage. Finally, he started walking, slowly, toward the ovoid, which lay there with its torn-open hull facing him, its innards hidden, shadowed by darkness.

Paul was quite close to the thing before he noticed the trail in the sand, leading from the ovoid's breached hull around to the shaded backside of the craft. Something had dragged itself from the wreckage...

Fifi leapt from Paul's shoulder and flapped off, disappearing behind the ovoid.

"Fifi!"

Paul chased after her without thinking. He found her behind the alien craft, perched atop what had crawled out of it. Trilling softly.

Paul slowly walked right up to the thing, unafraid, so overpowering was his surprise and curiosity. It was metallic, robotic and rather small, not much larger than his Davidic lyre. It was shaped rather like a mushroom, but with two short, flipper-like appendages at the base of its stalk. Lying on its side, it appeared injured, immobile. What looked like sentient compound eyes encircled its mushroom cap.

Artificial intelligence from another world... Paul concluded, his mind calm and lucid, his soul enthusiastically appreciative of this strange and unique encounter.

"I hope you're not in distress," Paul finally said aloud, addressing the mushroom with genuine concern, his suave, cultured mien exhibiting itself in his tone, in his posture, in his bearing.

The mushroom moved slightly, but remained silent. Fifi flapped back to Paul, landing upon his shoulder.

Paul slowly sat down, not wanting his height to intimidate the mushroom.

"I see your wings are broken," he went on, grasping for something to say, "like mine. I hope you don't mind my sharing this island with you. I know it's an unexpected inconvenience..."

The mushroom remained silent.

"You're quite different than what I had expected. Were you up there, in the stratosphere as a tourist? I was... in a way. I wanted to see things, that I hadn't seen before, so I set off on this damn voyage around the world..."

Paul felt himself being regarded by the mushroom's multiple electronic eyes. It made him feel a bit uncomfortable.

"I wish I understood you," he stated sincerely.

What looked like black granules poured out of the mushroom, like sand out of an hourglass. The small grains puddled atop the surface of the dried-up lagoon, and then the particles began to move. As if by magic, the grains assembled themselves into letters, then into words:

you must leave this island

"But," Paul stammered, "I'm marooned here. Like you."

The black grains reassembled themselves into new letters, into new words:

not like me
all that i am
and more
is also elsewhere

"I don't understand," Paul responded.

you do not need to

"But I want to."

all that you are exists only here
you must leave at once

"Why? Why must I leave this island?"

fusion bomb

"Fusion bomb?" Paul struggled with it. "A hydrogen bomb? What, a test? Where? Here?"

no
south of here

"The test, is it by you?"

no
by you

"Wait." Paul jumped to his feet and raced back to his balloon's gondola. Inside, he rifled through his charts.

Returning, he spread out a map of the central Pacific. Howland Island lay at latitude 0° 48' 24" N and longitude 176° 036' 59" W. To the south, a mere thirty-five miles distant, was tiny Baker Island, another uninhabited, desolate speck, like Howland.

Paul pointed to Baker. "Where? Here? Baker Island?"

yes
baker

"The magnitude of the explosion?"

100 megatons

"My God…" Paul thought of the old Soviet Tsar Bomba, the most powerful nuclear weapon ever detonated by man. It had a yield of 50 megatons… Its explosive cloud had risen over seven times the height of Mount Everest, well into the mesosphere—higher than his balloon had been! Buildings were destroyed over a hundred miles from ground zero. And this test on Baker, a mere thirty-five miles away, would have twice the yield…

"When?" Paul heard himself ask.

sunrise

you must leave this island

"How?" he barked.

The small black grains composing the word 'sunrise' disassembled, leaving only the words:

you must leave this island

Paul rose to his feet and looked about. But there was nothing but desolation, nothing to build a raft with. The envelope of his balloon was torn, ripped, shredded beyond repair. His gondola, even if he could drag it down to the sea—which he could not— would now sink like a stone, so damaged it was.

"I'm sorry," he said to the mushroom. "But I'm unable to."

In frustration he threw out a stone, and then slowly walked after it, pondering his fate. Fifi on his shoulder began to trill.

"Not now, Fifi," he said gently. "Not now."

~

As Paul wandered, he felt as if he were walking across a landscape without time, so barren and isolated was the tiny island, and yet he knew that the clock was ticking down…

He glimpsed the daytime moon, hanging there ghostly in the sky. And for the first time he saw it as something other than an object of beauty and wonder. Today it was a dreadful, far-off barren world. *Just like this desert isle!*

As he walked on, he noticed the columns of warm air rising from the sand flats. So intense was the upflow that he witnessed an approaching cloud actually split apart and move past the isle by flanking it on either side. Cloud formation was impossible over the island. No chance of rain. No lagoon. No fresh water source.

I'll die anyway in a week, after my rations run out...

Paul kicked at the sand, once, twice, three, four times before he uncovered the dead coral rock that made up the island. It would be impossible to dig any type of a hole to shelter himself in from the shockwave of the bomb... And even if he could, he would only die horribly later on from radiation sickness courtesy of the fallout.

There really was no way out of this situation...

Several dozen steps and Paul encountered a large sign, the size of a small billboard. It lay fallen down, flat upon the coral sand, facing up, its surface faded by years of overexposure to the equatorial sun. Even the twin posts that had once held the sign upright lay prostrate, decaying. Paul read the sign silently to himself:

Howland Island
National Wildlife Refuge
No Trespassing

"No trespassing..." And Paul laughed.

He then tried his best to compose himself. He even recited aloud a brave little poem:

"However low one may be
... It is holding oneself in sway
That is imperative..."

~

Returning to the ovoid, Paul made his way into the shade beside the alien robotic mushroom. He had carried with him from the gondola an assortment of dried food, a bottle of water, two bottles of wine, and his ten-string Davidic lyre.

"It's 114 °F in the shade," Paul said as he sat down. "I checked, back at my balloon."

Nothing from the mushroom.

"Do you intend to keep your identity a dark secret from me?" Paul asked the mushroom as he opened a bottle of wine. "What are you?"

The black grains, still present, rearranged to spell out:
the answer is complicated

This gave Paul pause, but only for a moment. "You, your kind. You're here because of this test? Because of our nuclear bomb madness?"

The letters remained motionless.

"How long?" Paul asked. "How long have you been observing us?"

The letters rearranged to:
hiroshima
nagasaki

This time Paul was silent.

The letters rearranged themselves again:
2431 nuclear bombs exploded since
why?

Paul did not have an answer.
to kill?

"No," Paul defended his planet, humanity.
no?

"No," Paul confirmed.

The black grains moved about, swirling, forming into new letters.

your last world war
50 million killed
1700 cities destroyed

Paul sighed, defeated, and he sort of gazed off across the barren landscape. "I know. If we're not careful, we could reduce our Earth to something like this island... only worse..."

The alien letters were motionless for a moment, and then the unexpected:

mars was once like earth
with an ocean
a significant atmosphere
life
intelligent life

A chill crept over Paul. "You're not from another star, are you?"

no
we are not from another star

"Are you a... Martian?" Paul stumbled with the word *Martian*, a name worn out generations ago and now some *thing* claiming it?

those of mars
became us
our progenitors left mars
long ago

"To where?"

the asteroid belt
and beyond

"... Why?"

those of mars
destroyed mars

"How?" Paul asked.

The black grains remained frozen for several heartbeats and then:

nuclear war
millions of years ago

And Paul's eyes became still, like glass, as the dread and enormity of the implications sank painfully into his psyche. *Mars sterilized, most of its atmosphere blown away millions of years ago... And now, man of Earth fully prepared to commit the same irrational madness?*

"... Is this the ultimate fate of us warring little things of flesh and blood?" Paul uttered the words softly, disappointment aching in his soul, his mind floating off. "Is that what you're telling me?"

The alien letters did not move.

Paul took a long drink of the wine, and then slowly his thoughts fled from the all-too-horrible-to-contemplate thought of unavoidable nuclear holocaust and turned inward, focusing instead on something smaller, on his own pending end.

"Do you believe in immortality?" Paul finally asked, shaken, his mind still far away and drifting farther. "... I want to believe that there's a chance, that something of me can be carried on, somehow, somewhere...

"I hate the idea of an end. I know it's inevitable, that it's what has gone before that matters. Not what can't go on after... but..."

And Paul looked at the mushroom, at its many eyes. Although they were mechanical, in them he thought he saw compassion and pity. And he became rather embarrassed.

"The art of a people always reveals their true soul," he said in soft defense of humankind, and he picked up his lyre, pressing its rosewood close to his heart. Leaning his face against its sidearm, he began to play notes generated by human emotion, by instinct and imagination. Fifi joined in, blowing soft, melodious fluted breaths. Like that night on the balloon, a hypnotic rhythm soon developed between them. The music was hauntingly that of man, of ancient man, so strongly did it echo the notes that must have sounded in his prehistory and early history, during the taming of agriculture and the raising of walls. The music brought to mind place names such as Jericho, Damascus, Jaffa, Byblos, Jerusalem...

But suddenly the music changed. The change came from Fifi. The notes she fluted were so unlike anything she had ever before produced that Paul could not help but look to her. He saw that her bright eyes were looking down at the sand between them and the alien.

The mushroom's communicative black grains were now in the shape of musical notes, shifting, swirling, changing. Fifi was reading and playing the mushroom's alien music. It sounded otherworldly and so very old, ancient beyond true comprehension. They were notes that echoed the earliest days of the solar system... so utterly distant were they of time and place.

Paul played on, allowing his mind and soul to be swayed by the alien music. And his music changed. It was no longer something representative of man's past alone, for it became an amalgamated reflection of two different histories: human and nonhuman.

The mushroom's notes soon altered too, and played by Fifi they complemented the new sound emanating from Paul's lyre. The emerging melody was magnificently different, weirdly unfamiliar and unreal, like something out of an impossible dream.

Paul and the mushroom went on composing together in a meditative trance, refining their composition, extending it, perfecting it. Shortly after sunset, exhausted and drunk on wine, Paul slipped into a deep and undisturbed sleep, the final melody haunting his subconscious all night long.

~

Paul awoke before sunrise to find Fifi perched nearby, inert, lifeless, her battery drained. He picked her up gently, sadly cradling her in his hands. *All hope is lost...*

He looked to the mushroom, which still sat there, leaning on its side, motionless. Its grains moved, forming letters, words, asking:

are you afraid?

"Sad," Paul answered. "It's not a light thing, being born a man."

being mortal?

Paul nodded. "Are you just going to lie there?"

i am also elsewhere

"... while all that I am exists only here..."

And then he thought of Mars and of Earth.

"Is there hope?" he asked forlornly. "For humankind?"

there is hope

Paul nodded slowly yet unsurely and walked off with Fifi, heading down to the beach.

He stood there at the water's edge, looking south. The explosion would come from the south...

He wondered how terrible the look of desolation must be on his face. He was thankful that he could not see it. To escape what was to come would require a supernatural miracle, and he knew that none would be forthcoming.

But who was he to expect anything different? After all, what was he when held against the backdrop of eternity? Against the faces of all those who had gone before?

Yet something stirred in Paul. For in his heart he still believed in humankind. Perhaps he had no future, but he felt that man did.

No... His mind rumbled defiantly. *No man has the right to die... when he can still leave something meaningful behind.*

71

As the sky lightened, ever so slightly—for the sun had still not yet risen—death focused his mind. *Do what you can, with what you have, where you are…*

And suddenly, he knew what he needed to do.

He raced back to the gondola in a mad dash. Within the cabin, he tore the place apart until he found sheets of music paper and a pen. Then he sat. Closing his eyes, he allowed last night's collaborative composition to flow into his mind. And he began to write the music down, closing his eyes when he needed to, to recall the strange melody created by the union of a human and a nonhuman mind; the first human and alien creative collaboration.

But he had to rush, for the sun would be rising soon. Yet he had to write the melody out correctly, in order to gift its magnificence into the future.

When he finally finished, he scribbled his signature and wrote at the bottom: Allow this melody to inspire mankind to embrace peace and shun war.

He then looked for that damn wine bottle that he had stepped on, that had sent him banging into the wall, knocking himself out. He could not find it. So instead he opened a new bottle and shook it like mad to empty it. Rolling up the sheet containing the melody, he inserted it into the bottle and recapped it, pushing the cork down flush. *The seawater will swell the cork. Make the seal airtight.*

He frantically ran back down to the beach. Looking over his shoulder, behind the silhouette of the Amelia Earhart beacon, he could see that the eastern sky was aglow, the rising sun about to show itself.

Splashing into the waves, he ran and then swam out some distance to get to the fringing reef. Climbing up upon it, cutting his hands and knees to shreds, he rose to stand. He then tossed the bottle as far out to sea as he could. He stood there for a long moment, until the current caught the bottle and started to carry it away from the island, floating it eastward.

"Ha!" he exclaimed, defiantly, victoriously. He had his chance for something of him to be sent on, somewhere. Into the future.

Bottles have reached across entire oceans!

And although he hated the idea of an end, he turned south to confront what was coming. As he stood there to face the inescapable, he thought of that tiny ballooning spider, and he wished he could loft himself into the heavens on a gossamer sail. But he had no such wings to save himself.

And he shed a tear, a single tear. Not out of fear or regret, but out of the sadness of standing there now, *so soon*.

And he heard his own last words echo forth:

"O heart! Imagine owning everything in this world,

Imagine your pleasure garden luxuriant,

Then imagine your being there like dew,

Appearing at night and disappearing at sunrise."

And the sun rose.

He lifted Fifi and held her gently and lovingly against his heart. In his imagination he heard his Fifi begin to whistle, to trill. And he drew strength from the beauty of her music.

The flash of light was blinding. But he did not close his eyes.

The shockwave came...

And then there was nothing.

~

No... Wait... There was something.

Paul suddenly felt himself conscious again, embraced by a cocoon of... *force*... Whatever it was, it engulfed him completely, inside and out, his body, his mind... He also felt the sensation of speed and movement. Upward movement.

Opening his eyes, he found himself wrapped within a translucent bubble, ascending straight through the troposphere and into the stratosphere toward what looked like a star, but brighter and much larger—a diamond-shaped star that was flashing intensely colored lights: red, green, orange, blue.

Paul looked for Fifi, finding her still there clutched over his heart, her serene eyes now alive, glowing.

"Fifi," Paul gasped, "we have another tomorrow..."

Fifi began to sing, gloriously.

And Paul slowly realized that these mushrooms who patiently watched would continue to carefully observe mankind and only intervene if absolutely necessary, and only at the last possible moment—as they had done with him. From this, he had learned to treasure life. Perhaps man could learn to do so as well? Perhaps this was the strategy of these mushrooms?

In any case, Paul understood that his being miraculously saved as he had been represented something far larger than himself, for it was a promise to all humankind: *there is hope.*

Paul again looked heavenward, to the colorful lights of the mysterious UFO awaiting him high above. He found himself looking forward to continuing his interrupted journey, to ballooning with those who were once Martians and now beings of artificial intelligence, aliens from the asteroid belt and beyond.

~

Recommendations

• *UFOs: Generals, Pilots, and Government Officials Go on the Record* by Leslie Kean, published in 2010.

• *UFOs and Defense: What Should We Prepare For? / Les OVNI et la Défense. A quoi doit-on se préparer?* An independent report written by the French association COMETA, published in France on July 16, 1999.

• This author recommends that readers who are interested in the poetry of Omar Khayyám acquire the book *Rubáiyát of Omar Khayyám.*

Niko Zinovii

Acknowledgements and Identifying Notations

• The present altitude record for a hot air balloon was set by Dr. Vijaypat Singhania, who achieved an altitude of 68,986 feet on November 26, 2005, over Mumbai, India.

• The description of the UFOs in this story is based on both the incident that occurred over Portugal on November 2, 1982, when Portuguese Air Force pilot Júlio Guerra encountered an unidentified flying object at 5,000 feet (witnessed by two additional Air Force pilots), and the September 18, 1976, Tehran UFO incident, in which Iranian Air Force pilots engaged unidentified flying objects over Tehran, the capital of Iran. Both of these incidents are described in Leslie Kean's book *UFOs: Generals, Pilots, and Government Officials Go on the Record*.

• When the protagonist in this story, Paul, recites aloud:
"However low one may be
It is holding oneself in sway
That is imperative."
he is reciting a Japanese haiku poem written by Japanese poet Iio Sōgi (1421–1502).

• The primary poem featured in the story is by this author's favorite poet: Omar Khayyám, the Persian mathematician, astronomer, philosopher, and poet who lived in Iran from 1048 to 1131.

• The phosphorescent glow of sea life and the mysterious, luminous deeper sea life encountered by the protagonist in this story are based on Norwegian adventurer and ethnographer Thor Heyerdahl's experience as described in his 1950 book *Kon-Tiki: Across the Pacific by Raft*.

• "Do what you can, with what you have, where you are" is a quote attributed to Theodore Roosevelt, the twenty-sixth president of the United States.

• Though the alien states *"2431 nuclear bombs exploded since,"* it needs to be pointed out that the official number of nuclear bomb explosions carried out by mankind is listed by various sources as being as low as 2,053 and as high as 2,400. This author used the fictitious number of 2,431, assuming that the monitoring aliens were aware of all tests carried out (there are a number of untallied alleged tests, e.g., the alleged covert joint Israeli and South African nuclear test of September 22, 1979, in the Indian Ocean) and that additional new tests had taken place between the present day and when this story takes place in the near future.

Why might there be new tests? Since the September 10, 1996, Comprehensive Nuclear-Test-Ban Treaty (CTBT), intended to ban all nuclear explosions, India and Pakistan have had two sets of tests in 1998 and North Korea has had four tests: 2006, 2009, 2013, and 2016. This author assumes in this story that such tests have continued.

This author furthermore suggests in this story, via the alien's written communication, that the nuclear test to be carried out on Baker Island is one of a pure fusion weapon, a hypothetical hydrogen bomb design that does not need a fission primary explosive to ignite the fusion of deuterium and tritium. A pure fusion weapon would require new testing by world powers.

• The idea of the possibility of UFOs originating from within this solar system's asteroid belt was stated in COMETA's *UFOs and Defense: What Should We Prepare For?*

The specific excerpt from the COMETA report: "We should point out that some people envisage another hypothesis, which is much debated: the UFOs do belong to a civilization located in the asteroid belt, but this civilization itself comes from our planet. Older than any known terrestrial civilizations and highly advanced, it supposedly disappeared from Earth (nuclear war, radioactivity, pollution, etc.) but resettled in the solar system."

• The idea that UFOs may possibly be concerned about Earth's future was also indicated in the COMETA report:

"It could be that, before 1947 and after, they (UFOs) have had fears for the future of earth, a future threatened by risks of nuclear war."

• Regarding Mars: In 2012, plasma physicist Dr. John E. Brandenburg claimed there was evidence of massive thermonuclear explosions on Mars in the distant past—that Mars was "nuked." As of the time of this writing, this claim of Dr. Brandenburg's has not been reported as having been discredited or substantiated by other scientists.

A Note from the Author

This author hopes the reader appreciated the many details woven into this castaway tale of a UFO sighting and extraterrestrial encounter and that these facts gave the story a welcome ambiance of realism.

The protagonist unexpectedly running into bad weather reminded this author of something entertaining that he had once read, namely that "weather forecasting is like horoscope reading."

Ballooning spiders are true spiders. They have been found nearly 1,000 miles from land in the sails of ships. They have also been collected in atmospheric data balloons at elevations of 16,000 feet.

There have been a number of cases of messages in bottles found at sea after having traveled considerable distances, some of them having been afloat for over 100 years.

Importantly, this author would like to thank Taylor, who gently nudged this author to provide a meaningful ending to this story.

This author will leave the reader with this thought: if a universal natural progression exists for intelligent biological life to develop AI (artificial intelligence), then it may be more likely than not that any extraterrestrial visitation of Earth might be by machine life empowered by AI, or perhaps some synthesis of biological and artificial life, as opposed to a visitation by purely biological life.

Niko Zinovii
Santa Monica, California
1 June 2016

Niko Zinovii

Umbrellas Up the Mountain

There in a thatched hut, hidden below misty mountain peaks, David found his privacy invaded by wandering white clouds. Stepping outside with his morning tea, he walked up to the small Buddhist temple atop the nearby hill. He smiled at the butterfly floating, fluttering above the temple's roof. And then, with such seriousness, he looked skyward at the ghostly seal of the early morning moon.

Lightning ran down inside lightning, and thunder rumbled. White birds flapped off and disappeared into the mist. Rain fell. In that shower, David bent to the words cut in stone before him. And he read aloud the Japanese script, in English, his voice richly textured, velvety:

"Passing through the world, indeed this is just a shelter from the shower."

By the time his focus returned to this world, the rain had stopped. He briefly looked up at the puff of cloud that had made him wet, then he sipped his tea and found himself quietly appreciating the drifting mist and the temple's splendor, both reflecting beautifully off the surface of the large puddle at his feet. Sitting there beside him, serenely gazing up the mountain, was a large toad. David too gazed up at the cloud-shrouded peaks. He thought how lovely the misty rain was, how this special mountain provided such peace for his heart.

"The bucket full of rain," he said aloud, to the mountain, respectfully, "is enough for today."

He then looked down at his own reflection, which wavered there, unsure, upon that flat puddle. And he stood there motionless for the longest time, just observing himself without bias, yet with considerable subjective interest. There on the water was the reflection of a wanderer...

A golden-haired drifter who had bounced clear around the world, his work always taking him from one location to another, most recently bringing him here, to this temperate rain forest within the Kii Mountains, on the southwest coast of Japan's island of Honshu.

His was a life of freedom. Renouncing society as he had, constantly traveling, moving here and there, always living close to nature. Walking through mountains. Sharing meadows with bees and dragonflies. Abandoning permanence and stability in order to do what he wanted, and not to do what he did not. Was this why he had entered into such an itinerate life? Or was his roving merely an unconscious search for a real home?

In any case, at the age of thirty-two, he had suddenly and unexpectedly found unimaginable fulfillment—in his latest work, here in this unique mountain sanctuary, in the privately owned Ōsanshōuo no Yama nature reserve.

He smiled at his first thoughts of this new day. He would keep them secret to himself.

He sipped his tea. It was quiet. All around him chrysanthemums were flowering. He meditated.

"David!" A voice intruded upon the tranquility. It was a young Japanese man, a colleague of David's. The slender man was escorting someone up from the valley below.

David closed his eyes, peacefully whispering to himself his thoughts in the guise of a haiku poem: "If only people would not come to visit me, in lonely mountains, where I have built my retreat from the world's many trials."

But then the woman being escorted forth stepped out of the nebulous mist as an image of loveliness. Her hair was an arresting ash blond, but more, there was a rare pleasant beauty to her, an unusual harmonious balance. Her walk, her mannerisms were so feminine, silken. Poetic.

"David," said the young man, his accent heavy, his tone formal, "this is Dr. Irina Fogel. Dr. Fogel, this is David, Dr. David Morrow."

She smiled when introduced. She presented as emotionally controlled, calm, cool, yet paradoxically something about her produced in David a sense of genuine warmth.

David noticed her eyes looking past him, off to where, beneath the vanishing moon, across the forest-clad mountain crests flew a line of wild geese. He saw the sincere appreciation of the beauty of the sight gently spread across her lovely countenance.

And he felt her further distraction as they shook hands, as a single dove sang out from deep in a ravine, searching for a friend.

"Such a lonely voice," she whispered. "It's so very beautiful here."

David suddenly felt himself drawn to her. He felt arousal.

He forced himself to turn to her escort. "Takahiro?"

The young man, Takahiro, responded. "Mr. Sato wants you to take Miss Fogel—Dr. Fogel—up the mountain, to see Kappa."

"Kappa?" David turned to Irina. "You're not here to see the birds?"

"Birds? No. I'm a geneticist, researching regenerative biology."

"Oh." David understood. "The accident."

She nodded.

"Still," David said to Takahiro, concerned, "we'll encounter our birds…"

"Dr. Fogel has signed all the required nondisclosure agreements," Takahiro volunteered. "At Mr. Sato's request."

She nodded to David, affirming the fact.

"Mr. Sato's sure about this?" David asked Takahiro.

"Very sure." Takahiro nodded, his voice suddenly somewhat cryptic. "He instructed me to give you this."

David took the envelope and opened it. It was a handwritten note, signed by Mr. Sato. David recognized the flamboyant signature. The note read:

Answer any and all questions Dr. Fogel may ask.

I'm granting Dr. Fogel complete access to our reserve.

Including our birds.

David folded up the paper, not knowing quite what to make of it.

"Dr. Fogel—" David started.

"Irina, please," she interrupted him. "When someone says 'Dr. Fogel' I find myself looking about for my father."

David smiled, and nodded. "Irina. It's quite a steep hike up to where we'll find Kappa…"

"I'm quite fit." She smiled.

David looked her lithe figure up and down; she was dressed appropriately for such a hike. Good sturdy boots, suitable attire, a pack, presumably containing a raincoat.

"Please," he said, "wait here at the temple. I won't be but five minutes."

~

David led Irina into a high meadow, beneath rain-laden clouds, across which they needed to pass before they could start up the misty mountain slopes. There was coolness in the air, and the sound of a distant bell, as it left the bell.

"Ōsanshōuo no Yama," Irina asked softly, "the name of this reserve, what does it mean?"

David thought for a second and then smiled. "The literal translation is 'giant pepper fish.' Mr. Sato's grandfather was the one who secured the sanctuary, the land. This mountain."

"How did you come to be here?"

"Sato's father," David answered, "the wonderful old man, he recruited me. When he interviewed me, he poured me his homemade wine, claimed it was the wine of the immortals. One cup and a thousand worries vanished; two, and I believed I had found heaven."

"And before?" she asked.

"Before?" David fell into subdued contemplation. "Before... my life was like a boat crossing a harbor, back and forth, leaving no mark on the world."

David stopped, looking up the mountain, calm, imperturbable. "Misty rain... can't see the summit. Interesting."

He then asked Irina, "Won't you come and see loneliness?"

As she stepped up to his side, he knelt and picked up a lone green leaf, four times the size of his open hand. "Just one leaf from the Kiri tree..."

The distant temple bell died out. But the fragrant blossoms remained, and the scent of chrysanthemums. And the sound of thunder—David felt as if it startled the magnolias to a deeper white...

David heard Irina's voice drawing him back from the meditative state that he had slipped into. He must have started to hum, unconsciously. "What are you doing?" she asked.

"Oh," he answered, his richly textured voice velvety, "listening to the moon. Following trails left by birds who vanished from yesterday's sky."

He waved for her to follow, and he started walking again across the meadow in Zen-like appreciative silence. He pointed out peony petals falling, piling one upon the other in twos and threes. He wondered if, after they had fallen, their image remained in Irina's mind as it did in his—those peonies.

He pointed to a bee staggering out from deep within a peony and departing reluctantly. Then he knelt, and she knelt beside him, and together they watched a camellia bending, spilling new rainwater, unloading its burden.

Moving on, he pointed to the mountains, to the sky, to tea flowers, white, yellow—to a hairy caterpillar beaded by dew.

The rising, overpowering hum of cicadas stopped them both in their tracks. David watched Irina as she listened to the buzzing and clicking of the multitude of insects, the soft lines of her face etched with a poetic appreciation.

"Nothing in the cry of cicadas suggests they are about to die…" she whispered, the magic of Ōsanshōuo no Yama overwhelming her.

She then bent and picked up something quite fragile, holding it out upon the open palm of her feminine hand. "A cicada shell," she said. "It sang itself utterly away."

And David felt himself wanting to lie down among the flowers with her, pillowed by her lap…

But there was a loud flapping of wings and a huge, white umbrella cockatoo landed heavily upon David's shoulder. Immediately the umbrella affectionately leaned against David, friendly, cuddly. Playfully, it rubbed its big black bill against David, let out a typical loud cockatoo scream, and then, in a typical cockatoo voice, it said:

"'I love you!' Such brief words, yet so hard to say them!"

The mimicry of the sound of human speech was not as perfect as a parrot's, but the inflection and tone were utterly amazing, completely human. It truly appeared as if the bird were actually speaking its mind.

"Kiss!" the umbrella then said, touching its bill briefly to David's mouth.

"Akio!" David greeted the umbrella, kissing the bird back.

David lifted an arm, and Akio hopped from shoulder to forearm, where he settled more comfortably. At once the bird focused on Irina. The wholly white crest atop his head rose high.

"Tell her," the umbrella screeched playfully, "I'm a persimmon eater, who likes haiku."

Irina stepped toward the umbrella, curious, looking into the bird's intelligent black eyes, which were encircled by light-blue skin.

The umbrella bobbed up and down, clowny, and then, ever so seriously, leaned out toward Irina, as if to tell her something very important.

"Life is like a butterfly," the bird said, "whatever that is!"

David smiled, appreciating once again that the umbrella cockatoo was the clown of the bird world, and how umbrellas knew exactly how to get one's attention.

"Akio," David introduced the umbrella to their guest, "this is Dr. Irina Fogel. But please call her Irina—if you call out 'Dr. Fogel,' she'll think her father is visiting the mountain."

Akio screeched out in laughter, screaming noisily as cockatoos do.

"I don't understand…" Irina responded, sensing something out of the ordinary.

"*Yo no naka ya, chōchō tomo are, kaku mo are!*" Akio responded.

Irina looked to David.

"You said you didn't understand," David held back his smile, amused, explaining, "so now he's telling you in Japanese, 'Life is like a butterfly, whatever that is.'"

Akio screeched and laughed and then asked Irina, "*Chōchōya—nani o yume mite, hanezukai?*"

Irina shook her head, unable to understand Japanese.

Akio took to the air and landed softly, gently, on her shoulder. The crest atop his great head lowered, calmly, and he whispered to her the translation:

"The butterfly—what are the dreams that make him flutter his wings?"

David sensed the goose bumps that rose up on Irina, and he wondered if it was inappropriate of him to allow her to be introduced to this mountain's secret so abruptly, so directly.

"*Kago no tori, chō o urayamu, mets uki kana,*" Akio went on, seducing Irina, his voice held low.

Irina waited for the translation. It came with charm:

"Ah, the sad expression in the eyes of that caged bird—envying the butterfly."

Akio made eye contact with Irina and held it, while adding enigmatically, "Irina, freedom is everything… Do you understand?"

Slowly, she nodded, yet she remained unsure if she truly understood the umbrella.

"You will understand," Akio assured her. "Kiss." Akio touched his bill to her lips and then flapped back to land upon David's outstretched arm.

"You'll have to excuse Akio," David explained, wondering about the umbrella's somewhat odd interaction with their guest. "Ever since I introduced him to haiku poetry, he's become infatuated with butterflies."

But Irina needed more, much more.

"Yes, I'm afraid I owe you an explanation," David admitted as he started walking again. By reflex he paused, briefly wondering how much he should reveal, but then he reminded himself of Mr. Sato's unusual instructions, which granted Irina complete access.

David began to explain. "After Sato's grandfather brought the original stock of umbrella cockatoos to Ōsanshōuo no Yama, from the island of Sumba in Indonesia, he asked a simple yet provocative question: 'Why only us?'

"He was referring to language. To our human advantage. He decided to gift this advantage to his umbrellas. It was already known to science that cockatoos, parrots, and the like, that these speaking birds had a larger number of neurons in their cerebral cortexes than mammals. Allowing their smaller bird brains to function cognitively on a level equal to primates'. These birds also had the FOXP2 gene."

"The language gene," Irina added. "Shared by humans and certain birds."

David nodded. "Sato's grandfather, by methods unknown to me, increased the density of neurons in their brains still further. And the overall size of their brains. In short, the Satos made their umbrellas smart enough to speak."

David paused to pet Akio, who cuddled back with great affection. "Akio here is just one of the hundred and ten umbrellas that live on this mountain. He's thirty years old. In this sanctuary, he should live well beyond a century. He's behaving himself today, but let me warn you, he can be as fickle as the weather."

Akio screeched in protest, and David stopped his stroking.

"More, please," Akio requested. David smiled and complied, moving a soothing hand over the umbrella's handsome white feathers.

"He's also extremely demanding. Sentimental. Fun loving. Friendly. Hyperactive. And he screams an awful lot."

On cue Akio screamed. And then laughed.

"Akio," David said, "I just realized. What are you doing down here? In the field?" He turned to Irina to explain. "He lives up at three thousand feet. Well?" David looked back to Akio. But Akio looked to Irina, focusing on her intently.

"Secret," he said. And he flapped back to Irina's shoulder. "'Lady butterfly, perfumes her wings, by floating over the orchid.' Bashō," Akio then added, identifying the haiku poet.

Once again Akio made intimate eye contact with her. "Irina, we need to fly."

She looked into Akio's sentient, dark eyes, trying to comprehend. The words meant something more than the mere words. They almost sounded like a plea.

"You will come to understand." Laughing, Akio then flew off into the mist, disappearing up the mountain.

David started walking again, Irina now keeping pace at his side.

"How intelligent is Akio?" she asked.

"Umbrellas have a different perception of the world… but these umbrellas, they're at least as intelligent as you or I. I believe even more so."

"And you," she put another question to him, struggling to put things together, "you're their… keeper?"

David smiled. "The anatomy of birds is a specialty. I'm an avian veterinarian. I'm their doctor."

And they too disappeared into the mountain's white cloud of mist.

~

Ascending the mountain, David and Irina jumped over a fast-flowing brook, ducking beneath pine branches hanging down.

Mountain rose petals, falling, falling—falling to the music of a distant waterfall. Fresh young leaves, the sound of that waterfall, both near and far. The loveliness of the mountain grew intoxicating.

David pointed out a pine mushroom with some kind of leaf sticking to it. And then a snail, waving its horns uncertainly.

"Climb Mount Ōsanshōuo no Yama, oh snail," David whispered. "But slowly, slowly."

Struck by a raindrop, the snail closed up.

They came upon a lonely pond, sleeping in age-old stillness. At the ancient pond, a frog plunged into the sound of water.

They continued forth in silence, together yet apart, neither intruding on the thoughts of the other.

Crossing another brook, Irina slipped on a moss-covered stone, falling into David's strong arms. He looked into her poetic eyes and sensed that within his arms she felt no worries, only safety. To him it felt as if the future would never come, as if all that existed at that moment was the timeless present.

It was then that Irina noticed the beautiful art on the surrounding rock walls, high up. It was reminiscent of the Cro-Magnon cave art at Lascaux, only outdoors and much more colorful, vibrant. The drawings were of the birds, monkeys, waterfalls, rainbows, clouds, frogs, toads, and salamanders of the Ōsanshōuo no Yama reserve.

"Painted by your umbrellas?" she guessed.

David nodded.

"Why?" she asked.

"The dawn of umbrella creativity," he answered, understanding its significance. "A release of creative impulses, their spiritual dawn. How they think. How they see the world. What they believe. What they want. Who they truly are... It's all up there."

"It's magnificent," she whispered, pirouetting to take it all in. As she did so, the moisture-laden clouds above began to release single water droplets, one at a time, small and large.

And the cockatoo voice of Akio echoed out. "A rain starting, and no hat—so?"

Akio screeched a typical cockatoo scream as he landed upon a moss-covered branch nearby. As did twelve other umbrellas—females and young with brown eyes, and males with eyes of black. The dozen new umbrellas at once began babbling, speaking a continuous flow of sounds, talking in Japanese, conversing with one another. There was no pause between words, only a tide of chatter.

"They all speak Japanese?" Irina asked, smiling.

"This is Japan," David answered gently. "Akio is the only umbrella whom I've taught English to so far. He's my indispensible translator. I'm still learning Japanese."

Another dozen or so umbrellas flapped in, perching upon surrounding branches and on the cliff face itself. Then eight to ten more joined, followed by others. Soon there were nearly fifty fluffy white umbrellas in semicircle around David and Irina.

"What are they doing here?" Irina asked. "Did they come to paint?"

"To paint with beaks. No," Akio answered her. "To see you."

"Why?" she asked.

Akio flapped down, landing upon David's outstretched arm. The crest atop his head rose high and fluffed out. And once again the large umbrella made meaningful eye contact with Irina, speaking words that seemed to carry an enigmatic message.

"'A caterpillar,'" Akio said to her, "'this deep in time—and still not a butterfly?' Bashō," Akio then identified the poet.

And Akio flew off, followed by the other umbrellas.

David and Irina both stood there for a while in silence, thinking.

"I apologize," David finally said, "I'm not sure what Akio is up to... Well, we had better move on, Kappa's not far from here."

~

The ascent steepened and the journey became difficult. David stopped to allow Irina a moment's rest. During the pause he heard far-off frogs, and he knew they were near their destination.

As they continued, passing young bamboo and the fragrant scent of white plum blossoms, David heard wings flapping within the trees and cockatoo whispers in Japanese, and he counted perhaps eight dozen umbrellas following him and Irina up the mountain.

What are they up to? he wondered.

David soon led Irina to a clear waterfall, where green pine needles fell into the ripples of the pool below. He glanced into the pool; its surface was decorated by flowering duckweed and yellow pond lilies—two clumps of them blooming in the light rain. A frog, swimming underwater, wavered unsteadily.

David walked along the bank of the fast-flowing stream, which emptied the pool, looking carefully between its many scattered rocks and deep crevices.

"I don't understand..." he mumbled to himself.

"What?" Irina asked.

"Ah," he exclaimed. "There he is, near the sazanka tree. There's your 'giant pepper fish.'"

Irina saw that up ahead of them, on the narrow pathway, spotted by fallen leaves, was Kappa. Kappa was a giant salamander.

David smiled to himself as he observed Irina's amazement at the size of Kappa. He was over five and a half feet long and he weighed slightly over a hundred pounds, remarkably near-human-sized—almost the same size as Irina, in fact.

"They spend nearly all of their time in the streams," David commented. "Lacking gills, they absorb oxygen directly through their skin, so fast-flowing water, abundant in oxygen, is where you find them. I wonder what he's doing on land?"

"I've never seen a Japanese giant salamander up close before," Irina commented, intimidated by the size of the amphibian.

"Actually, Kappa's a hybrid," David clarified. "Like most of the salamanders in the reserve. Japanese giants crossbred with Chinese giants. They're healthier, larger; they live longer. Kappa's ninety-two years old. Same age as Mr. Sato's father."

Kappa turned its massive head. Its eyes were so tiny, its vision poor. But its mouth was huge, spreading across the entire width of its wide head.

"Is he dangerous?" she asked.

David cautiously walked up to Kappa. Stopping a few feet before the giant, he sniffed the air and looked carefully at the salamander's brown-and-black mottled skin.

"It should be okay," he said. "When he feels threatened, he'll excrete a milky substance from his skin—smells like Japanese pepper."

And David knelt beside Kappa, running a gentle hand over the salamander's soft, supple skin. "Look at that coloring," David marveled, "perfect camouflage against a stream bottom. They've hardly changed in over twenty million years..."

Kappa slowly and hesitantly turned completely about to face them. Its left forelimb and hand were missing.

"How did he lose the limb?" Irina asked.

"Trapped in a flood gate, down in the valley."

Irina removed some medical instruments from her backpack and knelt next to David, examining Kappa's injury.

"Local cells have differentiated nicely," she commented, "forming a blastema."

"A blastema?" David asked.

"It's the blastema cells that will proliferate, and similar to embryonic growth, these cells will ultimately generate all the cells necessary to regrow the limb."

"Oh. How long will it take? For Kappa to regrow the limb?"

"Given Kappa's age and size, I'd estimate it would take well over a year."

"Ah." David now understood. "Thus Mr. Sato's concern. Missing that limb handicaps Kappa's ability to catch fish, frogs."

She nodded, spraying the stump of Kappa's limb with something. "A local anesthetic," she explained as she withdrew a syringe from her pack.

"And that?"

"A change of genetic instructions," she explained as she injected the salamander. "Kappa will now regrow the limb in under a month."

Kappa made a noise that sounded rather like a human baby crying and sprung away, astonishingly fast. Within seconds, it had put a distance of several lengths of its body between itself and Irina. It then paused.

"Wet with morning rain," David remarked, poetically, Zen-like, his eyes on Kappa, "I go in the direction I want."

But Kappa remained unmoving.

"Well," David continued his haiku-like talk, "which way should I go? ... The wind blows."

As if on cue, Kappa moved off, climbing up stone stairs covered by spring rain set into the mountainside.

David then noticed whispers.

"We've had an audience," he informed Irina.

They both looked up to see what looked like a hundred white umbrellas perched in the branches high above them. All the cockatoos were looking down at them, a few murmuring in Japanese, all the others silent.

"It looks as if only the elders are missing..." David observed. "Akio!"

Akio glided down, landing upon an open hand that David held out. The bird screeched once, in a typical cockatoo way, but then lowered his crest and looked to David with an unusual calm seriousness.

"What's this all about?" David asked.

"*Utsutsunaki tsumami gokoro no kocho kana*," Akio answered before hopping over to Irina's shoulder.

"What did he say?" Irina asked.

David thought for a second, shook his head slightly and gave the translation: "'Nothing actual? The feeling of holding in my fingers a butterfly.' Buson," David then added, identifying the poet by habit.

"I don't understand." Irina struggled with it, trying to find some deeper meaning.

"Neither do I," David remarked, a bit annoyed. "I'll take it up with him later. We need to start back down—"

"No," Akio squawked.

"No?" David asked, a bit startled, bewildered.

"No!" Akio affirmed the declaration. "We take Irina now. To Yama-Dera. Daikyōjō Hiroki will talk to Irina."

"Daikyōjō Hiroki?" Irina stumbled over the words.

"Their prefect," David told Irina quickly, and then to Akio: "Are you asking me or telling me?"

Akio's crest rose high, formidable. "Telling."

David could not believe what he was hearing.

"It's okay," Irina said, calm, cooperative. "I'll willingly go to Yama…"

"Yama-Dera!" Akio screeched.

David just stood there for the longest moment, looking at Akio, glancing up at all the umbrellas above. "Well," he finally said, surrendering to curiosity, "then we'd better start for the summit while we still have daylight."

~

Yama-Dera was an eleven-story pagoda, rising alone against the sky—a majestic, tiered tower built of the most beautiful wood, with a base of carved stone. The upturned roof of each level flared out dramatically, the structure in its entirety powerfully echoing the architecture of ancient Japanese Buddhism. The trees of pine surrounding the temple so naturally balanced Yama-Dera they seemed as important as the tower itself. Under the rain clouds, the blossoms of the planted plum trees seemed like stars, despite the daylight.

"Built for the umbrellas," David explained against the wonder of flowers opening and birds singing. "By the Sato family."

Yama-Dera sat quietly atop the highest point of Ōsanshōuo no Yama, overlooking the entire sanctuary. David felt the beauty of the mountain as never before, but more powerfully he felt the beauty of Irina… He found himself, for a brief moment, forgetting completely the curiosity engendered by his umbrellas, experiencing only a selfish want, wishing that he could somehow keep Irina there longer, with him, at this most special reserve.

Akio flapped past them, screaming loudly in his cockatoo voice. He then disappeared into Yama-Dera through its great open central doors.

David and Irina looked at one another in silence and then followed Akio's path. Within Yama-Dera, they stepped softly and respectfully into its great hall, which had above it multiple floors of other rooms spiraling upward around the pagoda's decorative central shaft. Along all the walls were paintings of umbrellas imagined as enlightened wisdoms representing the basic mandala of their kind, of the environment, of the cosmos: transforming anger, transforming ignorance and stupidity, transforming pride, transforming passion, transforming jealousy…

"The umbrellas—" Irina whispered to David, "they're Buddhists?"

"This is Japan," he answered her gently.

Akio introduced the umbrella elders by circling them in flight, one by one. All were large, old, black-eyed males, their sentient eyes encircled by skin of light blue. These were the cockatoos' adjunct prefects, their Gon-Daikyōjō. They were Junichi, Shiro, Ichiro, Daiki, Katsumi, Masato, and Kenji.

The seven Gon-Daikyōjō turned from David and Irina to look deeper into the temple, where sat perched over a throne their prefect, their oldest and wisest leader, Daikyōjō Hiroki.

Akio briefly alighted on Irina's shoulder and whispered to her ever so softly, "Butterfly sleeping on the temple bell. Soon to be awakened?"

Akio then flapped away, perching beside Daikyōjō Hiroki, whom David and Irina walked up to and stood before in reverence.

Hiroki looked at Irina, raising his great white crest ever so high. The prefect then spoke to Akio in a language that was not Japanese but old avian. And Akio translated for Irina.

"You are brilliant. Such depth. Such scope. You are the one we have been waiting for so very long."

Hiroki spoke again, in avian, and Akio presented it to Irina: "Please, set us truly free. Grow us hands?"

And David trembled. *My God*, he thought. Hands meant a freedom beyond flight, an awakening not unlike a caterpillar transforming into a butterfly.

As Irina answered with a resounding *yes*, David's mind spun as he suddenly understood Akio's enigmatic messages:

A butterfly sleeping on a temple bell... soon to be awakened...
Something actual...
A caterpillar so deep in time and still not a butterfly...
The need to fly...
Freedom is everything...
The sad expression in the eyes of that caged bird, envying the butterfly...
The butterfly—what are the dreams that make him flutter his wings...
Life is like a butterfly, whatever that is...

~

A cloud, kissed the mountain, and flowers bloomed.

Recommendations

• The scientific paper "Birds Have Primate-Like Numbers of Neurons in the Forebrain," by Seweryn Olkowicza, Martin Kocoureka, Radek K. Lucana, Michal Porteša, W. Tecumseh Fitch, Suzana, Herculano-Houzel, and Pavel Nemeca, published by the *Proceedings of the National Academy of Sciences* on June 13, 2016.

• *The Classic Tradition of Haiku, An Anthology*, edited by Faubion Bowers. Published by Dover Publications, Inc. in 1996.

• *Haiku, The Poetry of Nature*, edited by David Cobb. Published by Universe Publishing in 2002.

• *The Essential Haiku, Visions of Bashō, Buson, & Issa*, edited by Robert Hass. Published by the Ecco Press in 1994.

• *The Poetry of Zen*, translated by Sam Hamill and J. P. Seaton. Published by Shambhala Publications, Inc. in 2004.

Acknowledgements and Identifying Notations

• Many words, groups of words, sentences, and full poems were implemented into this story from numerous Japanese haiku poems and other poems written by numerous poets, some of whom were:

Matsuo Bashō (1644 – 1694)
Yosa Buson (1716 – 1783)
T'ao Ch'ien (365 – 427)
Kaga no Chiyo (1703 – 1775)
Kobayashi Issa (1763 – 1827)
Gozan (1695 – 1733)
Kōnō Kennichi (1241 – 1316)
Mukai Kyorai (1651 – 1704)
Tagami Kikusha-ni (1753 – 1826)
Mansei (circa 730)
Masaoka Shiki (1867 – 1902)
Arakida Moritake (1472 – 1549)
Musō Soseki (1275 – 1351)
Nishiyama Sōin (1605 – 1682)
Uejima Onitsuva (1661 – 1738)
Saigyō (1118 – 1190)
Senryu (?)
Shō-u (?)
Ikkyū Sōjun (1394 – 1481)
Santōka Taneda (1882 – 1940)
Inahata Teiko (born 1931)

• Kappa is the name of a Japanese mythological creature, likely based on the Japanese giant salamander.

A Note from the Author

This story, "Umbrellas up the Mountain," is this author's tribute to Japanese haiku poetry.

I've never before had such fun writing a tale of speculative fiction. I did so merely as an expression of creativity, having needed an artistic break from more research-laden writing, such as my previous story "Melody in a Bottle."

This story was inspired by haiku poetry and the scientific paper "Birds Have Primate-Like Numbers of Neurons in the Forebrain." And the recognition that high intelligence, language, longevity, and free hands with opposable thumbs (to manipulate the environment) are a few of the most important distinguishing hallmarks that combined to make our species, Homo sapiens, special.

Note of interest:

The Japanese giant salamander is a true giant of the amphibian world, second in size only to the Chinese giant salamander. The naturally occurring hybrid pairing of Japanese and Chinese giant salamanders has been very successful—so much so that the interbreeding is presently threatening the survival of Japan's purebred living fossil. The Chinese giant, introduced into Japan in the 1970s, possesses a more aggressive temperament than the calmer Japanese giant, and during mating selection the Chinese giant has been dominating the Japanese giant.

Niko Zinovii
Santa Monica, California
26 June 2016

Niko Zinovii

The Fall of Man

Year: 18,016 A.D.

Kal disconnected the safety cord from his belt as he carefully hopped off the moving sidewalk, feeling the need to momentarily step aside from the crowd in order to collect his thoughts, to try to analyze the troubling sense of unease that he felt rising in his intellect.

For a time he just stood there, staring blankly at the other pedestrians, at his fellow citizens moving to and fro. Everyone, like himself, was of medium height, narrow shouldered, slender, blond. In stature, musculature, body frame, both sexes appeared nearly identical, almost epicene. There was the visible distinction of the slight bulge of female breasts. And in general the faces of the women did present as a bit softer, projecting a subtle note of deeper femininity. But there was almost no masculinity evident in the men...

As a scholar, as a historian of very early man, Kal found himself momentarily wondering what it must have been like to have lived as a man 20,000 or so years ago, when there was such a pronounced difference between the sexes, physically and in temperament. When men were so very different from women: bearded, belligerent, daring...

But we are a content people... Kal told himself softly. And he nodded in approval of the strikingly healthy glow of those moving past him, at their universal look of youth and vitality. *And we have no worries. No concerns. Well, not until yesterday…*

Sighing, he gave a little shrug, straightened his clothing—a comfortable pastel, unisex jumpsuit, worn by all—and looked up at the breathtakingly beautiful towers and spires of the spectacular emerald metropolis surrounding him. As always, his eyes swelled with wonder and appreciation for humankind's achievements and promise.

It was a wonder absent in the eyes of his fellow citizens. But he realized that it was because of his vocation, of his unique learning, that he saw things differently than others. Sometimes, during moments of intense contemplation, he felt more akin to a time traveler from the distant past than a citizen of Thiopolis, the second of Earth's five cities. He understood that a society was composed of the personalities that it created, that people were unconsciously trained how to act, think, and feel, in order for all to share a similar and compatible personality pattern. People adapted their personalities to their culture and to technology, culture changing and adapting to the natural environment, to discovery, ideology, and to changing human physiology…

Kal's thoughts fell silent, and he looked to the omnipresent state media screens. All were reporting on yesterday's shocking, unexpected death, announcing that the formal open-casket viewing would commence at midday today. The viewing would continue for the next ten days—or longer if necessary—to allow all citizens the opportunity to pay their respects. Viewing would be by assigned number. Kal reached into his pocket and withdrew a small ticket. His number was 2,434.

As Kal walked off, he wondered if, due to yesterday's tragic death, changes to the leadership of the city's Grand Council might already be underway. And what the repercussions might be…

"Robot!" he called out to a slender, metallic machine with an expressionless silver faceplate. "A travel pod, please."

The robot summoned one. A translucent sphere arrived moments later, approaching silently, gliding along one of the city's many monorail lines. Kal climbed into the bubble and strapped the safety harness securely about his torso.

"Thank you." He nodded politely to the robot, and the pod automatically rolled off at a safe twenty kilometers per hour.

Leaning back in his seat, Kal closed his eyes and thought again of the remote past. Ramesses the Great, the third pharaoh of the Nineteenth Dynasty of ancient Egypt, had been buried in a lavishly decorated tomb in the Valley of the Kings. At the entranceway, there was the glorious image of the sun, flanked by paintings of goddesses and lily plants. The corridors, halls, and burial chamber held beautiful scenes reserved for pharaohs and nobility, images of deities and sacred canopic jars, guarded by the goddesses Isis and Nephthys. It must have been overwhelmingly lovely. Such splendor. While an Egyptian commoner was wrapped in a plain cloth and simply buried out in the desert…

And what of Thiopolis's pending burial? Kal wondered as he opened his eyes. *What will it be like?*

There was a series of slight bumps as Kal's pod reached the city's periphery and rolled across the larger rail lines that connected Thiopolis to her sister cities of Enopolis, Triopolis, Teseropolis, and Pendopolis. He could see a long transport rolling away, heading off to the west, to Triopolis, moving not much faster than his bubble.

And Kal's troubling unease returned, and he suddenly realized that his growing mental discomfort was intimately linked to how he had come to view his civilization, and to yesterday's unfortunate death. He found his psyche aching dully with apprehension.

As the travel pod left the city proper, Kal sat up, surprised by the sight of the thousands upon thousands of citizens, aligned one behind another in five separate queues stretching out across the grassy free space surrounding Thiopolis, heading out toward a distant ceremonial mound reserved for today's dedicated viewing.

Kal looked at his ticket again. It was a low number, due to his privileged status as an educator. He could continue to ride his bubble for some time yet, likely to near the mound itself, where the rail came to an end.

Halfway there, Kal's sphere automatically stopped, and he disembarked, stepping aside as two robots performed a routine safety check on the pod. Kal immediately looked opposite the mound, to view his city's cosmodromio and its first interplanetary spaceship. His eyes swelled with amazed admiration as he focused upon the gleaming rocket, which rose taller than any of Thiopolis's shining emerald towers. Kal nodded his head gently in approval as he felt in his heart just how extraordinary and marvelous the craft was. It was more than a technological achievement—it was a symbol of humankind's greatness and a reminder of humanity's unique potential. After being earthbound for untold millennia, men and women were finally again looking to the stars.

Kal thought of how many times he had taken travel pods out to this very spot, just to watch from afar the construction of the spacecraft, in the heat of the summer, in the rain, in the snow, even under gentle moonlight.

"You may proceed," one of the robots interrupted Kal's reverie.

"Oh," he responded, "yes, thank you."

As Kal rolled away, his euphoria slowly dissipated and was replaced by a subtle nervousness. He searched his mind for what he knew about the capacity to influence human behavior and the forces that drove people to reach out for various human potentialities… His people stood today at a unique threshold, for nearly every human and societal need, drive, and urge was sufficiently satisfied. They had no need for group and individual security, as war had been abolished centuries ago and personal violence was unheard of. The state's simplified political structure organized all interpersonal power relationships in a manner that curtailed the rise of any institutional self-interest. Material wealth was fairly proportioned in an incentive-based system to all citizens. The need for companionship was easily met, for Thiopolis had a population of over one million like-minded citizens. Science satiated the populous's intellectual need for understanding, and men and women drew psychological certainty from humankind's vast body of accumulated knowledge. They rationally understood what they could influence and what they could not. And their great spaceship now promised them the horizon.

Kal's travel pod stopped, having reached the end of its rail. He smiled as he noticed Lasha in the second line over, and he quickly made his way over to her. As he approached, she held up her ticket. She was number 2,435. Kal displayed his number to her with a mischievous smile: 2,434.

They kissed lightly on the lips, gently held hands, and then turned forward, focusing with genuine empathy on the grassy mound that loomed before them. Golden steps led up to a golden platform, upon which lay a single ivory casket adorned with bouquets of flowers. The coffin was open, and one by one the citizens of Thiopolis ascended those golden steps to momentarily stand before the casket to pay their respects.

"Kal?" Lasha asked, noticing the unusual concern etched upon his countenance.

But he merely shook his head slightly, withholding any explanation.

It was twilight by the time it was their turn to ascend the steps, which they did together. Kal felt a bit fatigued as he reached the top, where he straightened himself to stand there before the open casket. Having Lasha there at his side, still holding his hand, helped to mollify the unease that he felt as he looked down at the deceased. It was a man, an unfamiliar man with a kind face and soft golden hair. All in all an unremarkable-looking man. In fact, the deceased was not that unlike Kal himself in general appearance.

Kal looked off to the side, at the coffin's nameplate.

"Jon Day," Kal read the name aloud. He then turned about to look back at the lines of citizens extending all the way back to their fantastic emerald city. Many were now holding flickering, electronic candles in the dimming light of the setting sun. It was an awe-inspiring sight. All of these people turning out to pay their respects to a man probably only a handful of them had actually known. And this procession was being broadcast globally, to all five of Earth's cities. Everyone was watching, all humanity mourning.

Kal felt his psyche reel, and the world wobbled for him as he thought of how until yesterday, due to advances in science, no one on Earth had died in over 500 years… Aging had been stopped centuries ago. All diseases had long ago been eradicated, cured. Microscopic machines swam through their bodies, protecting and enhancing their health. Almost any physical damage to the body could be repaired. But there were still some rarities beyond the influence of their science…

So tragic, Kal thought. And more, it was such a stark reminder to all of them of their own still-fragile mortality.

It was as Kal was about to descend those golden steps that he heard the sound of his innermost fears manifest into reality. Mouth agape, he turned to view his city's cosmodromio. From the distance, silhouetted against the final waning rays of the setting sun, he could see robots beginning to disassemble the rocket.

"No…" he mumbled weakly. "No…"

Humankind's near conquest of death had ended all war, allowing for utopia to be realized, but at a price, for it also produced a careful populace, wary of risk. And a leadership that required but one small reminder of the vulnerable reality of life and death.

Kal's towering spaceship was suddenly stillborn, and coming apart before his eyes. He felt as if he were viewing humankind from the vantage point of the distant past, of some bygone age, looking forward through time and seeing a progeny that stood frozen, stunned by death and too afraid to truly live, voluntarily giving up their distinguishing need and urge to go to the horizon…

And Kal looked up at the rising moon, and he began to cry. For he understood all too well that as long as the human species was limited to its cradle, to Earth, it was doomed to face eventual extinction. And the promise of man would forever vanish from the universe.

Kal collapsed to his knees, sobbing at the bitter irony: the fall of one man had led to the fall of man.

A Note from the Author

This author hopes the reader found this short and simple utopian tale of the far future interesting.

Science has speculated in recent years that due to the reduction of cultural barriers and the increased ease of global relocation, the future human population of Earth may likely become physically homogenized toward dark hair and light brown skin. This story took the opposite approach, assuming some event(s) occurred during the 16,000-year span between the present day and the story's future setting, reducing Earth's population, bottlenecking it down to experience a founder's effect leading to an all-Caucasian, blond human population. The future is usually what is not expected.

The typical utopian look of the futuristic city of Thiopolis, with its gleaming towers, moving sidewalks, benign robots, and pod transports, was purposely selected by the author over something uniquely imaginative.

In conclusion, this author asks the reader to consider that 99% of all the species that have ever existed on Earth are now extinct. Due to various factors, extinction is the norm. Also, our fragile Earth will only be habitable for approximately another 2.3 billion years, after which it will be too hot to sustain life, due to the increasing luminosity that will be generated by the life cycle of our sun. If the human race does not colonize space, dispersing itself throughout our solar system and beyond, it will eventually face certain extinction.

Niko Zinovii
Santa Monica, California
22 August 2016

The Fall of Man

Niko Zinovii

The Isle of Pan

~1~

Midnight. The South Pacific, 260 nautical miles east-southeast of Suva, Fiji:

John David, polished, sophisticated, thoughtful, found himself slowly walking the main deck of the deep-sea cable-laying vessel *SS Venture*. Tired but unable to sleep, he strode the ship in an attempt to relax his mind. The sea was exceptionally calm, the night lit by the waxing moon. In the dimness, John could sense the full 324-foot length of the craft, due to the navigation lights fore and aft, port and starboard, and he drew some comfort from this, being able to distinguish the physical boundaries of the *Venture*. It steadied him, for he was far from home and surrounded by the unsettling vastness of the open sea.

Midship, John found himself slowing and stopping near the metal monstrosity that was the ship's cable-laying cage. Standing there gentlemanly, in silence, he slowly surrendered his mind to the rising discontent that lay in his heart, and his intelligent, soulful eyes turned inward, reflecting his solemn thoughts. At forty years of age, he was living the kind of life that he had thought he always desired: one of travel, intellectual fulfillment. He was distinguished in his profession. He had achieved international recognition. He had financial security. In these respects he was comfortable, at ease, but still there was that emotional restlessness stirring deep within him...

His rather solitary life of sojourning was stitched together by a single thread: his search for the ideal. For years he had hunted for perfection in man's past, immersing himself in archaeological digs in the Aegean, around the rim of the Mediterranean. Examining ancient fragments of pottery, art, unearthing long-forgotten settlements. Inquisitively peering backward through the veil of time, scrutinizing the lives and beliefs of those long gone. Disillusioned, he had recently turned his back on the past and found himself wandering... alone again.

John suddenly felt very lonely, very desolate, and rather friendless.

A soft hooting sound interrupted his troubled, weary thoughts. It was coming from nearby, from within the ship's cable-laying cage. For a moment John had no idea what the sound could be, but then he remembered.

"Oh, the gorillas," John said aloud in a cultured accent, his voice rich and resonant, unusually pleasing in timbre.

And John carefully stepped toward the three-story-tall cage, its circumference spanning nearly the full beam of the ship. In the moonlight he could see that the structure had recently been converted into a series of separate internal enclosures. It looked akin to an enormous aviary, but within this giant cage, rather than birds, there were nearly a hundred mountain gorillas, most sleeping soundly in the darkness.

A solitary female gorilla had her large head gently pressed up against the bars. Her flat nose and nostrils widened as she curiously sniffed the sea air while hooting meekly to John.

"You can't sleep either?" John asked compassionately, his calm, mellifluous voice settling the ape somewhat. And then John's eyes met the gorilla's, and a thoughtful sadness slowly palled his dignified, handsome features.

The intimate moment dissolved as John heard the sound of approaching footsteps, soft footsteps. Out of the darkness stepped a slender, blond-maned woman, her hair falling in magnificent, tousled cascades. John felt himself a bit startled by the striking beauty of the woman. It was as if he could intimately feel her femininity, her sexuality.

"The cage is difficult and unpleasant," she said softly, in a caring voice, as she stepped up to him, "but it's necessary for the transport."

"Actually," John responded thoughtfully, looking back at the gorilla, his suave voice like velvet, "I was thinking about how loneliness can take so many forms. You can be with your own kind, and still feel alone..."

Surprise lifted and dropped on the woman's lips, in her eyes.

"It's strange," John went on, pulled further into the moment by his intellect, "I can look upon a fish or a deer rather dispassionately, even a horse, but when I see a chimpanzee or a gorilla, there are differences to be sure, but there's also far too much that's like me, and I find that I can't build a wall in my mind that places these primates and myself on opposite sides. Somehow I get the feeling that we're both sitting on the top of that wall, facing opposite directions but nevertheless perched up there together."

"You have a sensitive mind," she responded slowly, her tone appreciative.

And John felt it again, her allure. He also sensed a kindness, a gentleness, in her that he found very appealing.

"You're not a member of the crew, are you?" she asked him. "In Suva we picked up a writer..."

"John David," he introduced himself, offering his hand, which she shook. "Actually I'm an archaeologist, a historian. I haven't written anything in some time."

"Talent can't be turned off for a writer," she commented slowly, eyeing him anew.

"And you're Dr. Evans?" John asked. "The primatologist I was told about?"

"Helena, please." She nodded. "We're transporting these three troops of gorillas to Fatu Hiva, an island six hundred fifty miles northeast of Tahiti."

"In the Marquesas Islands."

"Yes, that's right," she affirmed. "There are fewer than five hundred mountain gorillas remaining in the wild today. They're a critically endangered species. Our sponsors purchased Fatu Hiva, resettling its three villages onto the neighboring islands. We have the entire island to colonize with these gorillas, to offer them a sanctuary. We've spent the past five years planting the mountain slopes with gallium vines, wild celery, bamboo, thistle, bedstraw, senecio trees, all the vegetation the gorillas feed on in their natural habitat. Monsanto was very helpful in developing and adapting certain vegetation for the project."

"Ape Island?" John smiled politely.

"Still Fatu Hiva." She smiled back in a soft, lovely manner. "But our conservation post has been officially named Beringei, after the subspecies classification: *Gorilla beringei beringei*, the mountain gorilla."

John suddenly found himself wanting to share future moments of his mind with her. He imagined lying in a hammock with her, holding her, and speaking to her softly of distant thunder, distant rain.

"You're very lovely," he heard himself compliment her, charmingly.

"Thank you," she responded humbly, yet with appreciation, "but I think I may be an illusion to you. The pretty girl who is also the scientist."

"Scientists don't believe in illusions," he countered.

"You're not being very scientific," she kept the ball in play.

"But the heart of science is truth. Although all the men who have ever lived and died on this Earth did so in a world of illusions."

And she stopped to consider the deeper meaning hidden in his esoteric words.

They both turned to a rather ordinary-looking man, fortyish, who stepped out of the darkness. "Ah, I thought I heard voices out here," the man said, his smooth, confident tone carrying a hint of intellectual arrogance. "I'm Doctor Alan Neville," the man introduced himself, subtly eyeing how close John was standing to Helena. "I see you've met *my* colleague, Helena."

"Alan," Helena introduced John, "this is John David. He boarded in Fiji."

"Ah," Alan reacted, his voice tinged with cynicism. "Doctor John David, the archaeologist? Author of *The Dehumanized Man?*"

"Yes." John nodded, courteously.

"He who fights the future," Alan admonished, "has a dangerous enemy."

"Well…" John responded calmly, respectfully defending his work, "I can't help recognizing that modern man is being swept along in a stream of things that give rise to other things, at such a pace that no inward stability has been achieved."

"But the future is what we have invited," Alan retorted. "The forces that science have unleashed are inevitable forces beyond human control. Most are rushing to eagerly embrace the future, and yet you fear that man has no future?"

"It's not that I fear that man has no future," John coolly corrected Alan, remaining well mannered. "It's the nature of the future that I find numbing. Modern man is so dangerously close to bringing into existence a type of man who has less time alone than any man before him, so little opportunity to explore his own thoughts. He sits quiescently before a flickering screen while his cultural world dissolves. So he individually develops a superficial philosophy to carry himself over the surface of life. Soon he'll no longer think in the old terms. What has the family been reduced to? What will love be reduced to? Will man soon dispense even with art—and with man as we know him, as such art has made him?"

"One can't live in the past," Alan responded rather bluntly, a bit unprepared for John's intellectual depth and eloquence, for John's engaging, beautifully modulated voice which had the ability to color words. "Progress requires endless adaptation. Evolution demands it."

"But we've abandoned our past without realizing that without the past the pursued future has no meaning, it leads to—"

"—the dehumanized man?"

John nodded sincerely, his countenance reflecting that of idealism incarnate. "There must be another road into the future, a better path to tomorrow. One that embraces our past as we step forward. If a people don't embrace their history… well, they'll lose the ability to properly imagine what is indeed possible in the time ahead. And desirable."

"The past is prologue." Alan nodded with concealed appreciation, staring at John for a long moment, studying him. As he did so, a rather mysterious, nebulous fog rolled in across the deck, engulfing them, the flow of mist coming from the ship's bow.

"We seem to be moving into a fog bank," John observed.

"Alan," Helena said, "it's late. John must be tired. We're all tired."

"Wait," Alan responded, his focus still on John. "I seem to recall reading that you recently abandoned archaeology?"

"In a sense, yes."

"And yet you rank the past so importantly," Alan noted. "Before Fiji, you were traveling from where? If you don't mind my asking."

"Bhutan," John answered openly.

"A land struggling with the future..." Alan remarked. "An isolated mountain kingdom trying to remain forever locked in its traditional, past state..."

John had no response to offer.

"You're getting off at Papeete?" Alan asked.

"Yes," John nodded. "In Tahiti."

"Helena," Alan's smooth voice trickled critically. "I think I understand him now. I was once like him... An idealist. He couldn't find man's inner stability in the ruins of the past, so now he's looking for some lost garden, some Shangri-La, tucked away here in the present, in some lost corner of the world. To escape the future."

John made no reply. He suddenly felt quite fatigued and even a bit lost. It was true; from the fragments of past cultures he had found no ideal place of perfection and harmony. No vanished setting where his heart could imaginatively settle. He was indeed now rather desperately fleeing from man's modern world, yes, in search of a utopia. Where everything was for the best. Where he could truly live, where he could simply stand there in the middle of it all and feel that he was there, part of it. Part of something better, something different. Alan was correct. Only John had not fully realized this until now. It had taken a stranger to point it out to him.

John wobbled on his feet and stuck out his arms to balance himself. For a second he thought that it was only him, but then he caught Helena, preventing her from falling, while Alan stumbled on his own feet and tumbled to his hands and knees.

John then felt the vibrations in the deck, the terrible rumbling beneath his feet, accompanied by the dampened sound of a tremendous grating of steel. It was an awful sound, one that assailed the ears and portended something utterly disastrous.

"My God," Alan announced it, "we're running aground!"

Finally, after what seemed an eternity, although it lasted but the span of tens of seconds, the rumbling stopped, as did the ship. Alarms began to sound, and lights and sailors flooded the main deck in a mad commotion.

"My plants!" Alan uttered, and he rose and ran off.

"The hold is filled with second-generation vegetation," Helena explained quickly. "For transplant to Fatu Hiva. Alan's our botanist."

She then rushed off into the fog, circling the converted cable-laying cage, responding maternally to the ruckus being made by her awakened, panicking gorillas.

John was about to go after her when he felt something odd. It made every hair on his body stand on end. It was something in the air, a sudden change. It made him shiver. It made his mind ache. His senses suddenly felt infringed upon. Then he heard the whisper of an echoing voice calling out to him, seemingly from somewhere out at sea, out in the fog, off the port side of the *Venture*.

"Hear me," the voice called.

Startled, John stood unmoving, doubting what he had heard. Had he really heard it? It seemed almost as if he had instead *felt* it, in his mind. He tried to shake his head clear. Then, once more the strange voice called:

"Hear me."

John peered off into the fog, but he saw no one. Yet he felt absolutely compelled to respond.

122

"I hear you…" John answered, carefully.

"Tell the world that I am still alive," the voice whispered. Then there was a moment of complete silence, before the commotion of the sailors jarred John's senses back to a normal state.

He bumped into Helena.

"Did you hear that…" he began to ask, only to realize by the look in her eyes that she had heard nothing.

He noticed a deck officer, and he took Helena by the hand, following the sailor through the fog, up to the ship's bridge.

John entered the bridge with Helena to find the ship's deck officer, chief officer, and chief engineer assembling around the captain, who was receiving oral reports from other officers and crew who were rushing in and out of the room.

"Captain?" John asked in a concerned but civil tone.

The captain held up a hand, signaling them to wait. Finally, he turned more to Helena than to John:

"We seem to have run aground on a submerged coral reef," the captain answered. "There is no danger of sinking, but it appears that we're hopelessly stuck."

"How could this happen?" Helena asked.

"An uncharted reef," the captain explained, leaning over a large map, pointing out their location. "Our last recorded position, just before we encountered the fog, was here, latitude -18° 05' 28" S, longitude -175° 53' 15" W. As you can see, there's nothing here. Nothing for a hundred nautical miles in any direction!"

"You'll be radioing for assistance?" John asked.

The captain turned to the ship's second officer, who responded, "There's, um, some type of unusual interference. We can't transmit or receive…"

John watched Helena pull out her cell phone. No signal.

"Compass is also spinning like a top," the ship's chief officer added, bewildered. "Some type of magnetic disturbance."

"But even without transmitting an S.O.S.," John asked, "there will be a search for us, after we fail to arrive in Papeete as scheduled?"

"Due to weather," the captain responded, his voice level yet severe, "we were forced to deviate from our registered course. This course change went unanswered in Suva."

"So…" John took a second to put it together, speaking with extraordinary aplomb. "Nobody knows where we are?"

"Nobody," the captain confirmed.

At that moment a seagull flapped past the bridge's huge forward windows and then disappeared back into the fog.

"A gull?" the captain queried. "This far out at sea?"

A sailor, brandishing binoculars, rushed into the bridge. "Captain," he said. "Off the port side. A few hundred yards north of this reef, *an island…*"

~ 2 ~

At daybreak:

John, Helena, and Alan, along with a dozen sailors, were slowly lowered toward the lagoon in two lifeboats. The ship's chief officer was heading the landing party, the captain and other officers remaining on board the *Venture*.

As John's lifeboat jerked downward, he was able to see that the full length of the *Venture* was resting atop a wide, flat coral reef, which lay perhaps eight to ten feet beneath the surface of the sea.

"This is the damnedest fog…" Alan commented, perplexed.

And John took notice of the peculiar fact that the fog hung stationary atop the submerged reef, which appeared to completely encircle the mystery island. It was the oddest sight, the wall of mist, this fog that would not dissipate. It must have extended miles out to sea in every direction. Yet the lagoon within the reef was clear of any cloud cover, the sun sparkling resplendently off its translucent, tropical water.

But directly above the central island, there again floated the odd fog, immobile, hanging vaporously over the land, thin enough to allow the penetration of sunlight yet substantial enough to conceal the island from any aerial or satellite imaging. It was suddenly quite clear to John as to why this island was not on any map.

"I don't understand…" Helena commented, mystified. "What could possibly cause cloud condensation only over this reef and the island?"

"It's almost as if the island is…" John started but then stopped.

"As if the island is what?" Alan asked critically, challenging if John had any enlightenment to offer.

"I was going to say," John offered his thought unabashed, his resonant voice beautifully modulated, "it's as if the island is purposely… hidden."

There was a loud splash, the lifeboat rocked, and the three of them grabbed hold. As the boat steadied, it was disconnected from the winch lines, and sailors began to row.

John looked off across the lagoon at the cloud-shrouded island and wondered what awaited them. Helena pointed out something in the water. Dolphins. The pod surfaced and separated, playfully accompanying the lifeboats. The dolphins were small, sleek yet robust, and so beautifully, boldly colored.

John felt his rising smile drop almost immediately as he realized: "They're Mediterranean common dolphins…"

John had encountered this particular dolphin species so frequently during his time spent in the Aegean. He had swum with them. Played with them. He had grown to love them.

Their distinct bright coloration, the complex, crisscrossing hourglass pattern, the distinctive yellow panel along the flank, it was all unmistakably familiar to him. And so intimately was this type of dolphin connected to his investigation of the past. So often had they been recorded in Greek and Roman art and literature. They had a long history with man.

"*Delphinus delphis*," John added. "The short-beaked common dolphin. The classical Geek dolphin. The colors, the size, it's unmistakable—they're smaller than their Atlantic and Pacific cousins."

"But… what are they doing here?" Helena asked softly.

John simply shrugged, baffled. He had absolutely no idea what this species of marine mammal was doing so far from its natural range, hidden away in this uncharted lagoon, but he enjoyed seeing them. He smiled and then turned his eyes to the unmapped island, to the verdant, hilly mountain that rose up out of the sea where no island was supposed to be.

He could see the shore now, an idyllic, pristine stretch of sandy beach, gold and pink in color, shaded by lofty palm trees lazily leaning out over the lagoon. And behind the palms—

"*Pinus brutia*," Alan identified the medium-sized pine trees. "The Turkish pine. Native to the eastern Mediterranean…"

John lifted his own small pair of binoculars to his eyes. He could see the deep fissures at the wide base of the pines, in the thick orange-red bark. Within the yellowish-green needles hung stout, heavy cones, some green, others glossy red-brown. And behind these pine trees, growing up the craggy hillside, silvery-green, short and squat, trunks gnarled and twisted:

"Olive trees…" John said aloud, in disbelief. "On a tropical island?"

"Look," Allan pointed out. "Cyprus and oak."

Alan then pointed farther inland, to where, growing higher up the slopes, there was a great forest of huge, glaucous blue-green conifers standing over a hundred feet in height.

"Cedars?" Helena guessed.

"Lebanon cedar," Alan narrowed the distinction. "*Cedrus libani*, native to the mountains of the Mediterranean…"

Then all three fell silent, for they noticed something quite peculiar, a large greenish-brown pipe of odd design. It ran up out of the sea, stretched across the beach, and disappeared into the foliage. There was another farther down the shoreline. And another, and another, all spaced apart by several hundred feet. They appeared to encircle the island.

The pipes were clearly manmade. Yet the island showed no sign of habitation, at least not on this particular stretch of coastline.

The lifeboat ran ashore, jarring John, Helena, and Alan out of their puzzled state. Sailors went over the sides, splashing, dragging the boats up the beach. John felt himself step up and drop down into warm, knee-deep water. Immediately he made his way over to the incongruous pipe.

The pipe was huge; the top of it rose several feet above John's head, even though half of its circumference was sunken into the sand. Its diameter must have been in excess of twenty feet. The lagoon's water was uncomfortably cold near the pipe. John reached out and placed a hand upon its bumpy, metal surface, only to withdraw it quickly.

"It's cold," he explained to Helena, who had stepped up to his side.

"Like the water here…" Alan added as he positioned himself between John and Helena. "Next to the pipe…"

And all three were silent for a long moment, overcome by the strangeness of the pipe's appearance. Up close it looked rather uncanny, otherworldly.

The ship's chief officer was next to move up from behind. At once he visually scrutinized the greenish-brown surface of the pipe. "The color—this pipe, I think it's a copper-nickel alloy."

"A copper-nickel alloy, why?" Alan asked.

"Seawater leaves copper-nickel alloys practically intact," the chief officer explained. "The color of it, it's an oxide film that forms over time on the copper's surface. Stops further corrosion. The film gets thicker over the years."

The officer leaned forward, examining the pipe even more closely. He touched it, rubbed it, scraped it. "This must be really old," he added, puzzled.

"How old?" John asked in his cultured, calm voice.

"I'd guess… ancient," the officer answered, bewildered.

"Ancient?" Alan retorted. "But that doesn't make any sense."

"Neither does the flora of this island," Helena reminded him.

"Copper alloy artifacts," John interjected, "have been recovered in nearly pristine condition after having been buried for thousands of years…"

"What are you suggesting?" Alan asked sharply, his intellectual hackles raised by the seemingly absurd implications of John's statement.

"What could it used be for?" Helena asked the chief officer.

"Cold water intake?" the officer guessed. "Copper alloys provide superior thermal conductivity. These alloys are widely used for marine hardware: seawater supply lines, condensers, heat exchangers… You know, in a way, the coldness, it reminds me of an intake pipe of an OTEC plant, like the one in Hawaii."

"OTEC?" Helena asked.

"Ocean thermal energy conversion." Alan's confident voice went soft as he identified the acronym to Helena, taking the opportunity to display to her his breadth of knowledge.

"Yes, that's right," the officer confirmed. "It's a system that takes advantage of the difference between warmer surface water within the tropics and colder deep-ocean water to drive a turbine, to produce electricity. Maybe this island is a clandestine test location of some corporation?"

And the officer splashed off to join his sailors up on the beach. Alan followed, guiding Helena through the gentle waves.

John stayed behind for a few moments, wondering about the unusual pipe, about the unknown technology that it represented. He found himself thinking of the fictional castaways who had arrived on Jules Verne's *Mysterious Island*, fated to meet the self-exiled Captain Nemo. *And who is awaiting us on this island? Whose island are we trespassing on?* John heard himself asking, thinking back to the voice he had thought he heard calling out to him late last night...

As John stepped out of the sea onto the beach, looking up at the out-of-place Mediterranean flora, he noticed at once the heavenly, dreamlike quality of the island's air. Every whisper of breeze carried upon it the perfume of new blossoms, the spicy, resinous scent of cedar, of pine. Under the relative coolness of the white, misty cloud cover, John felt as if he were breathing eternal spring. He truly felt as if he had set foot onto another world. So completely different was this place from a normal hot, humid, sand and coral and palm-fronded South Seas isle. Classical dolphins, olive trees—a goat!

John ran to the landing party, where Helena had her hand outstretched to an approaching goat. It was a Vlahiki goat, the indigenous goat of Greece: small, hardy, with short legs, an adaptation to the Mediterranean's steep, rocky terrain.

As John stood there, staring at the goat, a man stepped out of the foliage and walked toward them, following the hoofprints made in the sand. The man was Caucasian, gray haired; he looked to be in his mid-sixties. His features were quite handsome, distinctive. He had a profile that could have been stamped upon an old Roman coin. His hair was curled in an interesting style, held in place by scented wax. He was barefoot, wearing a light, loose-fitting white tunic made from large squares of cloth pinned at the shoulders and belted about the waist, the traditional garb of ancient Greece.

The man placed a caring hand upon his goat and stood there, statuesque, before the *Venture*'s landing party—calm, appearing affable, alert yet completely at ease, projecting an image of intelligent, refined austerity.

John saw the man's eyes widen as he noticed the *Venture*, shrouded by mist, stuck out on the island's reef. In a stately manner, the man pointed out to the reef and politely asked in ancient Greek:

"You are from another world?"

"From across the sea," John answered in ancient Greek, a language that he had learned as part of his study of classical archeology. It was only then that John realized the voice that had called to him last night, the voice he had felt in his mind, had spoken to him in ancient Greek. But it was not the voice of this man...

The man looked at John incredulously and then spoke for a time. When he finished, he smiled, graciously, and motioned with an open hand toward the island.

"He's speaking in ancient Greek?" Alan half asked, half stated.

"Yes," John answered, unable to resist the subtle taunt: "You don't speak Greek?"

"No," Alan replied sharply, defensively, "Latin."

"Never mind that," the ship's chief officer interrupted coolly. "What's he saying?"

"His name is Agathon," John answered, his pleasing voice richly coloring his words. "He doesn't believe that we came from across the 'sea of waves.' His worldview is that the sea is endless. Beyond the sea there is only more sea. Forever. He says that we must have come from a *star*... Across the 'sea of darkness.' That the journey must have been long and difficult. That we must be tired and hungry. He welcomes us to *Arcadia*... as his honored guests, and he asks us to follow him to his village. Their settlement is inland. Living on the shore is forbidden."

~ 3 ~

John walked alongside Agathon. Helena and Alan kept pace behind him, followed by the *Venture*'s chief officer and half of his landing party—the other sailors having been left behind on the beach to guard the lifeboats.

John asked Agathon about the island's name, Arcadia, for the name stirred in John a feeling of hope. To him it represented an ideal, an earthly paradise. Arcadia had been a unique region of ancient Greece. It had lain in the central highlands of the Peloponnese, isolated ¡by mountains, uninfluenced by the outside world. Farmers and shepherds had lived there peacefully, in simplicity, in their fertile valleys and fields... until the Romans invaded.

"Our land," Agathon answered John quite seriously, "has always been named Arcadia. In honor of Arcas, son of Zeus and Callisto. Arcas was one of our early kings. And our greatest hunter."

John felt himself smile ever so slightly, completely surprised by the response, which invoked mythology as if it were fact.

The path narrowed as the growth of pines thickened and Agathon stepped ahead of John, taking the lead. The goat brushed by John, passing him. John noticed the animal's thick coat, which protected it from harsh weather. He wondered how severe, in terms of coldness, the weather on a tropical isle could possibly become.

The path turned and began to run alongside the strange pipe from the sea, which continued inland. John felt a chill in the air as they walked alongside the pipe. He noticed smaller pipes branching off from this main one and disappearing down into the ground. He thought about the cold seawater running through the pipeline (if the chief officer was correct in his guess of the pipe's function). How it must have chilled the surrounding soil. He wondered if the temperature difference between the roots in the cool soil and the leaves above in the warmer air might create something akin to microclimates. Might this explain how the temperate flora they had observed could survive and flourish in the tropics?

John momentarily glanced up at the misty cloud cover hanging stationary above the island, and he wondered if it too might somehow be produced artificially. Surely the fog was not delivered by the winds. It had to have an insular origin.

The forest thinned and opened up to a series of fields and wooded hillsides. They passed great old trees that were marked for felling. High above, men, similar in look to Agathon but young and dark-haired, were removing birds chirping in their nests. John asked Agathon about this, and Agathon described to John how the nests, handled with care, were to be placed in the branches of younger trees. Out of respect for the birds.

John caught the pleasant, bucolic smell of straw and old stables. Horses suddenly passed by, each with its rider—and behind them, skylarks followed. Nearby, disturbed from the fields by farming men, beautifully colored birds flew off toward the village that lay still ahead of them. Within nearby tea flowers, little sparrows played hide-and-seek. A cicada sang out, loud in the pine, the noontime heat never arriving under the mysterious, ethereal cloud cover. It was all remarkably lovely.

John found himself glancing back at Helena, who smiled at him.

They passed well-cared-for donkeys and mules, leisurely drinking water from troughs alongside the fields. John could see barely, beans, and lentils growing in profusion, as were cucumbers, onions, and garlic, almonds and walnuts. There were groves of fruit trees: apples, pears, and pomegranates. All non-tropical vegetation. Vines grew everywhere, and grapes were being crushed underfoot in giant vats to make wine. Shepherds and sheep dotted the hillsides, where olive trees grew wild. Agathon's goat ran off to rejoin its freely wandering herd.

Between the fields, great windmills with wonderful feather-shaped blades turned slowly and steadily in the breeze, providing energy to pump water, to irrigate the land.

John felt a state of mental calm descending upon him. The unfolding pastoral landscape was one of peace, the absence of complexity, the natural world embraced harmoniously and revered.

Agathon waved to men dressed as he as the landing party began to walk by attractive single-story houses built of coral, stone, and clay, the roofs tiled or covered by palm fronds. Like Agathon, these men kept their hair curled and carefully arranged, held in place by waxes and lotions. They looked aristocratic, yet they were men who worked the soil with their hands.

The women were lovely. Their colored tunics went down to their ankles, unlike the plain-white, knee-length garb of the men, and they wore their hair long, kept either in braids or ponytails, simple and unpretentious.

Children ran along barefoot, as walked most of the men. The women wore leather sandals. All appeared unusually healthy, physically and mentally at ease, spiritually content. Their outlook presented as carefree, optimistic, and remarkably happy.

Helena pointed up to a kite entangled in a gnarled tree. As she did so, a young boy ran up to John, tearfully tugging on one of John's pant legs, begging him to pick the full moon from the daytime sky and give it to him, in place of his lost kite.

The boy's mother soon appeared, apologized, and disciplined her son by tying him to the nearby tree. "The breeze will cool him down," she said to John with a smile.

And John looked back, concerned, but he saw that the child was already clapping his hands and playing happily beneath the shade of the tree.

They entered the village's center by way of a beautiful paved promenade, lined by colonnades of coral. Behind these pillars rose a wall decorated with painted images of nature in its most beautiful moods: the sea enlivened with fish and sparkling sunlight, wild flowers, birds, and deer of the countryside. There were also images of idealized human figures happily partaking in the mundane yet welcomed responsibilities of everyday life.

The public square was immense. It was left natural, carpeted by comfortable grass. Beyond it lay a grand theater open to the sky and several large earthen mounds topped by towers of white rock, temples of coral, and altars decorated with polished mother-of-pearl.

Behind the village center towered a lofty and beautiful array of copper panels. Shaped like gigantic petals, these solar cells were opened like blooming flowers, leaning toward the hazy sun, glowing dimly, converting solar radiation into electricity.

John stopped and stood there motionless, speechless. He wondered if it were all real. The village and its surroundings presented as possessing the technology needed to afford the comforts of modernity, while simultaneously being locked in the distant, timeless past. But more, Arcadia presented as a microcosm of an idyllic earlier time, of a bucolic utopian past state of living that had never truly existed. Yet this all did appear to exist. Here in the present. Hidden away on this remote, unknown South Seas island.

"How can this be?" John asked aloud, his voice a reverent whisper.

~ 4 ~

Hours later:

As John walked away from the impossible village and started up the nearby hillside, he glanced back to see Helena watching him leave, her magnificent, tousled hair glowing golden in the dimmed, ethereal sunlight. For a moment he deeply regretted not having asked her to accompany him, especially when he saw Alan stepping up to stand there at her side. But he had so much weighing so heavily upon his mind. He needed to surrender to the overwhelming urge he felt to simply be alone with his thoughts.

Agathon and the other elders of Arcadia's thriving community had provided a generous lunch for John, Helena, Alan, and the *Venture*'s chief officer and accompaniment of sailors. With an affable, calm politeness, the elders answered the many questions put forth by the landing party, all translated through John. Despite the honest answers provided by the elders, the origin of Arcadia remained a mystery.

The Arcadians appeared to genuinely believe that their island had existed since the genesis of this world, that they were the only people of Earth—that Arcadia *was* Earth, surrounded by endless ocean.

The Arcadians held a belief in a supernatural order and in a harmony of all things. To them, their interpretation of the natural world and of unexplained phenomena seemed most reasonable: there were superior beings who created, defined, and ruled the cosmos. These deities influenced man's fate and prosperity. The Arcadians felt quite vulnerable in this world that held them, but being under the protection of the gods they worshiped ensured their survival.

The Arcadians believed that the creation of the cosmos began with Chaos. Chaos gave birth to Mother Earth and to Eros, Erebus, and Night, who begat Air and Day. Thereafter came Death, Sleep, Dreams, the Fates, and Sky, followed by the birth of the Giants. From the union of Mother Earth and Sky, the Titans were born. The battle between the Giants and the Titans gave rise to the new gods who gained control: Zeus, Poseidon, Hestia, Demeter, Hera, and Hades. It was the Titan Prometheus who created the Arcadians.

The manners, customs, and beliefs of the Arcadians all appeared to have an authentic historical presence of thousands of years. Their oral history was steeped in the most ancient Greek myth but limited to the story of creation and the recognition of the earliest deities. Completely absent were the heroic sagas of Heracles, Theseus, the Argonauts, Perseus, Bellerophon, and others. There was no telling of the Trojan War. No Odyssey. Their beliefs appeared to predate and exclude all such later mythology, which was unknown to them.

As for their society, what they described staggered John's mind. They were a peaceful and cooperative people. A quasi–Bronze Age garden culture led by educated elders who ruled by reason, governing loosely, permitting the people to ultimately control their society in an individualistic and communal manner. Everyone was truly free. Independent thought prevailed.

Women enjoyed complete social equality. There was no concept of money. Individuals only did the work they enjoyed, contributing to the common good. They lived in harmony with the natural world. Completely absent was any technology that separated their humanity from nature. They shared a common religious philosophy, yet religion was unformalized.

They had temples for worship but no official ceremonies, only the informal, recurrent communal celebration of Arcadia's native god, which took place according to the phases of the moon.

To John, someone who had been searching endlessly for the ideal, Arcadia seemed the perfect utopian world. So much so that he felt completely overwhelmed, as if he were experiencing a troubling disassociation from reality. Thus his need to be alone: to walk, to think, in order to ground his psyche.

Everything seems to point toward some absent, directing intelligence pursuing some unknown purpose... John listened to his own thoughts as he walked. And then he shivered as he wondered again about that strange voice that had invaded his mind, calling out to him from across the darkness.

He thought again of the village. He could not stop thinking about that village and its people and their way of life, and the paradoxical austere elegance that it presented to him.

Continuing up the hillside, John noticed that as he climbed higher, he was afforded an increasingly interesting view of the island. It was a relatively small island, perhaps not more than thirty miles in circumference. In shape it was nearly circular, without bays, entirely surrounded by the fog-shrouded reef that lay offshore. The huge, otherworldly pipes from the sea did indeed encircle the island. Running inland, the pipelines netted the hilly surface of Arcadia, seeming to converge somewhere at the island's central, highest elevation.

John recalled how it was the chief officer's opinion that these pipes were of a significantly higher level of technology than that possessed by the Arcadians, whose windmills and solar panels, although interesting, were quite rudimentary.

John stopped as he noticed a fat toad, sitting there in the middle of his path. The toad croaked, and the swollen bubble beneath its neck sunk in, vanishing completely, as if it had just burped up a cloud so huge it could fill the sky.

And John once again glanced up at the eerie umbrella of fog hanging vaporously over the island. The more he thought about it, the more he became convinced that it must be the product of some utterly unknown technology. Perhaps the same technology that was producing this exquisite, heavenly air, laden with the scent of eternal spring.

John shook off his thoughts, suddenly content to just breathe in the cool, fragrant air. More than anything, its pleasantry symbolized to him all that Arcadia was. So very gentle was the upland breeze, it would not even disturb a butterfly, this soft spring air that wandered aimlessly through the pine forests and settled so gently upon the cultivated fields below.

"I've been waiting for you for so very long," John heard himself admit aloud, his voice velvety, resonating softly.

In his mind's eye, he pictured the ideal, perfect state of the society below, with its fields, its slowly turning windmills, and its austere yet elegant people. *Through embracing the past, they have assured the future.*

And as a small butterfly crossed John's path, moving as though unburdened by the world of desire, John felt his mind unburden itself, and he embraced the relief that he felt in his heart. For he had at last reached the place where his search would end.

He continued up the slope an unburdened man, his pace increasing, driven by sheer euphoria and mind-tingling curiosity.

~ 5 ~

John wrapped his arms about himself for warmth as he strode through Arcadia's great cedar forest, continuing his solo ascent. The temperature had dropped significantly with the rise in elevation, far more so than was natural for anywhere on the planet. He wondered if this might be due to the pipes from the sea becoming closer to one another with the rise in elevation, like the spokes of a wheel converging toward a central point.

The strong, resinous scent of the cedars filled the air to a near-intoxicating degree. Shadowed by glaucous blue-green leaves, John looked in appreciation at the thick, cracked bark and broad, level branches of the towering trees. And he smiled as he noticed wooden buckets resting beneath brass taps hammered into a number of the trunks—Arcadians harvesting cedar oil.

So many breezes wandering through these trees. John smiled. *But never enough.*

Squirrels ran the branches above. Rabbits hopped the forest floor. John altered his course, giving a crested porcupine a wide berth. He caught sight of a red fox, but it was gone in a flash. He spied wild goats in the steeper terrain, and he thought he heard wild boar somewhere down the mountainside. He watched as a resting doe, its chestnut-brown fur luxuriantly dappled by beautiful white spots, moved quickly to stand beside her calling fawn. On the fringe of the forest, he spied two bucks licking frost from each other's fur.

John noted in his mind how the roe deer, and the other animals, were all native to the lands around the Mediterranean, like the island's magnificent trees, and the ancient culture of the Arcadians...

John also saw a few animals that he could not identify. These animals left him with a haunting sense that he was perhaps seeing living ghosts from time past, species perhaps now extinct in the outside world but still very much alive here, enjoying sanctuary on this hidden island.

Climbing above the forest, John stepped out onto a grassy hillside overlooking the sea. A few snowflakes landed gently upon him, causing his eyes to flutter. It was then that he noticed the thin layering of whiteness up ahead. He moved to it and dropped to his knees, laughing like a child. Scraping the snow together, he packed it into three balls, placing one atop the other. And he sat back to look at the miniature snowman that he had built within the tropics, wondering how long it would last.

As John rose to his feet, he realized that from his new vantage point he could now see the island's central, dormant volcanic cone unobstructed. Half way up its time-worn slopes, the many pipes from the sea tunneled into the low mountain, disappearing from sight. As his eyes adjusted to the distance, he noticed a white vapor slowly rising out of the crater at the volcano's summit. Floating upward, this nebulous mist slowly merged into the mysterious cloud cover that umbrellaed the whole of Arcadia. John wondered about the secret and unknown technology that was housed inside the volcano.

Turning to the sea, he looked out at the fog hanging over the island's encircling reef. He wondered if there might also be something hidden inside the reef, perhaps a similar inexplicable mechanism. Was it this same mechanism that was playing havoc with the *Venture*'s compass? That prevented any distress call from being sent off? Or was that due to something else? Something designed to… keep them here…

John's thoughts could not help but focus on the even greater mystery: Who was behind Arcadia? What genius had modified this island? And why?

Slowly, the sound of an old woodpecker working a tree as the day turned to evening pulled John out of his contemplation. *How long have I been wandering, chasing the scent of pine?* he thought. *Time to return to the village.*

~ 6 ~

As John descended, finally at ease in his heart, contemplating and embracing a new future, he entered a meadow of wild landscape. He slowed as he heard pipes playing, the sound coming from somewhere in the surrounding woodland. The melody seemed to haunt the woods, so deeply did it reflect an unrefined aspect of nature, matching in rawness the untamed gurgling of a mountain spring, the rugged sparring of deer in rut. The music of the pipes unexpectedly stirred in John a primordial urge to roam, like a wild child of nature, surviving with complete abandon of civilization.

John fought against the feral mood, yet drawn forward by it, he pursued the sound of the pipes, venturing deeper into the woodland. It grew dim as the trees thickened, the foliage shadowing the land. John sensed a difference; the island seemed to have somehow changed... Or was Arcadia merely revealing itself to him more fully?

As John closed on the source of the music, he heard the voices of men. He slowed. The men sounded intoxicated, uncouth, wild. John considered turning back, retreating. For he sensed something that up until now he had not felt on Arcadia—the sensation of danger.

But suddenly he saw the men, for a fleeting moment, through a break in the greenery, and they saw him. The men were bearded, hairy, clothed only in rustic loincloths, and shockingly, they appeared disturbingly animalistic—each with a long horse's tail and ears. The world suddenly tilted on John, so much was his perception of reality assaulted, his view of Arcadia challenged down to its core.

These *men* dropped their flutes and wine and roguishly picked up knives of brass. John ran. Howling out in excitement, these ani-men of the woodland gave chase. And they were fast. John felt himself in another world, suddenly in a nightmare, and he ran as he had never run before, his heart pounding. He bounded across the meadow, down a hillside, and through a stand of pines. He tumbled down a rocky slope, rose, and kept running. As he fled, his mind raced too—wildly, franticly, the island so suddenly and jarringly having presented to him such a completely different and unexpected wild side. *How can this be? Who—what are these men?*

And John ran and ran.

Finally, exhausted beyond all endurance, John tripped and fell. Immediately he looked behind himself. There was no sign of his pursuers. He listened. There was only the calm susurration of the wind blowing through the trees, the melodious chirping of birds. The island appeared to have returned to its ideal, peaceful, gardenlike state. His mind also felt free of the feral mood that had temporarily invaded it.

What just happened? What did I see? He wondered if the group of... *men*... if they were perhaps wearing false attachments of ears and tails cut from horses... for some type of pagan ritual? *Yes, yes, it must have been... Yes, that must be it. This 'Mysterious Island' is not transforming on me into the 'Island of Doctor Moreau'!*

But John did not believe what he was telling himself. Deeply troubled, he rose.

Some time passed before he noticed the sea below. He was up on a high hill overlooking the beach, just east of where their lifeboats had made shore. Down on the sand he saw Helena, accompanied by Agathon, following two sailors of their landing party. The sailors were leading them toward a body that had washed ashore.

~ 7 ~

John stepped up to Helena, Agathon, and the sailors, doing his best to ignore the pungent, fishy odor that permeated the air.

"It's a… *merman*…" Helena stated, astonished, her voice but a whisper.

And John looked down at the merman, his perception of reality once again assaulted. His mind reeled, but he forced himself to focus on what lay before him, however unbelievable it was. He looked first at the thing's face. The creature's lifeless, open eyes still held a depth of power, a level of confidence, an arrogance that John had never imagined possible, not even in his dreams.

In form, the naked, fabulous creature was half manlike and half fishlike. It seemed something unearthly, yet paradoxically simultaneously something of this world. Designed for this world. Its dolphin-smooth skin was tinged a waxy, emerald green, its great shoulders barnacled by what resembled seashells… Its magnificent manlike torso tapered into a powerful fish tail, finned and scaled.

"This is incredible…" was all John could manage to say.

Agathon spoke in ancient Greek, in a low voice, racked by sadness. John translated:

"As our kind grows older still… our gods grow older with us… and most die…"

John looked again at the dead eyes of the deity lying before them, attempting to fathom the confidence and arrogance held by a *god*.

143

Their gods are real... And mortal? John heard his own thoughts rumble. "Who was this... *god?*" he asked Agathon. Agathon told him, and John told the others:

"It's the sea god Triton, son of Poseidon and Amphitrite." And John knelt to look up close at the huge conch-shell trumpet that Triton still held clenched in one of his odd, powerful hands.

"With that trumpet," Agathon informed John, "Triton could rile up the sea to punish us or calm the waves to save us. The shell could make a roar so terrible it would send giants fleeing. Triton protected us, in return for our love and worship..."

Agathon pried the heavy trumpet loose from Triton's still hand, placed it aside, and then asked John if the sailors could help carry the body to their village for the necessary funeral.

John sent one of the sailors off to get help. As they waited there, looking down at this amazing god, soaking in the reality of what lay before them, Helena noticed John's torn shirt, the bruises on his arms, the blood on his lip, all from when he had tumbled down the hillside.

"John," she asked, concerned, "what happened?"

"Oh..." John responded, his mind spinning, trying to recall what he knew of ancient Greek myth. Aside from gods, there were demigods in the forest... Spirits of nature... Worshipers of Dionysus who were mischievous troublemakers, chasers of nymphs... They were men with the ears and tails of a horse.

"Satyrs," John explained, forced to accept the unbelievable reality of his recent encounter, his mind going numb. "I think I was chased by satyrs..."

And there, under the diminishing rays of the setting sun, John's soul trembled. What was happening to his utopia? Was it suddenly slipping away from him as it further revealed itself to him? What was next?

~ 8 ~

Night had fallen. The waxing moon glowed eerily through the vaporous, ever-present cloud cover of Arcadia. The entire populace of the island had gathered in the grassy village square, which was lit by flickering torches and beautiful, reddish-gold electrical bulbs, huge in size but dim in radiance.

John was sitting beside Helena, who sat beside Agathon. Sitting amongst Arcadia's other elders and alongside his chief officer was the *Venture*'s captain, who had joined the landing party, leaving only his second officer, chief engineer, and two deck hands aboard their vessel. All the other officers and crew were presently seated amongst the islanders, staring in bewilderment at Arcadia's dead god, whose alien form now lay high atop a funeral pyre of stacked logs of oak and pine.

Satyrs, a son of Poseidon, a hidden ancient people—my God, how does this all fit together? John pondered, troubled, feeling the needling of growing distress. But he could not guess. So he temporarily let it go. Slowly, he allowed himself to be relaxed by the unusually soothing, poetic melody being played by the Arcadian musicians.

Once again, despite his newfound concerns, he felt himself being pulled into the utopia that presented itself to him. He found his eye drawn to the lyre player, who played upon a magnificent alabaster instrument, beautifully decorated with paintings of white swans. Next to this musician, a young woman played a small, elegant triangular harp. Behind her were men on flutes and pipes and other wind instruments. There were stringed instruments played by hand, as was a large, shallow drum. There was a girl on a curved horn. And standing before them all was a young man blowing a conch shell, a triton shell, in honor of their fallen god.

To John, the music symbolized love, the love the Arcadians held for their lost deity. John leaned across Helena and whispered to Agathon, asking him if the interpretation was correct. Feeling unexpectedly stirred and distracted by the warm touch of his arm against Helena's and by her pleasantly perfumed, gentle presence, John was unsure if he had heard Agathon's answer correctly amidst the rising music. He thought he had heard Agathon answer:

"Our hearts ache. We now have only the keeper of the winds and our native god to protect us."

John gently leaned to Helena and whispered softly into her ear, "I feel as if we've vanished into a mist and entered a dream, a dream of a world that ended long ago."

"It's not unpleasant," she whispered back, "but I feel… helpless… and frightened. I only want to wake up."

John remained motionless, allowing the pleasurable warmth of her breath to linger there in his ear as he considered her words.

She whispered to him again, explaining, her tone that of the scientist that she was. "The Arcadians, their society, the fact that they're so displaced in time… it's beautiful, but it's also so haunting. Disturbing. I realize you may not want to hear this, but at first, this island—it presents as a paragon of the perfectibility of mankind, but it's all an illusion. John, there's no true creativity here, no initiative. No forward development."

John felt his soul ache, his heart wounded by her incisive words. For her thoughts presented to him a lucid perception that he realized was likely far more objective than his own, which he knew remained clouded by his desperate, idealistic longings.

"John," she went on, still whispering. "This being, Triton… and the willed transformation of this island, how it's been altered and purposely hidden, the technology that's being employed to do so… I don't believe this represents a human achievement… I'm afraid."

John placed an arm around her, comforting her. As he reflected on her speculation, although he found himself pleased that Alan had still not made his appearance, he began to wonder just where the botanist might be. Alan was a rival in regard to Helena… but he was also a scientist, and John recognized Alan's sharp, penetrating intellect. John suddenly found himself very much wanting to discuss things with Alan, specifically the satyrs, and Triton.

Coincidentally, an Arcadian boy came up behind John and whispered to him that his friend, Alan, wanted to see him. That Alan was waiting for him "up there"—and the boy pointed to the top of a nearby earthen mound looming off in the darkness, to the towers of white rock standing atop it.

At that moment, the pipes and drums grew still louder.

"I'll be right back," John whispered to Helena. She nodded, and he left her there with Agathon.

~ 9 ~

John reached the top of the mound and squinted in the darkness. "Alan?"

"Over here," Alan's smooth, confident voice responded.

John walked toward where the voice came from, somewhere near the towers of white rock.

"Here."

And John turned to find Alan standing there in the coolness, between the towers, looking down at the lights, at the gathering below. Listening to the music.

"What are you doing up here?" John asked.

"Thinking," Alan answered.

"Alan," John started, "there are some important things you need to know."

"Funny," Alan replied, "that's what I was about to say to you."

John just looked at Alan, surprised.

"You're the only one I can trust with this," Alan went on. "Aside from myself, you're the only one of us with a measure of reflective insight. I spent the day talking to the elders, and to others."

"You learned to speak ancient Greek?"

"Don't be a fool," Alan responded sharply, with his typical arrogance. "They're bi-lingual. They understand Latin."

John had not guessed this. But it made sense. "And?"

But Alan hesitated, and then, carefully, calculatedly, he said in more of an appeal than an admission: "Our outside world, John, you were right. It's littered with the wreckage of war, worn-out philosophies, abandoned faiths. You fled from our world, John. You saw us rushing toward our own doom."

"I don't understand…" came John's slow response.

"John," Alan laughed out the words, critically, "don't tell me that you don't recognize this island as that lost garden you've been searching for. As the utopia that it is."

"I honestly don't know if I believe in utopia any longer," John said slowly.

"But you must!"

"Why?"

Alan turned John about to face the celebration down below. "What do you think would become of this society if we were to be rescued?" he asked John. "What do you think would happen if the outside world learned of Arcadia?"

John looked down upon the square, remembering what had happened when the Romans had invaded ancient Arcadia, in early Greece. It had spelled the end of ancient Arcadia.

"Go on," John said reservedly.

"We must remain marooned here." Alan stated it firmly,

unequivocally. "I need you to help me convince the others to stay. To scuttle the *Venture*."

For an instant, John saw a distorted reflection of himself in Alan. It made him fully realize that he needed to completely withdraw his heart from the embrace that he had all too quickly given to Arcadia. It forced him to fully acknowledge to himself that he needed to recognize that Arcadia, and the unfolding mystery that it was, required him to become stonily objective, more like Helena, to view things first and foremost as a scientist and not as a needy idealist.

"… No," John responded. "The captain, the officers, the crew. Helena, they all have lives, ambitions outside of Arcadia. They have the right to try to find a way off this island. To be rescued. Also, Arcadia—it's not what it first appears to be. I'm no longer sure what it really is."

"John"—Alan stepped up close to John, frustrated, ready to tell all, his voice trickling with controlled excitement—"you don't understand. There are edible plants here, herbs and flowers in this valley that don't exist anywhere else on Earth. These islanders, they don't know illness. They don't live and die normally like you and me. Living here, in Arcadia, breathing this air, drinking the water, eating the vegetation here, they live to be three, four hundred years old, even more. Agathon is nearly five hundred years old!"

"Are you certain?" John asked in utter disbelief.

"Of course I'm certain!" Alan snapped. "John, we've stumbled upon the fountain of youth. This *is* Shangri-La. And more, don't you see, it's a society in embryo. A seed in early germination. Something to be cultivated. Nurtured. Developed. We can guide Arcadia—evolve it toward a further ideal. Anything we want. And we would have centuries of time lying before us to do so."

And John thought about it dispassionately, scientifically weighing Alan's vision against what he had learned so far about Arcadia. "No," he said. "It won't work. There's an unknown intelligent controlling force behind Arcadia that won't welcome your interference. It won't permit it."

And this time John turned Alan about to face the celebration below. "I think you'd better come with me. Down to the square. The gathering, the music, it's a ceremonial cremation of an impossible dead sea god."

~ 10 ~

As John led Alan toward Helena and the others, images of satyrs and the dead god Triton danced in his mind. It was all such an enigma, the mystery of Arcadia. And now, near immortality too?

John tried to clear his thoughts. As he did so, the soft breeze flowing down from the mountains suddenly dropped, as if announcing the presence of something unseen. The musicians stopped playing. The Arcadians fell silent and turned to the largest of the surrounding earthen mounds. Atop it stood a single structure, a temple composed of limestone, ancient fossil coral, and red earth. Echoing out from within the temple came the sweet, piercingly sweet piping of a primitive seven-reed musical instrument. The distinctive sound of it incited the Arcadians to rise and to yell out excitedly, noisily, wildly.

"What's happening?" Alan grabbed John by the arm, so uncharacteristic was the behavior of the islanders.

John shrugged in response. A musky, goat-like odor then assailed his senses. It made him cough at first, so strong it was.

The odor initiated a sudden change. It could be felt in the air and in one's mind. For a third time, John felt his perception of reality tilt off kilter, warped this time by something unseen yet disturbingly palpable, real and present.

The Arcadians reacted to this with intense elation. The piping grew louder, and the Arcadians moved toward the mound like a flock being called back to the fold.

Then there was a shout from inside the temple. The voice pierced the spring air, and every hair on John's body stood on end. It was the same voice that had called out to him that night on the ship, from out in the fog.

And *something* leapt from the temple—a half-human form—running and jumping with the ease of a goat, its movements agile and swift—its form exhibiting the uncanny strength of and eliciting the reverent terror given only to a god.

Bounding into the moonlight, it stood there naked, arched backward, looking up into the sky as if having a love affair with the moon. It was an elemental figure, a kind of demon. Complete with horns, pointed ears, and a tail. Sexually aroused, it displayed a tremendous erect phallus—seemingly ready for any physical pleasure.

There was the click of cloven hooves as it swung its weather-beaten, bearded face to the crowd, lowering its pointed chin. John felt himself go dizzy under the gaze of those ancient eyes—startling, pale eyes slit horizontally by rectangular pupils.

On legs of a goat, this erection-toting horned god skipped down to the funeral pyre. There, it held out a branch of pine, and the Arcadians went wild, chanting their deity's name over and over.

My God... John silently mouthed the words, speechless. This divine he-goat, this great phallic god, it was the most revered, the most beloved god of ancient Arcadia. The pagan god of the shepherds. The god who watched over the flocks and the goatherds. The god of the meadows, pastures, forests, and mountains. The god of all wild things. It was the great god Pan.

"Pan! Pan! Pan! Pan!" the islanders continued to chant.

"This is impossible…" John heard Alan mutter in absolute disbelief.

"According to myth"—John's voice cracked, mirroring Alan's shock—"Pan was born and lived in ancient Arcadia… Pan is their *native god.*"

"John? Alan?" Helena stepped between them, having found them in the crowd. And the three of them stood together in stunned silence, their eyes on Pan.

Pan agilely hopped to a nearby torch. The flickering flame sent waves of firelight dancing over the god's hispid skin, which was crimson, the ancient color of strength.

Setting aflame the branch of pine, Pan looked up at dead Triton, lying there supine, high atop the pyre. He said something to Triton, in a low, respectful tone, in an unearthly language that John could not identify.

Pan then turned to the crowd, and in ancient Greek: "Time will never dare speak *my* name."

The Arcadians cheered, and the ancient god dropped the burning branch upon the pyre, setting it aflame. The oak and pine must have been soaked in an incendiary, for the fire roared almost instantly, sending up a massive pillar of smoke.

Pine resin began to crackle and pop within the flames, while sparks floated aloft. And Pan stood there before the Arcadians, their living god. But more, Pan was their umbilical to their natural world. He existed as the personification of the heart of nature, of Arcadia which embodied it. Pan's presence could somehow intimately be felt echoed in the trees of the forest, in the fields where the grass grew high, between the rocks, in the scent of the many wildflowers, in the sound of the island's gurgling streams, in the caress of its fragrant breeze. Pan was everywhere and with the Arcadians always.

As John stared at Pan in awe, he found himself wondering anew about these strange beings, Triton and now Pan. From where did their kind originate? Was it from a distant star, as Agathon had incorrectly surmised the *Venture* had originated from? But if so, why had these beings inserted themselves into humankind's early history? Why did they later create Arcadia? For what purpose did the few surviving gods remain here, hidden away on this remote island in the South Pacific? Worshiped by a population of anachronistic humans—whom these gods must have long ago transplanted here from ancient Greece.

In response to these questions, John's mind speculated wildly: Could these manlike, animalistic deities perhaps represent some impossible cross between godlike extraterrestrials and life on Earth? It seemed a possible answer. An exchange and recombination of instructions on a cellular level made possible by some alien, highly advanced science... to allow for survival on Earth, under this planet's specific gravity, breathing this world's unique atmosphere. Could this have been an extraterrestrial colonization attempt by proxy, somehow gone wrong and then abandoned? Its creations, designed specifically for life on Earth, then left behind to fend for themselves? Creatures that later avoided humankind as it advanced? And the satyrs—might they represent some impossible second-generation backcrossing between these designed-for-Earth deities and man?

The crowd parted, allowing Agathon to approach their great god. The elder Arcadian did so reverently, his eyes held obeisantly focused upon the gift that he held out to Pan. It was Triton's twisted conch shell, the dead god's trumpet.

Pan snatched it away and held it to his breast, cradling it as if it were a boon undreamed of, this horn from the sea.

Pan then relaxed in his goat-legged stance and stood there godly. Indiscriminately, he swung the trumpet toward someone in the crowd. The horn glowed. Pan blew the slightest whisper of air into the mouthpiece in the spire of the shell, a single, gentle puff. And something unseen and unnatural reached out from the mechanism. Barely audible, it sounded like the distant wail of a lost infant. This sound touched the Arcadian standing there in the forefront of the crowd. And the man collapsed into a lifeless heap.

"He's dead…" John heard a number of the islanders whisper.

As a murmuring wave of fear undulated through those gathered, John caught a glimpse of Pan's godly, pale eyes. He saw in those eyes power and intelligence coupled to uncivilized animal cunning. And as Pan stood there unchallenged, a shiver ran down John's spine. So indiscriminant was Pan's choice of the victim for the testing of the trumpet. It was completely random. Unselective. For the first time, John felt he truly understood the old statement that absolute power corrupts absolutely.

For when a god kills, there is no discipline from a higher authority. There is no response against the god. And when that god cannot even hear the scream of the victim… it must be incredibly corrupting. What happens when this can occur every day? It must become like walking over ants in the street.

Agathon guided the captain of the *Venture* forward, to stand there before Pan. The captain's officers and crew followed, hesitantly, standing at attention behind their commander.

Pan only half looked at the strangers, so focused was he on his horn, toying with it in his hands. But the he-goat did finally turn to Agathon, and the elder reacted as if he heard something in his mind.

"Brave men from afar," Agathon announced to the men of the *Venture*, relaying a message rather than speaking for himself. "From this day forward, you will be shepherds and farmers. May you thrive and live long here, in peace."

John translated it, emotionally numb.

"... Thank you," the captain said awkwardly and stepped back, relieved yet troubled.

"Why is it forbidden to live on the shore?" John then heard himself ask Pan directly, in English, all remaining hopes of utopia now completely torn from his heart.

"John, no," Helena whispered as John simultaneously received the harshest look of warning from Alan.

"No," John responded. "I want to know why certain freedoms are forbidden in utopia." John then repeated his initial question to Pan in ancient Greek.

"It was Poseidon's dictate," Agathon quickly interceded. "For our own protection."

"Why?" John asked Pan directly.

And Pan looked at John closely, for the first time. John felt his mind ache, and he saw something in Pan's goat eyes that he had not noticed before: wisdom.

John then felt something intrude into his mind. It was not something communicated or defined by words, but rather it was a complete thought that made its presence suddenly known:

"The future borrows its strength from man himself. It tricks it out of him. And then this strength appears outside him as the enemy that he must meet."

John recognized the thought. It was not alien to him. It spoke to his own observations and concerns, and to his belief in the numbing future he foresaw for humankind. And so John came to realize that Pan, like himself, had fled from some strange, unwelcomed future. To hide himself away in Arcadia, where he could embrace the comfortable past to assure a defined and controlled future. A future that he and the others of his kind did not want intruded upon by the outside world. John understood and sympathized with the sentiment. But where did this now lead him? He was suddenly uncertain, again...

Pan leisurely skipped over to the fallen Arcadian. The horned god touched the man ever so gently with Triton's trumpet, which glowed a dim glow, and the man sat up and gasped for air, suddenly alive again.

And hope arose reborn in John's heart. But then he watched the newly alive man rise to his feet, laughing and babbling like a feeble-minded idiot, his brain irreversibly damaged by the experience.

Yet the Arcadians cheered.

"Imperfect gods," John heard Alan whisper critically, worried, "in a perfect world..."

"With human frailties," Helena added, her whispering voice trembling with fear.

The music of Pan's pipes filled the air again as the god of Arcadia, the god of dance, leapt back into his more animal instincts, playing chaotic, spiritually fulfilling music. And the night's festivities began anew, Arcadia's musicians playing again, this time in accompaniment to their god's piping, as the islanders began to drink wine and dance lively upon the grass.

Amidst the rising commotion, John found his staggered, bewildered mind reeling, wondering about the fantastic science that Arcadia's gods displayed via their strange mechanisms: the power to transform the climate of an island, and now the power over life and death? He also wondered how Pan could project thoughts into the minds of others. Was it telepathy? John did not believe so, for he had once looked into telepathy and concluded that there was no known biological means that could account for the claim. *There must be some unseen mechanism at play,* John thought. *Could it be an implant for universal communication, something hidden inside Pan, created and gifted to him by an advanced alien technology?*

"That was irresponsibly foolish," Alan lectured John, gaining his attention. "Challenging that *thing* like that!"

John nodded and led Helena and Alan aside. There was much to discuss. But before he could speak, he sensed a change in Pan's music. He felt the new piping disturbing his brain, his senses. He felt the undisciplined instincts of nature arising within his psyche. It was intense: a freedom of spirit, the primitive drives of sinless love.

John saw that Alan appeared to be feeling something identical, although Helena seemed completely unaffected.

"What's wrong?" Helena asked the two of them.

But John only half heard her, so intense was the overwhelming sexual urge that Pan's music was stirring in his loins. It was then, as the blood flow to his genitals increased, that John remembered that Pan, this magic child of Arcadia, was also the uncivilized god of lust, the he-goat who chased after nymphs to seduce them for the pure sake of lust and carnal satisfaction.

John felt all the inhibitions generated by society and religion fall away and shrink to nothing, allowing his primal instincts to rise unbound. There was now only uncontrollable longing. Animal-like desire. All that remained was the intense want for grunting, groaning, moaning physical satisfaction in the filthiest form, guiltless and without shame.

And John felt fear tingling all over him as he sensed a soon-to-arrive moment of complete inability to control himself. He heard his own mind screaming to himself to grab the nymph, damn the consequences!

But Alan responded to the calling first, grabbing Helena, tearing at her clothes.

John grabbed Alan, and the two men struggled. John sent his fists striking into Alan's face and Alan tumbled backward, falling prostrate upon the grass. Rolling over, he looked up at John, who stood over him in a mindless fever, fists clenched.

"And I thought we had settled our differences," Alan said with sarcasm, wiping the blood from his lip, the pain of the confrontation apparently temporarily relieving him of Pan's influence.

John, also temporarily free, glanced about. Everywhere it was the same: Arcadian men fighting amongst themselves, indiscriminately chasing after their women, fornicating right there in the village square. While Pan played his panpipes, watching, enjoying.

"Run," John warned Helena, feeling the effect of the pipes again. "Run!"

She did.

And John gave chase, his psyche once more completely dominated by arousal and impulse.

As he caught up with Helena, he felt his sexual desire surge as it combined with a desire for power. He yanked Helena to the ground. He felt no anger toward her struggling against him, and he found himself using as little force as was necessary. This was an act of sex, not violence. Still, he needed to overpower her, control the interaction. Use his strength against her. And he did, pinning her, holding her down as he positioned himself atop her, preparing to rape her.

"Oh, John," she cried out, "not here, not like this." And she turned her face away in pure humiliation, degradation.

And the imminent rape forced upon John a distressing emotional strain. Suddenly he could see Helena's fear. Hear her sobs. It was impossible for him to ignore her copious tears, which soaked him, drenching him to the bone. She was a human being with rights. She was not to be held there, under the moonlight, trembling like a flower in a storm. He released her.

"Please go..." John mumbled to her, fighting against the music of Pan's pipes that still filled his head. "Get far away from me. Go..."

"Let me..." she answered, unsure. "Let me help you."

"No!" he yelled. Rising, he forced himself to run off. He ran and he ran, in a stupor, fighting against the influence of the Pandean pipes. As he entered the pine forest, he oddly felt overcome by feral elation, falling further under the possession of Pan. He felt as if he only wanted to run deeper and deeper into the woods and never return.

But as John distanced himself from the village, he distanced himself from Pan's spell. He stopped his legs and dropped into a seated position, in a daze, leaning off balance. A huge firefly, a little wobble on its wings, slowly fluttered past him. After the insect disappeared and the night dimmed again, John slowly came to his senses.

Why? John thought. *Why does he now want me to run off?*

Helena! John exclaimed in his thoughts, realizing the real danger that she was in—the only golden-haired woman on an island being savaged this night by an erection-toting horned god with an insatiable appetite for carnal pleasure.

~ 11 ~

By the time John arrived back at the village square, the chaos was over. The Arcadians were collecting themselves and walking off slowly, returning to their homes. Their communal celebration with their native god had ended. It had not lasted long. It was but a brief, intoxicating, wild moment of experiencing the complete abandonment of civilization. A ritual that apparently had become part of their culture, of their way of life.

The captain of the *Venture* was gathering together his officers and crew, who were widely scattered about. They all appeared baffled, shaken.

John looked for Helena but could see no sign of her.

Then he came across Alan, who was lying there upon his back in the grass, deeply disturbed, looking up at the clouds, the moon. At each of Alan's sides, their arms still wrapped about him in a lover's embrace, was a topless Arcadian woman.

"Alan?"

"Oh, go away, John," Alan replied with loathing, only glancing at John. "Go away."

"Helena's not here?" John asked him.

Alan sat up. "You ran off after her. She's not with you?"

"No." John shook his head. "I... let her go... Where's Pan?"

Alan rose to his feet, understanding the implication immediately.

"Captain!" John called, moving to the officers and crew of their vessel. "Did any of you see Helena?"

But there was only the shrugging of shoulders, the shaking of heads.

"She's in danger," John appealed to Alan.

An Arcadian woman shuffled up to the men, holding her torn shirt closed. She asked John if they were looking for the blond woman who had arrived with them.

John nodded, and the woman told him how she had seen Helena head off on the path that led down to the shore.

"She's gone to the boat," John quickly informed Alan.

The woman then added that after Helena had left, their great god Pan had asked the elders where this new woman was, with the golden hair. But they did not know.

"Pan's looking for her," John guessed.

"Well, John," Alan's voice trickled out with the deepest irony. "It looks as if you and I are united in a cause after all."

And the two men headed off toward the shore.

~ 12 ~

Only one of the two lifeboats remained on the beach. John and Allan took it toward the *Venture*. They rowed quickly but as quietly as they could, employing long, deep, even strokes of the oars. The moon was nearly full, and although filtered through the strange haze above the island, its glow lit up the surrounding sea.

John felt quite vulnerable as they traversed the lagoon, knowing full well that they could be easily spotted from the shore. How all-knowing and all-seeing was Arcadia's god? Was Pan watching?

As the two men rowed, in silence, John found himself occasionally looking at Alan and caught Alan from time to time glancing at him. John wondered what life experiences had shaped Alan's character, making the two of them as different as they were, given that they were both men of science. John wondered if under different circumstances he and Alan might have become friends. Was the friction between them solely because of Helena? A woman? Or was it something more?

Before long, the stranded *SS Venture* was looming there before them, rising high into the darkness. As they entered the periphery of the reef's odd, stationary fog, John felt some of the tension in his body ease, although his concern for Helena remained at its heightened state.

The missing lifeboat was there, roped up alongside the *Venture*. Had Helena taken it there? John and Allan secured their boat and immediately climbed the hanging service ladder up to the ship's main deck.

As John stepped down upon the deck, he found himself embraced by Helena. The embrace meant everything to him. She was safe, there on the ship. And more, she had forgiven him for the madness that had happened earlier. As he held her, he realized how powerfully relieving it felt to be fully in control of himself, unlike earlier.

"Hello, Helena." Alan's staid voice interrupted John's moment. "It's a relief to find you safe. Even if…" But Alan did not pursue stating the obvious. Instead he changed the subject: "How are our gorillas?"

"Fed, healthy," Helena responded. "But they're acting very unusually…"

Alan took several steps toward the ship's great central cage, which towered up into the fog. Within, all the gorillas were leaning up against its bars, silently staring out across the moonlit lagoon, toward the island of Arcadia.

"That's strange…" Alan commented.

"Pan," John offered. "He's the god of the forest. The god of all living, wild things."

"And?" Alan asked.

"Maybe they somehow sense it," John explained. "Pan's presence. In the breeze? By some unknown means? I've felt it myself. On the island. Pan's essence—it seems to haunt the mountain slopes. It's alluring, intoxicating."

"What are they doing?" Alan asked, pointing across the deck to the other side of the ship, where the vessel's second officer, chief engineer, and two deck hands were loading a starboard lifeboat with supplies.

"I told them everything that happened," Helena explained. "They're preparing the other two lifeboats for an extended stay at sea. Hoping that the captain and others will make their way back to the ship. So that they can lower the boats outside the reef, take their chances on the open sea. Make it to the shipping lanes, get rescued."

And Helena looked at her gorillas, deeply concerned.

The night breeze from across the lagoon suddenly dropped, leaving the air unusually still. In reaction, the gorillas began to move about uneasily, hooting softly.

"I've felt this before…" John commented in a deflating voice, with growing concern.

"Yes," Alan whispered. "And the last time it was a prelude for madness."

John picked up a pair of binoculars hanging nearby and looked toward Arcadia.

"Well?" Alan asked.

"Wait…" John murmured. "… Nothing on the beach."

The apes began to vocalize loudly, oddly, as if calling out to something unseen yet welcome.

"John?" Helena asked nervously.

"Oh no…" came John's response.

Alan ripped the binoculars away from John, affixing them to his own eyes.

"Oh no…" Alan repeated John's words. On a high hill overlooking the beach… there stood Pan, godly, on his goat legs, looking out toward the *Venture*. The horned he-goat lifted his primitive seven-reed panpipes to his lips and blew. Alan and the others could not hear the sound produced by the mechanism, but the gorillas apparently did, as they began to shake the bars of their cage in elation.

Pan next turned his pipes vertical and blew again, this time a narrowly directed piping, as if aiming at a particular target.

It took a moment for the *sound* to reach the *Venture*. When it did, it settled upon the ship's second officer, chief engineer, and two deck hands, all of whom reacted as if stricken by a sudden, blind panic.

John felt it too, but much weaker, being on the periphery of whatever it was that was sent across the lagoon. For John, it was a slight bewildering of his senses, a drive toward a mindless fear, which fortunately he did not feel himself stepping toward.

Driven mad by the music, the four sailors jumped off the starboard side of the *Venture*, splashing into the sea below.

John then heard sharply, piercingly, in his mind the echoing voice of a god:

"Leaving Arcadia is not permitted. You will remain here to be shepherds and farmers."

John instinctively cupped his hands over his ears, so loud was the voice in his mind. He saw that Alan and Helena were also receiving the same mental message. As were the gorillas:

"Your pre-men of the forest will live in my mountains in peace."

The apes howled out in triumphant happiness.

"I will watch over them, protect them. Love them. Forever."

John suddenly felt himself akin to a puppet, his attention yanked forcibly toward Helena, toward whom he found his head turned, yanked so by an unseen power. He saw the same happening to Alan.

"Your golden-haired nymph is *mine* to chase and seduce."

Suddenly it was over, and all three of them collapsed to the deck, their minds released, spinning.

John sat bolt upright, grabbed and focused the binoculars to see the great god Pan glare back at him with the ugly, surly face of an old pond frog. Pan then lifted Triton's glowing conch-shell trumpet to his lips and blew into it unrestrained.

"Get to a lifeboat…" John whispered to Alan and Helena. "Now!"

The *sound* that assaulted them came in a series of undulating invisible waves. The first wave blew over the ship with the terrible roar of a dark, wild beast. And the *Venture* shook in its entirety, from bow to stern, as the sea beneath it roiled, splashing violently.

As John, Helena, and Alan ran to the lifeboat on the starboard side, they lurched forward and backward as the *Venture* began to rise, floated upward by the swelling sea, which rose vertically as a great column of water.

The echoing of Triton's trumpet soon became as deafening as the roar of the rising ocean, the two mirroring each other in magnitude, one growing as did the other.

John picked up and dropped Helena into the lifeboat. As he did so, he saw that the *Venture* was now high above the reef, on a vertically rising swell of sea a hundred feet in height.

John lurched forward, tumbling into the lifeboat behind Helena, pushed into it from behind by Alan.

"What are you doing?" John yelled above the roar.

"Someone needs to lower the boat!" Alan yelled back. And he began to do so.

"Alan!" Helena cried out.

And Alan and Helena made eye contact in the storm of sound and sea that was all around them.

"You go," Alan yelled to her, his voice loud yet somehow soft in tone. "I can't go." And he shook his disturbed face as he glanced at John, communicating his heartbreak. "Besides, who will care for our gorillas?"

And the lifeboat jerked downward in a series of violent drops as Alan struggled to lower the craft with the ship's manual winch.

"Alan!" John tried again.

Alan just shook his head at John as they made brief eye contact. "I'll have time," Alan said to John, the volume of his voice dropping, unconcerned if John could actually hear him or not, "to turn the island... toward a true utopia."

The lifeboat hit the top of the swell that had lifted the *Venture* to such a dizzying height.

Above, Alan let loose the cables, which whirred by him, dropping into the sea.

At once, the lifeboat went soaring down the side of the swell, John and Helena hanging on for their lives. The boat splashed forcefully into the ocean below, but managed to remain upright. There, outside the reef, the boat slid away leisurely from the vertical column of elevated sea.

John and Helena stood. They watched as Alan waved goodbye and disappeared from sight.

What they could not see was Alan rushing over to the ship's central cage, which he threw himself upon, clutching and wrapping his arms and legs into and around its bars. He looked in at the gorillas within and then out at the island of Arcadia. "Hang on, old friends," Alan said to the apes, his voice trickling with fear mixed with hope. "I suspect this is going to be one hell of a ride."

John and Helena watched through the fog as the vertical swell of sea roared inland, carrying the *Venture* atop it. The wave dropped as it entered the shallows of the lagoon but remained strong enough to carry the ship up across the beach and a hundred yards or so into the forest, plowing down trees, before it settled there, upright, intact, undamaged.

As Pan's wave gently receded into the lagoon, the gap in the stationary fog closed, and John lost all sight of Arcadia. The mysterious, hidden isle of Pan was hidden once again.

~ 13 ~

Adrift.

The sunlight was bright, much more so than John had remembered it being, so accustomed had he become to the soft luminosity of the gentle sun beneath the ever-present cloud cover that shrouded Arcadia.

As he lay there in the lifeboat, cradling Helena in his arms, he looked at the rations of water and food on board. There seemed plenty for the two of them to survive for quite some time. But they were drifting at the mercy of the current, with no control of their destination. Would they be rescued? Or eventually die of starvation and thirst at sea...

John shuddered at the thought and closed his eyes, allowing his mind to turn inward. He considered how much was still unknown about Arcadia, about Pan and his kind. It was all still a mystery.

He wondered why Pan had called out to him that night in the fog, asking him to tell the world that he was still alive. Did he do so out of a moment of ego? Was he unable to resist reaching out to the passing ship? Was it so terribly painful for Pan that he lacked the worship of the outside world, from which he would remain forever absent, in self-exile?

Or could it be—did Pan somehow sense the *Venture*'s cargo of gorillas? And did he for some reason covet these "pre-men" of the mountains? And somehow lure the ship to strand itself upon the reef?

John slowly let the mystery go and found himself thinking of his enchanted walk up the Arcadian hillside, through the island's forests. He thought of the fragrant scent on the cool air, of the miniature snowman that he had built high upon that magical tropical island.

He then felt a twinge of envy for Alan, who had chosen to remain on Arcadia. Suddenly, safely distanced from the island in space and time, it did not seem as dreadful as it had been that wild night. It seemed, in John's mind now, to hold promise. Alan would discover if this was true or not. And Alan would have several hundred years of time to do so...

John smiled as he suddenly sensed the familiar smell of pine and cedar. It seemed so real—too real. He opened his eyes, alert, wary. No, he was still adrift, at sea. But… above him, there was a low, nebulous cloud, swirling, forming out of nothingness in the blue sky…

John sat up straighter, awakening Helena.

"What?" she asked.

John pointed at the odd, misty cloud.

Suddenly, John sensed something in the air. It made him shiver. It made his mind ache. His senses felt infringed upon. Then he felt a mild voice calling out to him in his mind, in ancient Greek.

"Do not fear. It is I, the keeper of the winds."

And John remembered and replayed in his mind the words of Agathon, from the night of Triton's funeral: "*Our hearts ache. We now have only the keeper of the winds and our native god to protect us.*"

Pan is Arcadia's native god, John's thoughts raced. *There's a second living god?*

Rising, John felt the rocking of the lifeboat mirror his reeling psyche as he witnessed a winged man flap out of the center of the materializing cloud. Kept aloft by great wings of feather, this god floated there effortlessly above them, like a myth brought to life, the embodiment of the air itself.

This god's face was soft, more that of a boy than a man, despite his maturity otherwise. His short hair was golden and wavy, with curled locks falling gently over his forehead. The white tunic that he wore, pinned at one shoulder, skirted at the knees, flapped freely in the wind.

John and Helena slowly smiled to each other, sharing an overwhelming sense that this god was benign and present to help.

"I am Aeolus," the god addressed them directly. "Son of Poseidon and Arne. Arcadia is Pan's island by decree of Zeus.

I am worshiped there, but I cannot interfere there. But here I can intervene..."

The god's face suddenly expressed extreme empathy as his tone changed, becoming grave.

"I cannot allow you to tell the outside world of Arcadia. I can now sink your boat… and you both will drown. Or you can accompany me to my island, to Aeolia, where you would need to remain for the rest of your days. It's a kinder and gentler place than Arcadia. The choice is yours."

John smiled. His adventure into utopia was continuing.

Recommendations

• *The Spring of My Life and Selected Haiku* by Kobayashi Issa, translated from Japanese by Sam Hill. Published in 1997 by Shambhala Publications, Inc.

Acknowledgements and Identifying Notations

• Words and groups of words were crafted into this story from the Japanese haiku poetry of Kobayashi Issa (1763–1828).

• When the protagonist John says: "It's strange, I can look upon a fish or a deer rather dispassionately, even a horse, but when I see a chimpanzee or a gorilla, there are differences to be sure, but there's also far too much that's like me, and I find that I can't build a wall in my mind that places these primates and myself on opposite sides. Somehow I get the feeling that we're both sitting on the top of that wall, facing opposite directions but nevertheless perched up there together."

It is assumed by this author that John had read and was influenced by marine biologist N. J. Berrill (1903–1996). In Chapter 3, "Patterns and Bones," of Berrill's 1957 book titled *Man's Emerging Mind*, Berrill wrote:

"I can look upon a worm or a fish dispassionately, or even a jackass, but when I see a monkey I don't know whether to laugh or cry. There is a difference to be sure but there is too much that is like me and I cannot build a fence that leaves monkey and myself on separate sides; somehow I get the feeling that we are both sitting on the top rail, no doubt facing opposite ways but nevertheless perched up there together."

• Words spoken by John, Alan, and Pan in respect to the present state of man and why one might seek out utopia were partly based on and influenced by material in Chapter 5, "How Human Is Man?", of the book *The Firmament of Time*, by anthropologist and philosopher Loren Eiseley (1907–1977).

• A few words describing the Arcadian village were based on the description of the ancient Minoan civilization as presented in Chapter 8, "Canaanite and Minoan Civilizations," of the book *The Evolution of Civilizations*, by historian Carroll Quigley (1910–1977).

• When the protagonist of this story contemplates the maxim of absolute power corrupting absolutely, his thoughts are based on a statement made by journalist Julian Assange when interviewed by journalist John Pilger in 2016.

• When the protagonist hears a voice call out to him from across the sea, this was based on a myth as told by a character in Plutarch's dialogue "On Why Oracles Came to Fail." A sailor named Thamus, as he sailed past the island of Paxi on his way from Egypt to Rome in the first century AD, is said to have heard a voice call out to him, informing him that the great god Pan was dead. This news was later spread through Rome. This proclamation of Pan's death is claimed to have announced the beginning of the end of paganism, during the rise of Christendom.

• The ship in the story being named the *SS Venture* pays homage to the vessel that visited Skull Island in the 1933 film *King Kong*.

A Note from the Author

This author hopes the reader found the unraveling of the mystery of Arcadia interesting, appreciating John's sensitivity to what presented itself to him in this mythic-utopian tale of speculative fiction.

In mythology, the winged god Aeolus, son of Poseidon, did found an island named Aeolian. Pan is not associated with any mythical island, although he did hail from ancient Arcadia.

"The Isle of Pan" is this author's fourth utopian tale to date, utopia being a subgenre that this author is drawn to given the dovetailing elements that often lend themselves to such stories: imaginative speculation and philosophical ideology.

The idea of transforming an island, such as Fatu Hiva, into a sanctuary for gorillas is purely the product of this author's imagination.

OTEC (ocean thermal energy conversion) is a technology that does exist, and it does produce the effect of microclimates, due to the creation of slightly lower air and ground temperatures around plants, allowing for temperate vegetation to be grown successfully in the tropics.

Genetically transforming humans in order to allow for the colonization of planets with different conditions than Earth's, as opposed to terraforming a planet to colonize it, is an old idea of science fiction. In this story, this author employed this idea, suggesting it as being the origin of the Greek gods of myth, i.e., that the ·deities were the product of such an abandoned extraterrestrial colonization attempt of Earth.

This story was inspired by a number of influences and experiences, one of which was this author's ascent of Haleakalā, the 10,000-foot eastern volcano of the Hawaiian island of Maui, where the continued drop in temperature with increasing elevation results in microclimates up the mountainside.

A second influence was the real-life incident that occurred on August 2, 1981, when the *Primrose*, a Hong Kong freighter, ran aground on the coral reef encircling North Sentinel Island, one of the Andaman Islands in the Indian Ocean. The ship's lookout soon spotted a group of hostile, spear-toting, naked islanders observing the *Primrose* from the shore. These natives began to build wooden canoes, but high seas prevented them from reaching the *Primrose*, whose crew was rescued by helicopter after a rather nervous week. Anthropologists suspect that the inhabitants of North Sentinel Island have been completely cut off from the rest of the world for over 65,000 years. The Indian government today enforces a three-mile exclusion zone around the island, preventing outside contact with the indigenous population.

Niko Zinovii
Santa Monica, California
8 Novemeber 2016

Niko Zinovii

Bimanous Quadrupedal Hexapods

Rudi Baumgarten came up the hillside as if he had stepped out of the rising sun itself. In look, bearing, and posture, he projected a strikingly cultured, European mien, blond, solemn, and intriguingly handsome. His piercing blue eyes reflected an uncommon depth of intelligence and awareness, set within a countenance echoing wisdom far beyond his mere thirty years of age.

Stepping forward, he allowed the grassy field and jungle beyond to engulf him, his intellect and soul embracing all nature's beauty, as well as her ineffable might. He felt the universe pouring through his senses. Yet he wanted to feel still more, to see even more clearly. He thought and felt, true, but he understood and accepted the limitations of man's senses and of his mind. He perceived himself as a tiny, self-conscious fragment of life, insignificant and lost somewhere within the infinite vastness of the eternal cosmos, struggling to grasp the depths of reality. And meaning, if meaning existed.

Rudi had inherited his scientific point of view from his father, an eminent biologist. Yet he simultaneously carried within him the influence of his mother, an acclaimed poet. He looked at the tall grass and heard himself reciting aloud:

"Summer grasses:
all that remains of great soldiers'
imperial dreams."

He then felt the scientist within him call out, and he bent and touched the wet blades of grass.

"A world of dew,
and within every drop,
a world of struggle."

And he thought of the transience of all things, including himself. He had been long engaged in writing a book that he believed he would never complete. When the opportunity had arisen to journey here, to Madagascar, to search for the subfossil remains of this unique island's extinct giant lemur, *Archaeoindris fontoynontii*, he could not resist seizing this moment plundered from life.

Archaeoindris was one of the largest primates to have ever evolved. These giant lemurs weighed up to perhaps 500 pounds—the size of an adult male gorilla. The only larger fossil primate was *Gigantopithecus blacki*, claimed by some on the fringe of science to be the ancestor of the mythical yeti and Sasquatch.

Radiocarbon dating indicated that giant lemurs had still been alive as late as 8,000 years ago. Rudi was intent on finding more recent bones that would prove that these giants had lived up to the year 350 BC, when humans intensified their settlement activity on Madagascar. For Rudi suspected that it was man the hunter who caused the extinction of Archaeoindris.

As Rudi walked along the edge of the forest, he imagined what Madagascar must have been like even just a few millennia ago, when ten-foot-tall elephant birds, monstrous tortoises, horned crocodiles, and possibly even giant lemurs roamed the landscape. Vanished giants of a lost world… Yet the past was alive for Rudi, in his mind, like the early notes of an eternal, ongoing symphony.

Rudi thought how he felt so alive, living his life at this moment purely for the sake of living. It gave his life individual meaning. But what about man as a species, he pondered—what meaning was there for man? Especially when viewed against the ephemeral nature of existence.

~

Rudi had set up his camp near a sinkhole that he had found, which opened into a deep cave below. In exceptional cases some sinkholes contained graveyards of lemur subfossils. But the sun had set, and Rudi felt it wise to cautiously put off any attempt at spelunking until first light.

He noticed the beams of arcing headlights before he heard the engine. Someone was approaching his campfire. He waited.

After some time, an all-terrain jeep jerked to a stop before him.

"Are you that paleontologist?" the driver asked in a congenial but raised voice, talking over the noise of the motor. "That Austrian fellow who came up from Toliara?"

Rudi nodded, and he felt the odd sensation that he and this man were like two raindrops on a train window that were destined to come together, and that there was no way to avoid this joining.

"Rudi Baumgarten," Rudi introduced himself as the man shut off the engine.

"I knew I'd find you." The man smiled, good-natured. "I'm Gideon Carroll, from that new coal pit, that open mine that everyone's complaining about. Deforestation."

Rudi smiled slightly but tried to hide it. This Gideon Carroll, seated there in the jeep, was such an untidy sprawl of a man, rotund and languid, he reminded Rudi of a jellyfish relaxed into lethargy, afloat upon a tepid, tideless sea. Gideon's facial features similarly hung slack. Even his British accent seemed extremely relaxed.

"Listen," Gideon said. "Would you mind coming with me? Back to the pit. It's not more than thirty minutes from here. Bumpy, I admit. But you see, we found something…"

"A fossil?" Rudi took a guess.

"Ummm, not really. You need to see it."

Rudi felt his curiosity stir, something about the look in Gideon's eyes.

"You're not going to tell me any more?" he asked Gideon.

"I don't know if I can," Gideon humbly admitted. And then, genuinely, with some desperation and humility: "I really could use your help. You see—please don't repeat this—I'm here on contract as their geologist, but I didn't exactly thrive in school. Failed, really. I seem to make a habit of not only doing things badly, but doing things badly with skill. I learn much more now every day than I ever did in school. Schools really should be there only to teach you how to learn, don't you think?"

Once again, Rudi felt a smile lift upon his face. "You don't have a degree? In geology."

Gideon shook his head. "Not a real one. Just between you and me, I'm more self-taught. If you're going to be a prisoner in your own mind, the least you can do is make sure it's well furnished."

Rudi surmised Gideon to be about his own age, yet he found himself quite taken by what he would describe as the man's avuncular charm, and his artlessness.

"Okay." Rudi nodded. "I'll come along."

~

After bumping along in the dark for approximately three quarters of an hour, Rudi found their jeep approaching a huge circular pit with shaley slopes, a moonscape-like scar on the earth. He eyed the runoff water from the mining operation trickling over the fine-grained sedimentary rock and pooling nearby into small craters devoid of life. To Rudi it appeared more than just deforestation; it seemed an assault on the biosphere itself.

Yet Rudi dismissed his ecological concerns, so curious had he become about what he was to be shown. Finding a fossil in a coal mine was not unusual; in fact, many such mines were rich in fossils, some a treasure trove of ancient secrets—as was this pit that they were now approaching. Over the noise of the jeep's engine, Gideon had described to Rudi how a catastrophic earthquake during the Permian had suddenly lowered a massive swamp over fifty feet, with the sea, sand, and mud instantly rushing in, covering, smothering, killing everything. In essence, the earthquake had frozen the swamp in time. Lush vegetation—scaly trees that looked like giant asparagus spears—river turtles the size of kitchen tables, a forty-five-foot long snake (five times as long as today's Amazon anaconda) were all preserved at this site rather elegantly.

But at 150 feet down, they had come across something quite unexpected.

Gideon slowed the jeep as they passed a dozen or so Malagasy laborers who were leaving the site, reluctant to share the road. Mud covered and fatigued, in the darkness they eerily looked like a group of man-sized elephants, worn out and walking off to find a place to die.

Gideon stopped the jeep, disembarked, and walked off. Rudi followed him. Together they approached a lean, hard-looking Caucasian man who seemed to be loitering with intent.

"My boss," Gideon whispered to Rudi.

"Ah, there you are," the man addressed Gideon, surly, preoccupied. "What took you so long?"

Gideon opened his mouth to explain.

"Never mind," the man cut Gideon off. "That was the last of the men leaving. And they're not coming back until that thing is out of there. And I can't blame them. What a goddamned hold up. Is this that scientist?"

"Yes," Gideon answered.

"Good," the man went on. "You stay here. Show him what we've got. See if he knows what to do with it. I'll take the drive back to Toliara, see about getting some crane equipment out here."

And the man walked off, muttering to himself, "Goddamned hold up." He climbed into Gideon's jeep and drove off.

"His virtue," Gideon commented to Rudi, "is that he always says what he thinks. His vice is that what he thinks doesn't amount to very much."

"That's not the only jeep," Rudi asked, suddenly a bit concerned, "is it?"

"Huh? Oh no, we have four. Well, come on, let me show you the um, the thing."

Rudi followed Gideon through the darkness, descending into the tremendous pit, which must have been over half a mile in width. As they did so, Rudi glanced at the stratums of sedimentary rock composing the nearby wall, stacked horizontally one atop the other, like layers of a cake. He was traveling backward in time.

The humid summer air grew slightly chilly and clingy as they descended deeper into the pit.

"At first," Gideon explained as he led Rudi still deeper, "I thought maybe it was a fossil tree. Not just a fossil trace, an imprint, but a whole petrified tree. I thought maybe a..."

Gideon made an effort to carefully pronounce the scientific name correctly. "A *lycopsid*. Seemed close to the right size. The books say these lycopsids grew up to a hundred twenty feet in height, with trunks many feet in circumference.

"After the dynamite, we used a high-powered saw to cut away what remained of the surrounding coal. Then we sprayed it down with hydrofluoric acid—that was my idea—to dissolve any silica or carbonate. But then suddenly, it didn't look like a tree any longer..."

"What did it look like?" Rudi asked.

"Like that..."

Rudi stopped dead in his tracks, absolutely frozen, speechless. Before him, in the darkness, stood something... unnatural. Eerie. It rose approximately forty feet in height. It was leaning oddly, slightly to one side... In shape, it resembled an opened umbrella, standing upright, with a huge bulb of a handle half buried in the ground. Only the parasol-canopy was proportionally much smaller in diameter than that of an umbrella's, and the shaft much thicker.

Rudi felt the pinpricks of fear tingle over him as he noticed the glossiness of the uniformly smooth surface of the uncanny object. A shine not unlike metal...

"It's an artifact..." Rudi whispered. "How old did you say this stratum was?"

"About two hundred fifty million years."

"Around the time of the Permian-Triassic extinction."

"The Great Dying." Gideon nodded. "Yes, I've read about that. Our planet's most severe extinction event, when well over ninety percent of all life on Earth died out."

"It's made out of metal?" Rudi asked.

"Hmm, I don't think so. Looks like metal, doesn't it, but it doesn't feel like metal. Doesn't sound like metal when you hit it."

Rudi took a step forward, to move toward the mysterious umbrella, but stopped, keeping his distance.

"It's a bit frightening," Gideon agreed, "isn't it? Creepy. What do you suppose it is?"

Rudi shrugged his shoulders, and he felt himself grin. Short periods of intense awareness were worth more to him than an eternity of dullness. He held such glimpses of truth at the highest value, for such truth was beauty.

Rudi began to pace around the object. Gideon followed him.

"You and I, Gideon"—Rudi allowed the confluence of his thoughts and feelings to flow freely, poetically—"we're such petty players, living and breathing somewhere within eternal time. Our lives are so piteously short. To think that long before man ever appeared, this thing stood here locked inside a block of coal.

"And millions upon millions upon millions of years passed, achingly slow, until eventually things such as us slowly rose up to become the preeminent giants of this tiny planet, the masters of our Earth. And in our conceit, we think ourselves so large… forgetting the immensity of this universe. How ancient the cosmos really is. Oh, to what heights did *other* things rise, long before our distant ancestors even crawled out of the sea?"

He stopped.

"You agree, then"—Gideon timidly pointed a single finger upward—"that it's not of this Earth?"

"It's the only explanation."

"I was afraid you'd say that." Gideon nodded. "Do you think it was an extraterrestrial landing gone wrong? That it landed in the swamp. And then the sudden earthquake…"

Rudi nodded slowly as he considered it—it sounded reasonable.

"So," Gideon asked apprehensively, "there are dead aliens inside that thing?"

Rudi's eyes shot open wide. He had overlooked this obvious conclusion. He turned to the object's huge bulb that protruded up from the earth. Was the base unit the capsule? Inside of which the remains of these ancient astronauts lay.

"How much more of it is there?" Rudi asked in a voice near a whisper.

"I had workers dig down around it," Gideon answered. "It seems to go down another twenty feet or so."

Rudi stood there silent, thinking, his mind racing.

"But how come it all didn't crumble away into nothingness over the years?" Gideon asked him. "Did the coal somehow protect it? Or is it what it's made out of?"

"I don't know," Rudi answered, mystified. "Being encased as it was would have protected it from weathering, but…"

A few moments of silence ensued between the men as each wondered about the spacecraft in ways formulated by their individual capacities.

"Do you think we should try to open it?" Gideon asked. "Before my boss comes back tomorrow. The mine owners, they'll likely take it away. Bring it somewhere to study it. Or sell it. I doubt we'll ever see it again."

Rudi considered it.

"We have a diamond-core drill here," Gideon offered. "Or do you think that drilling… might blow it up?"

"Or release extrasolar bacterial or viral contaminants," Rudi added.

"Can germs survive for two hundred fifty million years?" Gideon asked sincerely.

Rudi rolled his shoulders. "No, I don't see how…"

"Well," Gideon offered, "I'm an optimist at heart. And the point of living and of being an optimist is to be foolish enough to believe the best is yet to come."

"Get the drill." Rudi surrendered to curiosity and opportunity, reminding himself that from conception until death, he, as well as all life, literally burned like a candle. And that he would eventually, all too quickly, be consumed by life's flame. *Embrace the present*, he told himself.

~

It had taken them most of the night to haul down and set up the heavy and cumbersome drilling apparatus and anchor it securely into place near the bulbous aft hull of the umbrella-shaped craft from another world.

They had both been quite excited when they had selected the drill spot, a point within a recessed seam that appeared to suggest the outline of a large hatch. But the drill had had no effect on the hull. Not anywhere on the hull. Whatever the uncanny ship was made of, it was harder than diamond.

"Well," Rudi said softly after Gideon turned the loud drill off for the final time, "I believe we've solved the puzzle of why this thing didn't corrode, disintegrate over the eons."

Gideon nodded. "Now what?"

Rudi shrugged, and they both sat down and leaned back on the fold-up chairs they had brought down into the pit. Gideon twisted open the bottle of brandy that he had liberated from his boss's shack of an office. He took a swig and passed the bottle to Rudi.

"Still," Gideon commented, "it's nice to be interested in something you're engaged in."

"And often frustrating," Rudi added, taking a mouthful of the brandy.

"Do you think they were benign?" Gideon asked, signaling Rudi with his hand to pass back the bottle.

"Resources are limited—it's the reason for all conflict. Nothing we've observed in the cosmos alters this. Nature develops strong drives in life, to attack, compete. Intelligence empowers the focus on satisfying these drives. And technology enables superior drive satisfaction. It may very well be a good thing that these beings, whoever they were, whatever they were, wherever they were from, arrived here two hundred fifty million years too early…"

Rudi waved for the bottle, and Gideon handed it back.

"But," Gideon proposed, "maybe they could have been both tough *and* gentle. I suggest to you that to be gentle, tolerant, wise, and reasonable requires a goodly portion of toughness."

Rudi looked at Gideon, surmising that the man was presenting a portrait of himself. He also saw in Gideon that this man probably never accepted the world as it was offered to him. Rudi smiled, feeling the brandy, but also believing this quality to be important in a man or a woman, for such people often possessed independent minds, minds that thought differently.

"What do you think they looked like?" Gideon asked.

And Rudi thought about the question. "Nature is orderly," he answered slowly, reasoning it out. "She does not deceive. "

He then fell silent for a second as he recalled how he had once estimated—and he believed accurately—the mass and weight of an extinct giant lemur using only the midshaft circumferences of a subfossilized humerus and femur.

"Observations," he continued, "if correctly made… our interpretations and conclusions that follow should allow us to answer that question."

"Despite our prejudices?" Gideon wondered.

"Despite our prejudices," Rudi assured him. "Our brains may be hampered by certain limitations, and there are certain philosophical questions that may forever lie beyond our grasp, but we carry within our minds a torch that can light almost any darkness, I believe."

187

And Rudi leaned forward, seated there in the coal swamp, and he began. "All life evolves, following the same fundamental rules of mutation and natural selection. And convergent evolution is one of the strongest indicators of the power of natural selection. When confronted with similar environments, animals tend to evolve in remarkably similar ways. Even when they are of extremely different ancestries."

Rudi thought of the long-extinct marine reptile the ichthyosaur and how today's dolphin shared with it the same basic body plan, the dolphin being a hunter in the sea, the same environment the ichthyosaur had pursued its prey in. Reptile or mammal, it mattered not. Evolution had converged their morphology. The earliest ichthyosaurs went back to 250 million years ago...

"We can expect extrasolar life to evolve into similar forms as we find on Earth," Rudi concluded.

"Could they have evolved to be human, like us?" Gideon asked.

"Let's review what we know," Rudi suggested. "Man was a long time coming, step by step, rising up slowly over the millions of years. From the fullness of all possibilities, from the many potential paths of evolution, we had to be a mammal. We had to be a primate. We were not inevitable, but we were forced to take the shape that we did."

"You mean," Gideon sought clarification, "because of our hands, and our big brains?"

Rudi gave a tilted half-nod of his head, maintaining his focus. "And let's examine what we can surmise about these extrasolar visitors. We can state as a fact that they are far older than man of Earth. And that they were intelligent. We can also say with confidence that they communicated ideas to one another and joined in efforts to create things."

Gideon glanced up at the strange umbrella-shaped craft looming over them as Rudi went on.

"And we must assume that they came from a planet suitable for life, favorable in terms of atmosphere, temperature, gravity. A world perhaps not unlike our own. But a different Earth, a distant Earth.

"Here, on our Earth, never has there arisen a single, integrated, intelligent life-form that covered a large geographic area. Animal life has shown itself to be relatively small, self-contained, and highly mobile. We must presume that this applies to our aliens. Are we in agreement?"

"They wouldn't be like trees." Gideon nodded in agreement. "Rooted in one place."

"Yes, they would have motion," Rudi went on. "This would necessitate structure, senses to navigate successfully, a system of nerve impulses. They must have begun their evolution as we did ours, in the sea, in water. From this we can conclude that bilateral symmetry would have emerged, also a head end. And a tail end as well. Senses would have been close to the main center of the nervous system, the brain. We can conclude that our aliens have a head."

"Why not two heads?" Gideon asked, quite seriously.

"Two heads offer no advantage over the one," Rudi replied matter-of-factly.

Gideon nodded slowly.

Rudi continued, "I think we can safely say that our visitors each have but one head, one brain. But we do have examples of life here on Earth that come in more than one form—bees, ants."

"And caterpillars," Gideon added, "turn into butterflies."

"But I think we should place a limitation on the possible range of characteristics," Rudi responded, "and focus on what we know of vertebrate evolution. Let's step back for a moment and observe that on Earth the spectrum of life falls into three categories: marine, land, and airborne animals. Could our aliens have evolved from life in their sea and then developed intelligence and technology in the sea?"

"They would never have tamed fire under the water," Gideon pointed out.

"A key to a technological civilization," Rudi concurred.

"And fins," Gideon added. "How could they ever build anything without hands?"

"Yes," Rudi agreed. "Appendages suitable for developing tools and manipulating the environment would be an absolute necessity. Is there, on Earth, an equivalent of human arms and hands under the sea?"

They both thought about it.

"No…" Rudi stated. "But I imagine it's conceivable that octopuses could develop the ability for tool manipulation with further evolution… But they would need to invade the land to tame fire…"

Gideon glanced rather nervously at the alien craft. "Alien octopuses?"

"It's a possibility," Rudi admitted.

Gideon fidgeted uncomfortably.

"Some crawling creatures of the ocean floor," Rudi further suggested, "might possibly evolve the equivalent of human arms and hands. But they still could not develop fire under the sea…"

"What about aliens that evolved intelligence on land?" Gideon asked, appearing to wish to distance himself from the thought of octopuses and crawling creatures. "Do you think our aliens might have been standing creatures? That they walked around like us? On two legs. *Bipedal.*"

Rudi smiled slightly to himself, as he sensed that Gideon slipped in the term *bipedal* to display his self-acquired book knowledge.

"Let's get there in steps," Rudi suggested. "The key struggle of our evolution was getting to hands. Arms and hands suitable for climbing trees, and later for creating and manipulating tools and weapons. But bipedalism and hands were not inevitable.

"When the lobe-fins and amphibians evolved to keep only four limbs out of an original larger number of fins, this could have permanently prevented the opportunity for the rise of hand-using vertebrates such as us. Hands only came about because we evolved to balance on two legs. To have hands, there was no other choice. I suggest that bipedalism and hands are likely rare in our universe.

"But what if fishes and amphibians had kept their original six fins? And if the forelimbs were sufficiently adaptive for evolution to select to maintain them... It's conceivable that there might have arisen many intelligent, four-footed, two-armed, hand-using animals on Earth."

"Centaurs?" Gideon asked, quite surprised.

"Centaur-like," Rudi corrected him. "Four legs, two arms, and two hands. Would this require too much coordination as opposed to four limbs? I don't think so. Centipedes run their arms in teams.

"I suggest to you that our aliens are centaur-like. That most intelligent, technological life in the universe is centaur-like. That centaur morphology dominates. There will be manlike extraterrestrials in form, having a head, being bipedal, with two legs, two arms, and hands, like us, but few in proportion to centaurs.

"And we need to include the possibility of octopus-like sentient beings, but adapted to a terrestrial existence. The same for intelligent ocean-crawling forms."

"What about elephant-like?" Gideon proposed.

This insight caught Rudi off guard, and he thought about it.

"Four-footed," Gideon explained, "but using their trunks to manipulate the environment. To make and use tools."

"Let's add elephant-like to our list." Rudi smiled. "It's a sound possibility."

"And birds?"

"Birds are problematic," Rudi responded. "Flight requires birds to remain physically small. Such small body size cannot support a large enough brain to produce an intelligent, technological being."

"And they have wings instead of hands," Gideon added.

"However…" Rudi thought it out. "If you had flying vertebrates of the centaur lineage, they could have hands."

"But they'd still have small brains," Gideon reminded him.

"What if they evolved on a dwarf planet, or a moon?" Rudi postulated. "A world with a low gravity? Allowing for large 'birds.'"

"It sounds possible," Gideon admitted.

"So we add elephant-like and birdlike to our list of possibilities. Giving us six possible morphological structures for extrasolar intelligent animal life:

centaur-like

manlike

octopus-like

lobster-like

elephant-like

birdlike

And we agree that our aliens are most likely centaur-like."

"I defer to your judgment," Gideon said. "But what do we call our centaurs? Our aliens? We should give them a name."

Rudi smiled. "How about bimanous quadrupedal hexapods?"

"Bimanous quadrupedal hexapods," Gideon repeated it.

"I like it." And he said it again, with emphasis—"*Bimanous quadrupedal hexapods*"—rather pleased with his instant mastery of the seemingly complex term.

"Of course," Rudi qualified their conclusions, "this assumes extrasolar beings would be carbon-based life as we know it, and that such life would have evolved in a liquid medium, as life on Earth did."

Rudi noticed Gideon eyeing the umbrella-shaped spacecraft.

"How big do you think they might be?" Gideon wondered. "How many bimanous quadrupedal hexapods do you suppose are inside that thing? Their remains, I mean."

"There's a correlation between brain size and body size." Rudi thought it out. "For a brain large enough for intelligence, a body probably could not be much smaller than half the size of a human. Greater physical sizes require an enormous supply of energy and the development of disproportionately thick and strong legs. If they have four legs, larger sizes would be possible. Up to the size of a horse, or larger. I'd guess the range of size would be from chimpanzee sized to elephant sized."

"And our bimanous quadrupedal hexapods?" Gideon asked, the term rolling off his tongue with a certain pleasure.

Rudi eyed the alien craft. "If we remain strictly scientific, I have to admit it's impossible to estimate with any accuracy."

"If you had to guess?" Gideon asked.

"Pony sized." Rudi smiled, before growing most serious, his blue eyes swelling with intellect, reflecting insatiable wonder. "But the deeper question is, why did they visit our Earth two hundred fifty million years ago? And do they still exist, somewhere out in the cosmos? Or are they now an extinct race? What was the meaning of their existence? What is the meaning of ours? What meaning is there for man?"

And Rudi cautioned himself, recalling in his mind the words once spoken to him long ago by his archaeology professor and mentor, a man whom he held in great esteem:

"As humans, in all times and all places, we observe the world around us, process what we have observed, and then we question it. We attempt to understand the reality around us, to give meaning to our world and our place within it. As humans, we insist there is more to it than simply we are born, we live, and then we die and disappear. We feel we are deeper than this, that we are part of something awesome and eternal."

Rudi felt such depth for man. In the fiber of his being he felt it. Yet intellectually he knew and accepted the reality of the world. Just as individuals were born, lived, and died, so did species. Extinction was the norm. Ninety-nine percent of all the species that had ever existed on Earth lay in the dim, dusty cellar of time, extinct. Life was temporary and fleeting. Nothing was lasting. Even the Earth itself would one day be reduced to a lifeless, burnt-out cinder, perhaps even swallowed by its expanding sun.

Rudi shrugged his shoulders and shook his head and mumbled aloud, "Did we really rise up so far to think and to feel, to build and to destroy, to live, and to do it all without purpose?"

The dawn broke, and the rising sun cast light down into the pit.

Rudi and Gideon did not notice it at first. The glow. The shine. But then it intensified, heightening to an unnatural degree. It was then that it drew their attention.

Looming eerily, forty feet above them, the parasol-canopy of the extrasolar craft was aglow with sparkling, shimmering sunlight, light that swirled uncannily, moving back and forth across the surface of the opened umbrella in undulating, surging waves.

Awestruck, both men stood and began to slowly back up, putting a safe distance between themselves and the alien craft.

"The photons from the sun are somehow activating it," Rudi observed. "After having been locked in darkness for two hundred fifty million years… it's coming alive."

The alien structure began to pulsate, emitting a loud throbbing sound. The top of the structure slowly opened like a blooming flower, and a butterfly-shaped balloon, broad winged, long and slender, gently floated aloft, its mechanical structure sparkling with all the colors of the rainbow.

"A—a bimanous quadrupedal hexapod?" Gideon stuttered.

"No," Rudi said. "I think your caterpillar turning into a butterfly."

And Rudi smiled as he watched the beautiful butterfly balloon, finally set free, rise higher and higher, for he was confronted by an intense awareness, a glimpse of truth, of beauty. And he allowed the moment to engulf him, to pour through his senses. He could suddenly see more clearly now.

"I hadn't considered it…" he said, his voice low and reverent. "But there was another possibility. We could be living in a post-biological universe… Though planets may birth us ephemeral creatures of flesh and blood, the preeminent giants of the cosmos, the masters of the universe, are machines of artificial intelligence… And it's the role of us small, fragile, biological things to give rise to these thinking machines. That is our purpose…"

Rudi and Gideon watched the glorious butterfly balloon continue to rise straight upward, higher and higher, until it was but a point of colorful light hovering high above the Earth.

Rudi was later to learn that this floating butterfly from another world, displaced 250 million years in time, floating high above Madagascar, was transmitting to the whole of mankind the answers to all the unknowns that thinking beings had pondered. Knowledge was not allowed to perish in the universe. It was passed on.

Man of Earth would not need to repeat all the discoveries of knowledge that had been attained elsewhere in place and time. Man of Earth would not have to climb that ladder step by step, duplicating what others had done. Artificial intelligence saw a great efficiency in this. It was also how this intelligence expressed its appreciation to the catalyst whose purpose it was to birth its kind. It was its symbiotic *thank you* to biological life. It had been this way for untold billions of years. Earth was now part of this.

Recommendations

• The article "The Evolution of 'Humans' on other Planets," by anthropologist William Howells, which appeared in the June 1961 issue of Discovery magazine.

• The 1966 book titled *Intelligence in the Universe*, by Roger A. MacGowan and Frederick I. Ordway III.

Acknowledgements and Identifying Notations

• When the protagonist recalls the words spoken to him by his archaeology professor and mentor, these are actually the words of real-life archeologist Kenneth L. Feder, from his 2017 book titled *Ancient America: Fifty Archaeological Sites to See for Yourself*. The original poetic and insightful words in their fullness, in Feder's book (page 153), refer to why the rock art at Little Petroglyph Canyon is important:

"These places, all of them, are repositories of physical manifestations of the great creativity and imagination that characterizes the human mind. More than simple art galleries, though they are impressive and, indeed, important as such, these places also are windows into the human soul, however you want to define what that is. As humans, in all times and all places, we observe the world around us, process what we have observed, and then we question it. We attempt to understand the reality around us, to give meaning to our world and our place within it. As humans we insist there is more to it than simply we are born, we live, and then we die and disappear. We feel we are deeper than this, that we are part of something awesome and eternal. We think, we dream, and we imagine. Part of what makes us human is the impulse to make those thoughts, dreams, and imaginings concrete, to paint them on canvases, sculpt them in clay, record them on paper, and, as seen so often in our fifty-site odyssey, to scratch, etch, pack, or paint them onto soaring stone cliff walls."

Kenneth L. Feder is also the author of *Frauds, Myths, and Mysteries: Science and Pseudoscience in Archaeology*.

• When the protagonist in this story recites aloud:
"Summer grasses:
all that remains of great soldiers'
imperial dreams,"
he is reciting a Japanese haiku poem written by Japanese poet Matsuo Bashō (1644–1694)

• When the protagonist in this story recites aloud:
"A world of dew,
and within every drop,
a world of struggle,"
he is reciting a Japanese haiku poem written by Japanese poet Kobayashi Issa (1763–1828).

• It was assumed by this author that the protagonist of this story was familiar with and strongly influenced by the writings of marine biologist N. J. Berrill. The author attempted to show this via the protagonist's thoughts and dialogue.

• Some of the dialogue spoken by Gideon Carroll was based on quotes attributed to the actor and writer Peter Ustinov (1921–2004). Specifically:
"I learn much more now every day than I ever did in school. Schools are there to teach you to learn."
"If you're going to be a prisoner of your own mind, the least you can do is make sure it's well furnished."
"Her virtue was that she said what she thought, her vice that what she thought didn't amount to much."
"To be gentle, tolerant, wise, and reasonable requires a goodly portion of toughness."
"The point of living and of being an optimist is to be foolish enough to believe the best is yet to come."

• The speculations on the possible morphology of intelligent extrasolar beings were primarily based on:

An article by anthropologist William Howells titled "The Evolution of 'Humans' on other Planets," which appeared in the June 1961 issue of *Discovery* magazine, on pages 237 to 241;

Chapter 11, "Characteristics of Extrasolar Intelligence," pages 236 to 245, of the 1966 book titled *Intelligence in the Universe*, by Roger A. MacGowan and Frederick I. Ordway III. (Chapter 11 was prepared primarily by the co-author Roger A. MacGowan.)

• Bimanous Quadrupedal Hexapods:

Bimanous: Having two hands distinct in form and function from the feet. From New Latin *bimana* two handed, from *bi-* + Latin *manus* hand.

Quadrupedal: Four footed. An animal, especially a mammal, that has all four limbs specialized for walking. From Latin *quadrupēs*, from *quadru-* (see *quadri-*) + *pēs* foot.

Hexapods: Six-footed. Greek *hexapod-*, *hexapous* having six feet, from *hexa-* + *pod-*, *pous* foot.

A Note from the Author

This author hopes the reader found the science-based speculations offered on the possible forms that intelligent extraterrestrial life might take thought provoking. The speculations are based on a 1961 science article by anthropologist William Howells, a 1966 nonfiction book by Roger A. MacGowan and Frederick I. Ordway III, and a few of this author's own thoughts. (See "Recommendations.")

William Howells suggested the possibility that the centaur-like form might dominate alien morphology. He coined the term *bimanous quadrupedal hexapods*. Roger A. MacGowan and Frederick I. Ordway III disagreed with Howells on this point, believing that evolution would not preserve six limbs, since it required greater coordination and would not initially provide a selective advantage.

Roger A. MacGowan and Frederick I. Ordway III concluded that there were five possible morphological structures for extrasolar intelligent animal life:

1. manlike
2. centaur-like
3. elephant-like
4. dolphin-like
5. octopus-like

In this story, this author altered this list based on his own beliefs and suspicions and for purposes of entertainment.

The idea of artificial machine intelligence dominating the universe is that of Roger A. MacGowan and Frederick I. Ordway III, as is the speculation that knowledge may possibly not be allowed to perish and may be passed on from civilization to civilization throughout the universe.

This is the second story by this author presenting these ideas on alien morphology and machine artificial intelligence. The first was his 2012 novel *The God Antenna*.

Niko Zinovii
Santa Monica, California
22 December 2016

Bimanous Quadrupedal Hexapods

Niko Zinovii

Outgoing Tide

~1~

D r. Anthony Thin strolled rather leisurely from the ship's dining area, walking out upon the promenade deck, where he stopped to overlook the dark, moonlit Caribbean. As he stood there in silence, appreciating the quiet night, the tranquil sea, he drew inquisitive stares from other passengers. This was not surprising. At six foot three, Anthony cast quite a striking figure, being tall, dark, and handsome.

But it was more than his physical appearance that drew attention. There was also an unusual silent and defining strength to him, a dignity that echoed forth from his countenance, projecting a sense of decency and conviction. In a way, he seemed the moral conscience of the human race somehow made manifest in a single man.

At first, Anthony was unaware of the elegant woman standing nearby, who had paused in her walk to also look out at the sea. But as a delicate cloud drifted tenuously across the full moon, he ever so slowly became cognizant of her presence, and finally he glanced over at her.

She returned his look with a soft, relaxing smile. And there was an immediate flicker of attraction between them. Anthony felt himself involuntarily stand a bit taller, while she appeared to suddenly look a little flushed, her face softly aglow.

Anthony found himself nodding hello, politely. In response, the woman unconsciously touched her face, gently pushed back her silvery hair, and gracefully walked over to him.

"May I say hello," she said with a demure dropping of her eyes, her voice soft, her European accent quite pronounced.

"Of course you may," Anthony smiled, the tone of his voice respectful, warm, inviting. Up close, Anthony could see that the woman was clearly fifteen or so years his senior. He guessed she was in her early sixties. Yet he found himself drawn to her. He gazed into her lovely eyes, which reminded him of the sea after a storm, calm and alluring.

"I'm Countess Klára Conti," she introduced herself.

"Italian?" he guessed as he shook her hand, feeling the almost imperceptible caressing of her fingers.

"No, Hungarian. Italian by marriage," she answered openly, adding with some hesitation, with some shyness: "I'm a widow."

"I'm sorry to hear that," Anthony responded, genuinely.

"Thank you. It was long ago."

Anthony nodded and proceeded to introduce himself. "My name is—"

"Anthony Thin," she interjected, gently. "Dr. Anthony Thin."

"I feel highly complimented, but how do you…" Anthony stumbled. "Well, I know we've never met. I would have remembered."

And their eye contact deepened as the intimacy between them grew.

"Thank you." She accepted the subtle compliment elegantly. "But I think you're too modest. Yes, I know who you are. The paleontologist."

"Ah." Anthony understood. "But I'm actually an ophthalmologist."

"An eye doctor?" she asked, surprised.

He nodded.

"But I had read that… You are Anthony Thin, aren't you?"

"Yes, I am," he assured her. "But paleontology is just a hobby of mine, not my profession."

"But your discovery of that fossilized fish, it made you famous. I've seen your face on the covers of magazines, in newspapers. If you're an eye doctor, why are you so interested in fossil fish?"

Anthony turned slightly, looking out to sea as he explained. "My father was a paleontologist. I learned a lot from him. Before going my own way in life. Whenever I miss him, I dabble in paleontology."

"Oh," she whispered with understanding.

And Anthony turned back to face the countess, his exclusive interest focused once again on her. "How do I properly address you?" he asked sincerely. "Is it Countess? Mrs. Conti? Klára?"

"Klára, please," she answered. "Just Klára."

Anthony noticed the pupillary dilation of her lovely eyes. He wondered if his pupils were also widening with growing emotion. There was also the small increase in tear production in her eyes, which now glistened like the shiny eyes of a lover.

"Klára it is, then," he said, his voice softening, reflecting what he was feeling as their eyes remained locked in a prolonged, unbreakable gaze.

"Please, tell me more about your fossil fish," Klára asked, fully transparent that she had little interest in paleontology but was instead exercising a strong desire to engage him. "If you don't mind."

"I don't mind," he answered her, the tone of his voice making it clear that he would much rather look up at the moon with her, and perhaps whisper sweet nothings into her ear.

"Um, well, did you know that the gill regions of a developing shark and a developing human appear practically indistinguishable in the earliest stages of the embryo? It's true. And when we follow the gill arches through development…"

He gently reached out and touched the side of her lovely face as he continued, moving his hand to correspond with his words. "We follow the origin of our jaw, larynx, throat, ears… All the bones, muscles, nerves, arteries, they develop inside these gill arches. It's the window that allows us to see our inner shark. We're all just modified fish."

Klára smiled and then laughed quietly. And he laughed with her, softly.

"Well, it is true," he defended himself with a smile.

She then said some words, and he said some words, and the evening deepened. Soon, as they stood there together, high above the moonlit Caribbean, they fell nearly silent, mostly speaking without words. And Anthony came to realize that the most powerful and mysterious experience that one could ever have was the emotional upheaval of unexpected romantic love.

~2~

After having walked the countess to her cabin, where she had retired for the evening, Anthony found himself wandering the ship's promenade deck, his mind continually reliving the polite handshake the countess had given him before discreetly kissing him goodnight upon his cheek, so softly, like a whisper. Yet he had felt that delicate kiss make its way to the depths of his soul. This evening he had seen charm, and beauty, and unfathomable grace in a face that he seemed to have been waiting for. He felt a bit bewildered.

"Anthony," someone said, intruding upon his thoughts. "Are you okay?"

"Oh, Philip," Anthony acknowledged the psychiatrist whom he had met on board and befriended shortly after the cruise ship had set sail from Miami. "Sorry, I didn't see you."

"Well, I saw you earlier." Philip smiled inquisitively. "An old friend?"

"What? Oh, no," Anthony responded as the two of them began walking together. Comparable in age and level of education, they felt quite comfortable with one another.

"So, a new friend?"

"I don't know..."

"Well, she's certainly a beautiful woman," Philip remarked. "Is it her age?"

Anthony stopped abruptly. "You are frank, aren't you?"

"It makes life more interesting," Philip answered, his smile returning. "And less complicated. Well?"

Anthony nodded and they resumed their walk. "Yes, she's a beautiful woman." And he left his words hanging out there in the air for some time before slowly opening up. In his dark brown eyes stirred reflections of the serious, restrained, and intelligent nature of his character, coupled to his virtuous soulfulness. Reserved, he appeared rather like an American version of the stiff-upper-lipped gentleman, but one with heart.

"We wouldn't grow old together..." Anthony admitted. "We're at different stages in our lives... I imagine there would be difficulties in terms of relating to one other. Our expectations of the future would differ... But the chemistry is overwhelming, I've honestly never felt anything like it."

"But what happens after the initial excitement fades?" Philip asked candidly, growing serious, his voice reflecting the genuine concern normally reserved only for a dear friend. "For a man, becoming involved with a woman who is significantly older—it can be particularly challenging for a lasting relationship. After the excitement dissipates, you're left with who each other really are. And there are certain physical realities regarding attraction and intimacy. I think one needs to be cautiously mindful of what the relationship holds down the road. Of where it leads.

"Also, a man's natural desire for immortality, his need to leave something of himself behind... This would need to remain unsatisfied. There would be no children. Our only means of immortality."

Anthony digested the direct advice for a moment or two and then nodded, sedately. "Thanks, Philip, I appreciate your honesty."

~3~

Later that night, Anthony slipped into bed, still thinking of the Countess Klára Conti. He had left the blinds open, and the night sky was lit by the splendor of the moon. As he lay there, he felt as if he had fallen and found himself unable to rise. It was so strange, and so wonderful, the helplessness of love. Yet he felt pained by uncertainty. *I'm forty-five years old*, he thought to himself. *She's likely... sixty-three?*

A warm breeze flowed into his cabin, carrying upon it the scent of the sea. The odor brought Anthony's troubled mind welcome relief as it triggered within him the memory of his recent expedition to Ellesmere Island, in the Canadian Arctic, where he had found the fossilized fish that had produced his new-found fame.

As he slowly drifted off to sleep, in his mind's eye he recalled the windswept, desolate landscape of Ellesmere. It was a bleak, rock-strewn, frozen wasteland. He remembered imagining how the land must have appeared 375 million years ago. It had been a subtropical river delta then, straddling the equator, a warm watery world of swamps and streams and pools, all abounding with aquatic Devonian life.

It was there where, all those millions of years ago, an intrepid fish had dared to crawl up upon the dry land for the first time. Every reptile, every bird, every mammal alive today was descendent from that ancient, transitional fish. Including man.

Anthony had felt a thirst to learn more about this distant ancestor of humanity, to shine greater light upon that pivotal point in the history of life on Earth. So he had journeyed to the high Arctic, to hunt for fossils hidden in ancient rocks.

Specifically, he had set out to search for an earlier transitional fossil than those already discovered. He had reasoned that due to the widespread vertebrate speciation of the late Devonian, he would find such a fossil. And he did: a 380-million-year-old primitive fish that possessed tetrapod characteristics, marking it as the earliest evolutionary form of the transition from fish to amphibian. A creature that had colonized the undeveloped land, populated then only by algal mats, early terrestrial vegetation, wingless insects, and the first arachnids. In such a wide-open territory, this daring ancestor of man's had flourished.

~4~

The next morning, Anthony found the countess standing beside the ship's rail, staring out to sea. She was wearing a tasteful sunhat and a stylish dress, which nicely accented her elegance and refinement, as well as her attractive, slender figure.

Anthony silently walked up to her and stood beside her. "You seem to be lost out there," he commented, the tone of his voice low, pleasant. "What is it you're looking for?"

She turned to him and smiled softly. Her eyes fluttered for a moment, and once again the two of them gazed longingly at one another. Anthony noticed how in the light of day her age showed more clearly upon her face, fine lines marking a lifetime of experience. He wondered if perhaps she might be closer to sixty-four or sixty-five years of age... Yet she looked truly lovely.

"The promise on the horizon," she answered him, somewhat enigmatically. "And the red dawn. It delights me."

Let go of your worries, Anthony told himself. *Listen to your intellect and you'll only run away, afraid of drowning, drowning in a sea of love. Why not allow yourself to be drawn in? How can love lead you astray?* And he suddenly realized that love's aim was to experience.

"I'm glad I found you," he confessed. "Klára, I want to arrange to see you again, somehow, somewhere. You see, the next island—it's my stop. It's where I get off."

"The island of Olvidado?" she asked, surprised.

He nodded. "I'm paying a long-distance house call to the owner of the island."

She looked at him in disbelief.

"No, it's true," he explained. "Shortly after publishing my find, that fossil fish, I was contacted by a representative of the island's owner, who contracted my services at a fee I simply couldn't turn down. All expenses paid. Airfare. This cruise... Why are you smiling?"

"Olvidado," she answered, "is also where I disembark."

"How is that possible? I mean... my understanding is that it's a private island."

"I'm visiting Spa Fuente. It's an exclusive beauty spa on Olvidado, by invitation only."

"Really?"

"Yes, really, it's true."

~5~

That afternoon, Anthony stood with Klára amongst a half dozen other passengers, all couples in their late sixties, seventies, eighties, all affluent, all waiting for the water taxi that was slowly motoring toward the cruise ship from the verdant island of Olvidado.

The island was far more substantial than Anthony had anticipated. He had imagined it as a low-lying cay, but the opposite was true. A beautiful cliff rose up from the shore and lined the cove's crescent stretch of pristine beach. Anthony could see impressive stone buildings high above within the foliage, shaded by broad-leafed trees. And there was an incredible red-domed castle that terraced its way down to the sea, where there was a modern wharf. The sight was quite impressive.

The water taxi docked, and porters began to load their luggage on board. Anthony and Klára were the first to board, and they stood together at the bow as the craft motored off to Olvidado. The turquoise sea was crystal clear. Klára gracefully pointed up to the circling seagulls, whose bellies all appeared greenish-blue due to the bright upward reflection of the tropical sun off the sea. They smiled together, at that moment being two individuals but one in soul. Time seemed to stand frozen for them, but then there was the bump of the taxi against the wharf. They had arrived.

They disembarked last and followed the others as island attendants dressed in stylish white spa uniforms led the group down the long pier. As they walked, Anthony glanced at the beach they were passing, feeling its beauty and mystery. It was a low-tide seashore of rocks and little pools and shallows of crystal-clear water, shadowed by vegetated dunes and cool grottoes. The air above was astir with seagulls, their evocative calls accenting the sense of remoteness emanating from Olvidado. The island seemed a world apart. Anthony could not help but think of the watery Devonian world of his fossil fish, and how timeless and unhurried was the way of nature.

Beyond the beach, Anthony and the countess followed the others up a wide stone walkway that led to two sets of diverging stairs embedded into the cliffside. Anthony leaned close to Klára, pointing out to her that the island's cliff was actually a petrified reef, like certain cliffs in Jamaica. That a hundred thousand or so years ago, when the sea was much higher, Olvidado's cliff was an underwater, living reef, composed of coral, sponges, algae—populated by thousands of species of wondrous sea creatures, all long-ago engaged in life's constant struggle for survival.

At the foot of where the stairs diverged, Anthony and Klára were respectfully asked to surrender their cell phones and any other electronic devices they might have in their possession. The confiscation was explained as being a standard security measure on Olvidado. Anthony quietly complied and placed his cell in the large basket that contained the relinquished items of the other guests.

A dark-skinned young man, uniformed in white, politely approached Anthony. "Dr. Thin?" he asked.

"Yes?" Anthony nodded.

"This way, please." The man motioned to the stairs on the left. "To the castle."

Anthony glanced at the other passengers, who were being escorted up the other staircase.

"That leads to the spa," the young man explained.

Anthony turned to Klára. "I'll come to see you after my house call?"

"Please." She gave him a light kiss on the lips, as if to awaken him fully to their moment of love, and they parted company.

As Anthony watched the countess gracefully walk off, he felt as if he always wanted to see her in his life, to hear her distinctive soft voice. To sense her scent when he entered a room that she had just left... Silently, he listened to the rumbling of his own poetic thoughts:

You think you're alive because you breathe air? Shame on you that you've been alive for so long in such a limited way...

~6~

Standing before the open door of the castle, blocking entry, was a small but handsome golden-brown capuchin monkey wearing a bright-red bellboy cap. Anthony turned to his escort.

"On Olvidado," the young man explained, "our trained monkeys wear service hats. They assist Dr. Munday. They work in the spa. Retrieving objects, turning lights on and off, opening drinks. Dr. Munday considers them nature's natural butlers."

"Oh?" Anthony remarked, surprised.

"This is where I leave you, Dr. Thin. The monkey will escort you to where you'll find Dr. Munday."

"I follow the monkey?" Anthony asked.

The young man nodded. "I see you have your medical bag with you. I'll have the rest of your luggage brought up as soon as possible."

Anthony nodded and followed the monkey into the castle, smiling slightly, amused by the fact that he was following a capuchin butler.

The capuchin led Anthony into a small elevator, pushed in on a large, brightly lit button, and received a small treat from a slot in the wall. There was an initial jerk, and they slowly descended a number of floors. When the elevator finally stopped, Anthony guessed that he was likely back down at sea level, or slightly above it.

Following the monkey out of the elevator, Anthony stepped into a cavernous room with walls of polished stone supporting a high, impressive vaulted ceiling. There were a multitude of large, extremely detailed charts of the Caribbean seafloor lying about flat and orderly upon high tables, and one enormous area map taking up a full wall. Nearby, hundreds of books stood precisely stacked in place beside a large, ornate desk that was exceptionally neat, clean, with nothing atop it save a computer.

Anthony wondered to himself, *If a cluttered desk is a sign of a cluttered mind, of what, then, is an empty desk a sign?* He found the suggestion of this thought quite paradoxical, even preposterous, as he knew very well that the man he was visiting was considered a giant in his field, a genius.

Directly behind the desk was an exquisite painting of a green sea turtle in flight beneath the waves, with several large remoras (suckerfish) adhered to its shell, along for the ride. Anthony looked for the signature of the artist. It was that of his host. Impressed, Anthony read to himself the title of the painting: *Coexistence.*

The capuchin scampered down a set of wide marble steps, and Anthony followed. Descending the stairs, Anthony caught the smell of exotic burning incense and the salty scent of the sea. The chamber transformed into an immaculate oceanographic laboratory on its lower level, with huge arched doorways open to and overlooking the Caribbean. Enormous aquatic tanks of various shapes and sizes decorated the room, containing exquisite creatures, beautiful and delicate, unreal—as well as others that exemplified ugliness, appearing as if they had been squashed by the unseen, torturous forces of the greatest depths of the sea.

There were deep salt-water pools in the floor, containing larger specimens of fish. The monkey was careful to avoid these. Anthony noticed the form of a shark in one of them and understood why.

Anthony stopped as he noticed a tall, lean man, middle aged, rising from a microscope and turning toward him with ramrod straightness, his emperor-like head held rather high, thrown back. In posture he was statuesque, but then he started toward Anthony and this majestic illusion vanished, as he walked like a man with rickets, slightly bent kneed and flatfooted, on legs that presented as fairly insubstantial.

The capuchin scurried to this man and leapt up into his arms, stopping him in his tracks. There the monkey received a tasty treat as a reward for services rendered.

"Dr. Munday?" Anthony asked.

"Leonard. Please call me Leonard," Dr. Munday insisted, his voice eloquent and unusually distinctive in sound, seeming all cello and woodwind, muffled in silk.

Munday gently placed the capuchin down upon the floor and walked the remaining steps to Anthony. Keeping a distance of several feet, Munday focused on Anthony like an eagle, comprehending all in a single glance.

"There's something about you," Munday observed. "Something photographs don't capture. You seem the living embodiment of virtue…"

"Thank you." Anthony humbly accepted the compliment. "I'm not sure what to say."

"Then let's simply say hello," Munday suggested, offering his hand to shake.

"Leonard," Anthony acknowledged his host.

"Dr. Thin."

"Anthony, please."

"Anthony it is."

As they shook hands, Anthony sensed in his host a vivid, passionate, yet sedate and sad demeanor. In a way, Munday seemed to Anthony a reflection of a tragic character from some lost Shakespearean play, someone too exposed to certain realities of life and half in love with the painful suffering that his experiences and perception engendered. This was not what Anthony had expected of this luminary of genetics, of this outstanding talent of the field of molecular and cellular biology.

Anthony also sensed something different in the handshake. It prompted him to glance down at his host's large, boney hands. They were six fingered. Perfectly symmetrical, there was nothing monstrous about them. They appeared quite normal, in fact, except that each hand had a sixth digit, an extra finger.

"You noticed the Greenland shark?" Munday asked.

"Yes," Anthony nodded, snapping out of his surprise, his eyes flickering back at the deep pool he had just passed.

Munday pointed back toward his abandoned microscope, his arm movements a bit stiff. "Actually, I have something here you might very well appreciate, given your profession, your specialty."

Anthony followed Munday over to the microscope, where his host lit a handsome sandalwood pipe with an incense stick and began to puff on it, filling the air with the rich scent of vanilla.

"That Greenland shark is three hundred ninety-two years old," Munday stated. "Plus or minus a hundred twenty years. This makes the species the longest-lived vertebrate on Earth."

"How can you tell?" Anthony asked. "I mean, the age of the shark."

Munday explained. "The age of a fish is normally determined by examining its otoliths, its ear stones. But sharks, as you know, are mostly cartilage. They lack this hard, calcified tissue."

"So how can you tell a shark's age?" Anthony asked, drawn in, intrigued.

"The Greenland shark has a unique eye structure," Munday answered. "The lens of its eye continues to grow throughout its life. The more layers added to the lens, the older the shark. These layers can be counted, similar to tree rings. Except, in this case, the layers are removed, one at a time, until the embryonic nucleus of the lens is reached. Radiocarbon dating then reveals the age."

"Interesting," Anthony remarked with genuine appreciation.

"Would you like to view the Greenland's eye lens nucleus?"

"I would."

Munday offered Anthony the microscope. "The surgical removal of one of the shark's eyes was necessary, of course, but it has provided valuable knowledge to science."

Anthony took his time over the microscope. As he examined the lens nucleus, he half listened to Munday, who went on:

"Such incredible longevity is also found in a number of species of Pacific rockfish. I have a shortraker in my collection, the large orange fish you passed on your way in. She's nearly two hundred years old, yet displays negligible senescence. Not even a decline in fertility. Oogenesis continuing into advanced age."

Anthony rose from the microscope. "Did you partly ask me here, to Olvidado, because you suspected that I might be intrigued by this lens nucleus?" he asked, guessing, still quite curious about the circumstances surrounding his being contacted.

Munday shook his head. "No." He then puffed on his pipe, reached back into his memory, and quoted aloud:

"'What occurred three hundred and eighty million years ago, when the first fish crawled onto dry land, affected everything that came afterward. It affected the fact that we *Homo sapiens* are here. This intrepid transition from water to land set forth the evolutionary steps of investments that shaped the core of our humanity.'"

Munday stepped closer to Anthony, making meaningful eye contact. "You wrote those very words. I wanted to meet the man who appreciated so profoundly the reality that you had expressed, the depth recognition. Surely such vision can grasp the unrestrained horizon of man."

"The unrestrained horizon of man?" Anthony asked.

Munday pulled back, reserved, patient. "I also asked you here because I read that you paint, as do I."

"It's your left eye?" Anthony suddenly asked.

"Down to business so quickly?"

"I'm sorry, I couldn't help noticing," Anthony explained. "You're blind in your left eye, aren't you?"

"The retina was detached during the biopsy, which confirmed the diagnosis. Intraocular melanoma. The one eye." Munday stated it matter-of-factly.

"The retinal detachment can be repaired by surgery," Anthony stated as he looked more closely at Munday's sightless eye. "With intraocular melanoma, a biopsy of the tumor is rarely needed. Who ordered it?—Never mind. Is the melanoma of the iris?"

"No, of the ciliary body."

"The thickness?" Anthony asked, immediately concerned, knowing that intraocular melanoma of the ciliary body was often larger and more likely to spread to other parts of the body.

"Two millimeters."

"Did your symptoms include a change in the position of the eyeball in the eye socket?"

"Please," Munday responded calmly. "All the necessary equipment has been assembled in our clinic, all is ready for you to operate. But first, I want to see your reaction to something."

Munday moved to a nearby wall and activated a communication device, speaking into it fluently in another language. "*Sendu Marko al la laboratorio, tuj. Mi kredas ke li estas en la maro, proksime.*"

Munday then turned to Anthony. "I've sent for someone. He should be here shortly. I want you to see him."

"That almost sounded like Spanish..." Anthony remarked, curious.

"Esperanto." Munday identified the artificial language rather casually. "Do you know how many different times a complex, image-forming eye has independently evolved since the Cambrian?"

"At least forty," Anthony answered.

"Yes, that's right," Munday acknowledged, impressed. "Good eyesight, in and out of the water, I'm sure you know, is quite rare in the animal kingdom. When we humans swim under the water, with our eyes open, it's difficult; our vision works poorly in that medium. Dolphins, on the other hand, have excellent eyesight both in and out of the sea."

"Yes," Anthony nodded, "when a dolphin surfaces, the lenses and corneas of its eyes correct the difference in the refraction of light. Otherwise dolphins would be nearsighted on the surface."

"Humans and dolphins," Munday stated slowly, "share a common mammalian ancestor. One that lived approximately sixty to sixty-five million years ago."

Anthony nodded, wondering where this was all leading. At that moment, a young man, Caucasian, dripping wet, wearing swim trunks, stepped into the laboratory, having entered through the open doors overlooking the sea.

"*Markon, venu ĉi tien,*" Munday said to the young man. "*Tio estas doktoro Maldika. Mi volas lin vidi viajn okulojn.*"

The young man walked over and stood before them.

"This is Marc," Munday informed Anthony.

Anthony noticed Marc's eyes. They were most unusual, a handsome but uncanny blue-black in color and brownish-tan where normal eyes are white.

"May I?" Anthony asked Munday as he reached into his medical bag to withdraw a penlight.

"By all means," Munday responded.

"There's an unusual oily, tear-like film lubricating his eyes," Anthony observed.

"Excreted from glands at the inner corners of his eye sockets," Munday explained.

Anthony started a pupil test. What he saw amazed him. Marc's abnormally large, round pupil transformed from round to a U-shaped slit, and then, as the brightness increased, the slit closed, leaving only two pinholes in the temporal and nasal parts of the iris.

Anthony turned to Munday, perplexed.

"If you had your instruments," Munday informed Anthony, "you'd also find that Marc's corneas are significantly thicker than those of a normal human eye. You'd notice that the choroids and vascular networks are more highly developed. The eyeballs are slightly flattened, as are the corneas. The eye lens is almost spherical. Light refraction and the focusing of images on the retina are performed almost entirely by the lens."

"Dolphin-like eyes…" Anthony stated aloud. "But how can a man have dolphin eyes?"

Anthony looked to his host, but Munday simply stood there ramrod straight, puffing on his pipe, his emperor-like head held higher than high, silently observing Anthony's reaction.

~7~

That afternoon, Anthony had been shown to his guest quarters, where his luggage awaited him. After he had sufficiently rested and prepared, he had operated on Munday, surgically removing the malignant tumor and reattaching the damaged retina, restoring his host's lost sight. The operation had been a complete success.

The surgery now behind him, Anthony relaxed his focus, allowing his thoughts to unwind as he stood on his room's balcony, watching the sun set. As his mind calmed, he thought of the dolphin-like eyes of the young man he had examined. He reflected on their remarkable blue-black color, on the uncanny contraction of the pupil.

But his mind was tired, too fatigued for serious contemplation. So he temporarily let go of the mystery. The moment he did, he thought of Klára, and he felt a longing to see her lovely face again, to look into her eyes.

He smiled as he considered how he was contracted to remain on Olvidado for the next two weeks as Munday's guest and personal physician, monitoring his patient's healing, a safeguard against infection and unexpected complications. Through sheer serendipity, this turned out to be a godsend. He would have two full weeks with the countess before he was to leave on the next cruise ship scheduled to stop at the island.

Anthony wanted that time with Klára. He needed it. For although he yearned to touch her, to kiss her, to feel her love, he still had troubling doubts about where such an affair would lead, given the difference in their ages.

Yet the passion he felt was intense. Her very presence filled him with desire. It was as if she were a goddess from another world, bringing with her the essence of love, infusing it into his life. He needed to see her. But he would have to wait until the morning, when he had been told such a visit would be arranged.

He peered off in the direction of Spa Fuente. He could see the complex's many rooftops through the foliage. As the sun disappeared below the horizon, seemingly sinking into the sea, and the world darkened and cooled, he fancied going off his balcony like a cat, following the ledge around the castle, finding his way down to the ground unobserved, to sneak off under the cover of night to pay a surprise visit to the countess. He smiled that he actually considered carrying out the whim. If he were younger, he might have.

Retiring to his bed, he went to sleep thinking of Klára, longing to have a precious moment with her under the moonlight, with only the stars watching. Alone, he suddenly felt a bit lost, as if love were the bridge between oneself and everything...

Restless, from time to time he awoke briefly during the night, on each occasion noticing the movement of the moon across the sky. In his sleep he must have heard the surf far below, for in his dreams he felt haunted by ghostly waves from somewhere far back in time. It brought to him a great sense of unease. And an inexplicable concern for Klára...

~8~

The next morning, beneath a sky of billowing, threatening clouds, Anthony was escorted to Spa Fuente, where he was asked to wait outdoors in a luxuriant, exceptionally beautiful flower garden.

As he waited, he thought of the mandatory nondisclosure agreement he had signed that morning, properly witnessed and notarized. He had been surprised that the document included all of Olvidado, and not only the spa and its proprietary health and beauty treatments. He found himself wondering if this was perhaps to prevent him from revealing his awareness of the dolphin-eyed young man.

As he turned to view the sea, he heard the lovely accented voice of Countess Klára Conti call out to him. "Anthony."

He moved to her rather quickly, for he had awakened for some reason feeling fearful that somehow during the night he had lost her. But instantly he found her enchanting eyes, looked into her soul, and all seemed right again.

He smiled as he noticed her hair, wet and flat, pulled straight back and held in a ponytail. He could see all the basal black roots of her silvery hair this way. This surprised him, as he had assumed she was naturally gray.

"It is me," she remarked a bit shyly, her eyes dropping demurely.

Although her hair worn this way was unflattering, it presented her face in full, without framing or concealment, and Anthony welcomed this. He found himself gazing at her with strong desire, his heart pulsing with love. She looked so extra lovely today, beautifully aglow. Lively. Refreshed. *Maybe she's only sixty... fifty-nine?*

"Yes," he remarked. "It is you."

He reached out and gently removed a patch of loose skin from her cheek. "You're peeling," he remarked.

"A full-body exfoliation"—she smiled—"followed by a mud mask, coconut scrub, and a honey and walnut body polish, ending with a lavender moisturizer."

"Oh." Anthony smiled back, laughing softly, feeling so good to be with her. But then he noticed the small adhesive bandage on her left arm. "Since when does a spa take blood?" he asked, curious.

"The treatment is unique," Klára offered.

"Unique?" he asked, as he further noticed a small red pinprick on the side of her right shoulder, where vaccinations are usually administered.

A large raindrop splashed off Klára's forehead, and she laughed in surprise. "I think we're going to get wet," she warned him playfully. "Here, follow me." She took him by the hand and led him quickly across the grass to a small gazebo, which they entered to escape from the pitter-patter that began.

Seated inside, Anthony found himself thinking how pleasant the touch of her soft and feminine palm felt against his own. He found himself gazing into her eyes, his heart swelling with passion. He only wanted to become irretrievably lost in her eyes, yet every part of him felt as if it were soaring off in a different direction.

"Last night," Klára said softly, her lovely voice almost lost in the roar of the downpour that commenced, "I was lying on the rooftop, thinking of you. I saw a special star and made a wish upon it."

"What was your wish?" Anthony asked, completely ignoring the cloudburst, focused solely on her.

"I wished for you to kiss me," she whispered, her eyes glistening.

"I've been kissing you since I first saw you," he whispered back, and he took her in his arms and kissed her. He wanted to love a lifetime in that moment. To never let go, to never be separate from her. He only wanted to love her. And he let himself go completely, willing to drown in the sea of love.

~ 9 ~

Some time later, the sun came out and Anthony found himself escorted back to the castle, where he was left at the main entrance. There, curled up, taking a siesta, he found one of the estate's handsome capuchin monkeys, its bellboy cap dipping down over its closed eyes.

Anthony smiled and headed down toward the sea, lured by the sound of the waves. Halfway, he noticed an attractive stone path leading toward one of the castle's many terraced levels. On that terrace, he saw a young, blond-haired, Caucasian man in swim trunks sitting upon a boulder, sunning himself beside a number of round bathing pools and decorative rocks. Anthony made his way over to the sunbather.

"Good afternoon," Anthony introduced himself as he neared the young man. "My name is Dr. Anthony Thin."

But Anthony momentarily fell silent as he noticed the man's eyes. They were a handsome yet unnatural blue-black in color, brownish tan where normal eyes are white. *A second man with dolphin-like eyes?* Anthony found it astonishing. He then noticed that the fingers on this man's hands were webbed, as were the toes on his feet. Anthony did his best to react indifferently about these observations.

"Nice that the day cleared up," Anthony said casually as he stepped up to the man, whose pupils were contracted into uncanny U-shaped slits.

"Yes," the man responded in a thick European accent, the delivery of his words quite stilted. "The sun feels good, so warm, after spending so much time in the sea. My name's Patryk. You're a colleague of Dr. Munday's?"

"Leonard—Dr. Munday—introduced me to Marc yesterday," Anthony answered, sidestepping the question, probing indirectly. "I'm an ophthalmologist. He asked me to examine Marc's eyes."

"Is Marc all right? It's still so early for him. I hope he's adjusting well. He only left the spa a few weeks ago."

"Oh?" Anthony remarked, continuing to fish for information. "I just came from the spa. Did Marc… work at the spa, before?"

Patryk sat up. "I haven't seen you on Olvidado before…"

"I only just arrived yesterday," Anthony explained, wondering madly about Patryk's eyes. *It can't be a mutation, not with the two of them having the same eyes… Transplants? No… And webbed hands and feet? Marc's hands and feet were normal…*

"So you're not working with Dr. Munday?"

"I'm interested in his work," Anthony admitted honestly. "I'm visiting Olvidado as a guest of Dr. Munday's. I'll be here for the next two weeks."

"I knew you were too young for the spa." Patryk smiled as he got up and started toward one of the nearby small, round pools.

Anthony followed, smiling politely, although he perceived that he was missing some hidden deeper meaning in the humor. He noticed that Patryk's skin, up close, appeared unusually smooth, sleek, and thicker than normal, almost exhibiting a rubbery texture.

Anthony also caught a glimpse of the inscription on the medallion worn by Patryk. It read: "*Estu Preta.*" It was only then that Anthony remembered that Marc had also been wearing such a medallion.

Patryk leisurely stepped forward and dropped into one of the pools. He allowed himself to slowly sink down to the bottom, fifteen feet or so beneath the surface, where he sat and calmly closed his eyes, as if meditating.

Anthony knelt and scooped up a palmful of the pool's water in his cupped hand. *Salt water.*

He then stood there waiting for Patryk to surface. But Patryk remained submerged. After a few minutes, Anthony looked at his watch, noted the time, sat himself upon a nearby rock, and waited, rather bewildered.

Anthony checked his watch again. It was now approximately six minutes since Patryk had gone under. *Remarkable.*

Anthony suddenly sensed the familiar aroma of fragrant, vanilla tobacco. A shadow moved over him, and he turned to find Dr. Munday, his left eye bandaged, stepping up from behind, calmly puffing on his pipe.

"Good afternoon," Munday said evenly, his woodwind-like voice silky. "I see you've met Patryk."

"Eye to eye…" Anthony responded, glancing at his watch. "He's been under water now for nearly seven minutes…"

"Yes," Munday stated, leaning forward, lowering his emperor-like head to peer down into the pool. "It's noon. He's likely reflecting on his oath of chivalry. It encapsulates the code of values held by our society."

"By your society?"

Munday nodded "The classic virtues of knighthood—*prouesse*, *loyauté*, *largesse*, *courtoisie*, and *franchise*—are how we here balance man's dual nature. You see, the evolutionary process has placed man in a most challenging state of inner turmoil. Our most honorable attributes exist side by side with our most ignoble. This human condition, gifted to us by evolution, by the forces of natural selection focused simultaneously on the individual and the group, will always be with us.

"But imagine a society that optimally balances our evolved social traits—honor, virtue, duty, altruism—with our individually adaptive traits—selfishness, cowardice, hypocrisy, deviousness—so that we accept our human condition of inner turmoil, yet through mastery over ourselves, by embracing a knightly code of conduct, we make it possible to rise to the most honorable of heights."

"Chivalry?" Anthony felt himself intellectually stimulated yet so very confused. "Dolphin-like eyes? Webbed hands and feet?" He looked at his watch again and shook his head in disbelief. "Meditating like he is, how long can Patryk hold his breath?"

"Why do you assume he's holding his breath?" Munday asked.

Anthony just stared at his host, absolutely wordless.

"Please come down to the laboratory an hour after sunset," Munday instructed Anthony, and he walked off.

~10~

An hour after sunset, Anthony, wearing the silken robe and slippers provided to him by Munday's staff, took the elevator down to Munday's study. There, in that commodious cavern of a chamber, it was dark and quiet, tranquil, much the opposite of Anthony's mind, which was tingling with curiosity, a commotion of questions.

As Anthony walked past the room's nautical charts and stacked books, he felt cool air and he heard the distant *drip-drip* of water, both coming from below. He paused briefly to admire Munday's painting, Coexistence, before descending the wide marble steps that led down to the oceanographic laboratory.

The air below was filled with the scents of the sea and exotic burning incense. Anthony hardly glanced at the many species of unusual and bizarre fish that he passed, so focused was he on his rendezvous with his enigmatic host. He was careful, however, to walk cautiously around the deep salt-water pools in the floor. He had already forgotten which one of them contained the centuries-old Greenland shark.

He was about to call out for Munday when he noticed the doctor on the balcony, beyond the laboratory's huge, arched doors that opened to and overlooked the dark, moonlit sea.

He walked up to Munday, who was also in a white silken robe, silently standing before a stone well, its bucket recently raised, dripping cool fresh water down into the unseen depths far below. Munday nodded to Anthony, took the chilled bottle of wine from the well's bucket, and proceeded to uncork it.

"A year after I relocated to Olvidado," Munday recounted, staring wistfully out to sea, his breathy, hollow voice calm and solemn, "there was a terrible hurricane. A ship wrecked itself on the reef out there. All its rats swam ashore. In less than six months, they exterminated all the island's native birds. This paradise of birdsong became a wilderness of silence."

Munday pulled out the cork with a slight pop and motioned to Anthony to retrieve two nearby glasses. Anthony did so.

"There was this one bird," Munday went on. "It's song was like the distant tinkling of bells, so exquisitely beautiful. And now, the quietness of death reigns where all was once melody.

"But it was that stony silence that had descended upon Olvidado that compelled me to notice the eternal song of the sea. The ancient rhythm of the waves meeting the land… It called to me like a siren, so powerfully did it tempt me, lure me."

Munday poured the wine, a cool white wine, as Anthony listened, restrained, serious.

"I called a question down into this well one night," Munday said, cryptically, "and from the bottom echoed back my own unhurried voice, from which I divined my answer. The knowledge I needed, to do what I intended, was hidden, but it could be freed, in time, by science."

Anthony handed Munday one of the glasses. Munday took it and proposed a toast, his words earnest, unaffected. "To world peace."

"To world peace." Anthony repeated the words and they sampled the wine.

"You never asked me about my hands," Munday stated, holding out and opening and closing one of his six-fingered hands.

"No, I didn't," Anthony admitted. "It would have been bad manners on my part."

Munday nodded appreciatively. "A congenital abnormality, supernumerary fingers and toes."

"Polydactylism?" Anthony guessed.

Munday nodded in affirmation, once again impressed by his guest's breadth of knowledge. "Developmental genes are crucial during embryogenesis. One particular gene, sonic hedgehog, sends out a key signal responsible for shaping the array of digits in the hands and feet. When there's a mutation that increases the effect of that signal, more digits form."

Anthony nodded a bit impatiently, wondering where this was all leading.

"This single gene," Munday continued, "performs the same function in other animals... We can trace this gene all the way back to life in Earth's ancient oceans. This gene that determines the shape of our hands also shaped the fins of our most distant fish ancestors."

Anthony's dark-brown eyes stirred, as did his intellect. "... Our inner fish runs deep."

"Precisely," Munday said ever so slowly.

Munday kicked off his slippers, and Anthony felt his eyes drop down to his host's feet. Like Munday's hands, his feet had a sixth digit. They were perfectly symmetrical, not monstrous or deformed, simply different.

My God, Anthony's thoughts rumbled as a flash of insight slowly descended upon him. Had Munday somehow shrunken the barriers that separated species? Had he somehow squashed millions of years under his heal? Did he unshackle man from time and set free life's connectedness? Was this what Munday had meant by "the unrestrained horizon of man"?

"Marc and Patryk," Anthony asked, "their eyes... Patryk's webbed hands and feet... genetic manipulation?"

Munday nodded. "Will you join me?" he asked, with a wave of his six-fingered hand motioning toward the nearby whirlpool bath sunken into the balcony floor, its underwater jets gently swirling its hot, steaming water.

Munday slipped out of his robe and, naked, he walked slowly, bent kneed and flatfooted, toward the pool, carrying along his glass and the bottle of wine. "It's a bit chilly tonight. I hope you don't find the nudity offensive, do you?"

"Ah, no," Anthony responded, although he found the unexpected situation uncomfortable. As he slipped out of his own robe, he found himself saying, "But all the same, I'll keep my bathing suit on."

"As you wish."

Anthony followed Munday into the pool, sinking down into its comfortably heated, circulating water. As he did so, he felt his mind racing rather madly over the questions and implications that arose from what had just been revealed to him.

"Patryk can actually breathe under water?" Anthony asked, starting with what was unclear.

Munday nodded.

"And Marc?"

"Not yet," Munday answered. "Anthony, empty your mind for a moment. Relax, float, feel your near weightlessness. Move up, down, left, right, submerge, surface... Can you imagine what it must be like to be a dolphin?"

"No, I can't, not really," Anthony answered truthfully. "Except that..."

"Go on, please."

"Except that as a dolphin, it must be limiting, even frightening, to have to breathe air. To be so tied to the surface for survival. Patryk doesn't have that fear, that limitation."

Munday nodded appreciatively. "The most daunting difficulty of making liquid breathing possible was increasing the surface area of the lungs. Extracting oxygen gas dissolved in heavy seawater is very difficult. Seawater has twenty times less oxygen than the same volume of air. And humans have much higher oxygen demands than cold-blooded fish. Altering the lining of the lungs was another challenge. Fortunately, all the solutions were already available, hidden away in nature."

"Deliberately redesigning the genetic code of man?" Anthony questioned it aloud, quietly pondering how such an act flew in the face of all existing political, ethical, and moral beliefs. How this fundamentally challenged religion and government. And everything that he knew and had been so comfortable with…

"Although most still fail to recognize it," Munday soberly pointed out, "Earth is no longer solely Darwin's world. We have entered a new age, an age of unnatural selection and nonrandom mutation. Present technology allows for the cutting, pasting, and editing of the genome at will. The applications are limitless, due to the interconnectedness of life. Traits from other species can easily be transferred into man, drawing upon the wealth of four billion years of life experiments."

"But"—Anthony struggled with it—"you're redesigning the future of humanity."

"A segment of humanity," Munday corrected him.

"Human speciation?"

"*Homo aquaticus.*" Munday allowed his emperor-like head to rise, holding it thrown back high above the surface of the pool.

And Munday fell silent, allowing Anthony a moment or two to consider it. Munday then sank slightly and awkwardly splashed over closer to his guest. Munday's words came out in a vibrating flow of air, his tone unusually controlled, as if a calculated appeal.

"Armstrong's first step on the moon," Munday said with excessive seriousness, "was one small step for a man but a giant leap for mankind. That fossil fish you found, it took small, unsure steps out of our ancient sea to allow for the giant leap forward of the future of evolution on land. Now imagine man's return to the sea... All that freedom to breathe, all the what ifs..."

"It's intoxicating..." Anthony admitted quietly, fully realizing the magnitude of it. The sea was such a vast, untapped frontier. He further understood and appreciated very much the analogy to the pivotal point in the history of life on Earth when a fish had transitioned into an amphibian, colonizing the undeveloped land, flourishing in that new wide-open territory. As would *Homo aquaticus* in the sea... "But—two human species?"

"It would simply mark a return to the normal condition," Munday stated sedately. "There were at least four Homo species simultaneously populating Earth when our direct ancestors migrated out of Africa fifty to eighty thousand years ago."

Anthony watched Munday look up to the glowing moon as the man continued passionately, visionary, prophetic. "In this emerging new age of ours, I foresee multiple Homo species arising, beyond what's happening here on lonely Olvidado. People will make choices to alter themselves, to expand certain capabilities. And this will be a positive thing. For having in existence multiple closely related species of man will make our evolutionary branch much less vulnerable to extinction."

"But," Anthony found himself politely challenging his host, "Neanderthals, Denisovans, Flores man, these related species of man all became extinct, apparently due to our competitive presence. Even within our own species, between different races, different cultures, human beings have treated other human beings in extraordinarily cruel and inhuman ways. How can recreating the increased competitive condition of multiple human species be morally justified?"

And Anthony and Munday entered into a lengthy intellectual discussion on this topic. Munday admitted that although he hoped for a peaceful coexistence in the coming era of human speciation, the canons of Darwinism would still wield influence. As an outcome, there would be winners and losers. Munday defended this on the grounds that it was the natural, inescapable condition of life. A condition that had existed long before man had ever appeared on the scene, a condition that would continue and reign on long after man's eventual demise.

The many peoples of Earth would undoubtedly all react differently to the technological ability to redesign the genetic code of man. For moral, philosophical, and religious reasons, many societies might choose not to engage in such manipulations. Others would embrace doing so. Manifold factors would coalesce and contribute to shaping the coming diversity of continued human evolution. But no factor would prevent human speciation from occurring. It was inevitable.

Munday also expressed a great hope that in unlocking the secrets of nature, something unexpected would emerge that could potentially alter man's perception and influence humankind to embrace world peace...

After their words wound down, Munday stood up, ramrod straight, and moved to exit the whirlpool. Anthony followed, averting his eyes from his host's nakedness.

"Why are you telling me all this?" Anthony asked. "You trust me to keep this secret?"

"Yes, I do," Munday answered honestly. "You realize that if it's stopped here, it will only happen elsewhere. One cannot stop the tide from going out. Besides, I'd like you to consider playing a role in our society, as you are, unaltered. I can provide greater details if you decide you're sincerely open to discussing this. Please take these coming days to consider this offer."

Anthony nodded, and there was a brief silence as the two men slipped into their robes.

"How many others are there, aside from Marc and Patryk?" Anthony then asked, curious.

"Less than a hundred thousand years ago," Munday answered in a roundabout manner, as he pushed his feet into his slippers, "the human race came within approximately two thousand individuals of complete extinction. Our society presently has that number, all adapted well beyond what you've seen in Patryk, who is still in early transition."

"A few thousand?" Anthony found it difficult to believe. "But I've only seen perhaps a few dozen individuals on Olvidado."

"Why do you assume our society is on Olvidado?"

"Where, then?" Anthony struggled with it. "... Under the sea?"

Munday stood there silent, his head held high.

Anthony noticed that Munday wore a medallion hung about his neck, like those he had seen worn by Marc and Patryk.

"*Estu preta?*" Anthony asked, recalling the words he had read on Patryk's medallion. "It's Esperanto, isn't it?"

"Yes, Esperanto is our society's adopted language," Munday answered. "*Estu preta* means 'be ready.'"

"For what?"

"The future, of course," Munday answered, preparing to leave.

Anthony felt his mind reeling. "Wait, how—I mean, where do you get your recruits? Do you invite them here, to Olvidado, like you did me?"

"Yes," Munday stated. "It's by invitation only... Goodnight."

As Munday turned and left, Anthony felt his heart begin to pound as a horrible feeling of shortness of breath overcame him. He felt as if he were choking, suffocating, being smothered alive. He was dizzy, trembling, shaking. In his mind, he heard Klára's words from the ship, before they had arrived on Olvidado:

"I'm visiting Spa Fuente. It's an exclusive beauty spa on Olvidado, *by invitation only*."

~11~

The next morning at sunrise, Anthony was waiting in the luxuriant garden beside the main entrance of Spa Fuente. At Anthony's request, an attendant had gone to retrieve Countess Klára Conti.

Anthony paced for a bit, but he then sat himself in the garden's small gazebo. He had not slept last night and he felt quite tired. He found his mind straining to focus.

By invitation only. The words haunted his thoughts. As did his love for Klára. He felt himself longing to see her, to kiss her soft lips. For he felt that he had found elegant outer beauty coupled to the inner beauty of the soul, the only lasting beauty. But was he now to lose this treasure? Was Klára to be taken away from him by human speciation? Had she been invited to Olvidado to be willingly transformed into an amphibian? Into one of Munday's new *Homo aquaticus* specimens? It made absolutely no sense to Anthony. *Why on Earth would she want to do such a thing?*

"Anthony," called the soft voice of Klára.

But Anthony hesitated to look up, fearing that he might find Klára walking toward him with the blue-black eyes of a dolphin, with uncanny U-shaped pupils. The thought horrified him, but he gathered his strength and raised his head to face her.

There before him stood a vision of loveliness. Klára's charming eyes, calm and alluring, were unchanged. She looked absolutely radiant, her face like the freshness of spring flowers.

He stretched out a hand to her, and she took it with a pleasant smile and a graceful, feminine gentleness. He quickly glanced at her hand—no webbed fingers, just a normal, wonderful hand. He suddenly felt quite foolish.

Slowly, she leaned into his space and, in his early dawn of happiness, gave him three soft kisses. Anthony found himself feeling at that moment that it was her face, her fragrance that intoxicated the garden, not the surrounding flowers, and he realized then and there that true lovers did not finally meet somewhere in life, they were in each other all along.

"What is so important?" she asked him.

Anthony stood, feeling his stress leaving him completely, as if a great wave had collapsed and subsided. "Let's go for a walk," he answered.

She smiled, and he smiled, and holding hands, they wandered off.

~12~

As lovers tend to do, they soon got lost, finding themselves somewhere along the edge of the island's high cliffside within the grounds of a long-ago-abandoned garden, its flowers now growing wild.

"I was concerned," Anthony admitted as they stood together amongst the flowers, overlooking the beauty of the sea, feeling the oneness an individual can never know by reasoning.

"Why?"

And Anthony found it difficult to explain himself intelligently, so focused was he on her attractiveness. She seemed to be growing more beautiful each time he saw her. He was so in love with her. The way she pursed her lips and then let them part just the slightest bit, so lovely. Love was lifting his soul into the sky. He only wanted to know the joy of her whispering "more."

"Why?" she repeated, laughing softly, playfully poking him to gain his attention.

"Something led me to believe," he explained, "that Spa Fuente might not be an ordinary beauty spa, but something else entirely."

"Oh," Klára said softly, oddly lowering her eyes, backing away a step.

"What?" Anthony asked, sensing the sudden change in her, his suspicions resurfacing. "Spa Fuente?"

But she said nothing.

"Please tell me, what is it?" he asked. "Please."

"When I complete my treatment at the spa," she explained, hesitantly, "some important things will be different, about me. For one, I'll leave the spa without the title of countess, penniless."

"I don't understand..."

"It's how Olvidado is financed," she explained. "All visitors to Spa Fuente sign over one hundred percent of their wealth. Everything."

"But why?" Anthony asked, absolutely baffled.

"Secondly," she said ever so slowly, "I'll also be... different. After I leave the spa. Physically different."

Anthony felt paralyzed, speechless. It seemed his worst fear was coming back to life. He brought a trembling hand to his face and, feeling faint, he turned and misstepped. Slipping, he accidentally tumbled off the side of the cliff.

Anthony heard Klára scream out his name from above as he fell, and fell, and fell, his face in a mad rush of air.

Something suddenly hit him, stopped him. It was the beach. Pain shot through his entire body. He had landed flat, upon a wet carpet of sea moss, on his stomach. His face was turned toward a number of shallow pools left behind by the outgoing tide, and beyond, the gently receding waves of the Caribbean.

As he fought to remain conscious, he dimly heard Klára calling from above, something about her going for help. Then there was only the sound of the waves and the beating of his heart.

Each time he tried to move, he started to black out. So, he lay there still, on the shore, that place of man's most distant ancestral beginnings. His head against the wet moss, eye level with the waves, Anthony seemed to sense how his fossil fish might have felt, leaving the sea to venture out onto that ancient, alien frontier of dry land so long ago. He found even deeper respect for the bravery of that fish that was his ancestor. And more, he strangely felt, and knew, that that fish was still within him. That he, like all humans, was a modified fish.

The waves weakly collapsed, one after another, marking the passage of time. On and on the waves broke, and slowly drew back into the sea.

How much longer would he have to wait? When would help arrive? Already it seemed as if it had been a thousand years that he had lain there helpless, racked in pain. Finally, he heard the sound of men and women approaching. It was at that moment that his vision dimmed and he slowly lost consciousness, his final thoughts filled with fear. Would he recover only to find his Klára transforming into an amphibian? And what of himself? Would he be taken advantage of in his current helpless state, to awaken with dolphin eyes, webbed toes, and thick, rubbery skin?

~13~

Anthony awoke under the sea. He knew this because he could see the Caribbean above him and before him, dancing resplendently within beams of sunlight, teeming with tropical fish of a multitude of sizes, shapes, and colors.

But he was lying in a bed, in a recovery room of some sort. One with a transparent ceiling and forward wall, both of which looked out into the beauty of the sea. He was somewhere under water...

Elastic compression wraps were wound about his chest. He must have broken a number of ribs in his fall. And his right arm—it was in a cast.

He sat up and, with difficulty, swung his legs out to sit on the edge of the bed. It was then that he noticed the mirror on the near wall, and his reflection in it. The top of his head was bandaged. To his relief, his eyes were normal, unaltered. But his face was covered with perhaps seven or eight weeks of beard growth...

The chamber's door slid open, and two individuals entered, a man and a woman, both dressed in professional white uniforms, like doctors. Both were young, European looking, with attractive blue-black eyes, dolphin eyes, with abnormally large, round pupils.

Anthony could also see that their hands were webbed, as were their bare feet. And their skin, like Patryk's, appeared abnormally thick, slightly rubbery in texture, yet unusually smooth, sleek. There was also a faint bluish sheen to their skin and to their hair, something Patryk's had lacked.

These two individuals also appeared strikingly stronger than Patryk or Marc. They were well muscled, powerful, but with stunning aesthetic symmetry. Like beautiful animals of nature, these vibrant humans of the sea were impressively attractive. Anthony knew at once that he was looking at two of Munday's fully altered amphibians, two representatives of the new species *Homo aquaticus.*

"How long?" Anthony asked, his voice but a dry whisper.

The man said something to the woman in Esperanto, and the woman left the room. She returned shortly with Dr. Munday, who with ramrod straightness walked over to Anthony.

"You've been in a coma for nine weeks," Munday informed Anthony. "It's quite relieving to see that you've finally come out of it, that the coma wasn't irreversible. You suffered trauma to the brain. Fortunately, according to our doctors, there should be no lasting ill effects."

But Anthony was only half listening to Munday, so focused was he on Munday's eyes. The doctor's eyes appeared to be somewhere between normal human eyes and *aquaticus* dolphin-like eyes.

Munday noticed Anthony's stare. "Yes," Munday acknowledged. "I'm in transition. I had to wait until after you operated on me, removed the tumor, reattached the retina."

"Where's Klára?" Anthony demanded. "Is Countess Klára Conti still on Olvidado?"

"No," Munday answered matter-of-factly. "She completed her treatment. She's presently here, in Nova Ateno, our undersea city. She's been very concerned about you."

"Take me to her, now," Anthony insisted.

"As you wish," Munday said ever so slowly, his hollow voice silky.

~14~

Anthony, fully dressed, quietly followed Munday as the doctor led him down a short, tubular corridor. Although silent, Anthony found his soul screaming, every fiber of his being on the edge of panic, his heart racing. He felt as if he were standing on the precipice of the most terrible shock, sadness, and heartache. *Nine weeks*, he thought, wondering how long it took to fully transition from human to amphibian.

"She's changed?" Anthony heard himself ask Munday, unable to endure the suspense.

"All will be clear to you soon," Munday answered cryptically.

Munday led Anthony into a long, transparent tube that ran away from the medical facility and toward the center of the undersea city. The view outside amazed Anthony. Like the spokes of a great wheel, other such tubes, perhaps a dozen in all, similarly ran from outer facilities to the center of Nova Ateno, which lay beneath a huge transparent, clam-shaped geodesic dome.

The sea outside was busy with activity. Hundreds of amphibian men and women were farming, fishing, carrying out construction, making art, swimming to and fro—all breathing underwater, completely at home within the sea.

"It's amazing…" Anthony remarked.

"It took ten years to build," Munday stated. "And billions of dollars."

Questions raced loudly through Anthony's mind. *Why would wealthy men and women voluntarily turn over their vast fortunes to be transformed into a species of underwater humans? Why? Why?*

Anthony followed Munday blindly, lost in wild speculative thought, overpowered by fear and anxiety.

As they entered the center of Nova Ateno, Anthony could not help but look up, stunned by the dome's magnificence, its translucence, its architectural grandeur. It was then that he heard Munday announce:

"Allow me to present to you the *new* Klára Conti."

Anthony felt his heart sink as he slowly and deliberately lowered his vision, bringing it down from the splendor of the heavens beneath the sea, down to the woman standing before him. As he laid his eyes on the new Klára, he felt utter shock and confusion.

"Anthony," Klára said softly, the tone of her soothing voice carrying an uncertain plea. "I feel as if I've been with you, a part of you, from the beginning of me. Please don't allow this change to separate us. Stay close to my heart. Please don't give myself back to me…"

And Anthony rushed forth and embraced her fully in his arms, feeling drenched by a flood of love and relief. He kissed her with his whole life, and he felt his heart touch the sky.

He then held her at arm's length to look at her carefully. Wait… Was it really Klára? Yes, yes it was his Klára, only a different Klára—a youthful Klára, who appeared to be only twenty-two or twenty-three years of age, her fuller figure sculpted, shapely, her skin blossom soft, her eyelashes sweeping, her hair thick, midnight black, cascading over her shoulders...

Anthony hesitated, found her enchanting eyes, and looked into her gentle soul. There, within, he recognized her—she was indeed his love, somehow transformed, rejuvenated.

"You and I," Anthony whispered to her passionately, "no matter what your age, will be together until the universe dissolves."

But how had this miracle happened? He turned to Munday.

"You remember my Greenland shark?" Munday asked rhetorically. "My specimens of Pacific rockfish?"

"Negligible senescence…" Anthony recalled the descriptive term Munday had used. His mind jolted, startled into realizing the reality of the situation. "You genetically… unlocked the Fountain of Youth?"

Munday nodded ever so slightly, his staid, emperor-like head held high, thrown back. "*Homo aquaticus* is biologically immortal."

"Your recruits," Anthony asked, "Marc, Patryk…"

"When they arrived at Olvidado," Munday answered, "they were old men, facing but a handful of remaining years of declining life. The clock had wound down on them. I offered them, and the others, a choice. In exchange for their wealth, renewed life, a second life, immortality as a new species of man."

"But…"

"Some declined," Munday explained, nodding to Klára, "accepting instead the second offer on the table: rejuvenation in exchange for their fortunes. Remaining human, youth restored, but to age thereafter normally. More time, but once again a limited life. Only the full treatment, only transforming completely into *Homo aquaticus*, assures negligible senescence. Of course, one could have repeated rejuvenation treatments…"

Munday paused to allow his last words to sink in before adding, "Rejuvenation and the full treatment both also restore fertility, oogenesis."

Anthony looked at Klára.

Klára nodded. She would be able to have children. Another miracle.

Anthony started to smile, but then his dark-brown eyes stirred with realization, and he grew gravely serious. "No… Untold millions suffer the effects of aging and eventual death.

It plagues our entire world. A discovery of this magnitude, of this importance—to limit the benefits of this to a small, select group of the elite is wrong. It's immoral. It's cruel."

"Why do you assume I aim to keep my discovery secret?"

Anthony fell silent, wordless.

"Recall my offer to you." Munday said ever so slowly, calmly, his voice seeming all cello and woodwind, muffled in silk. "I'm hoping to have you as my emissary, as the official envoy of Nova Ateno. To arrange gifting this discovery to the world, to all *Homo sapiens*, from their new brothers of the sea: *Homo aquaticus*. Such a gift, I believe, will potentially alter mankind's perception of the value of individual life, and ensure world peace…"

Acknowledgements and Identifying Notations

• The description of Dr. Munday's desk was based on the quote:
"If a cluttered desk is a sign of a cluttered mind, of what, then, is an empty desk a sign?"— Albert Einstein

• Some of the story's opening narrative was based on material in the public domain, specifically the episode "The Doctor and the Countess" of the 1952 to 1956 television anthology series *Four Star Playhouse.*

• Romantic descriptions in "Outgoing Tide" were influenced by the poetry of the thirteenth-century Persian poet Rumi (1207–1273)

• References to mankind's inner fish were based on paleontologist Neil Shubin's 2009 book titled *Your Inner Fish: A Journey into the 3.5-Billion-Year History of the Human Body.* The story "Outgoing Tide" fictionally speculates that the protagonist, Dr. Anthony Thin, finds an earlier transitional fish than Shubin's find, *Tiktaalik roseae.*

• Speculations on the redesigning of humanity were partly based on the 2016 book titled *Evolving Ourselves: Redesigning the Future of Humanity—One Gene at a Time*, by Juan Enriquez and Steve Gullans.

• *Homo aquaticus* is a term coined by famed French underwater explorer and scientist Jacques-Yves Cousteau, who in 1963 introduced his vision of *Homo aquaticus* to the World Congress on Underwater Activities held in London. Those interested in learning more of Jacques Cousteau's prophecy of *Homo aquaticus* might start by reading the April 21, 1963, *New York Times* article "Portrait of *Homo Aquaticus*," by James Dugan. An alternate version of this article was later published by Dell Publishing Co., Inc. in a 1966 paperback titled *Edge of Awareness: 25 Contemporary Essays*. James Dugan's essay in the book is titled "Portrait of *Homo Aquaticus*."

• Regarding the term *negligibly senescent* used by Dr. Munday in the story: Negligibly senescent animals do not have measurable reductions in their reproductive capability with age, or a measurable functional decline with age. Death rates in negligibly senescent animals do not increase with age.

• The bird life of Olvidado being exterminated by rats was based on the real-life 1918 incident of the steamer *SS Makambo* running aground on the north shore of Lord Howe Island in the Tasman Sea. Black rats escaped to the Lord Howe, where they multiplied and caused the extinction of fourteen species of the island's endemic birds. Evolutionary biologist Dr. Ernst Mayr described the incident thusly: "This paradise of birds has become a wilderness, and the quietness of death reigns where all was melody."

• Olvidado is a fictional island, the product of this author's imagination.

Niko Zinovii

A Note from the Author

This author hopes that the reader appreciated this speculative, quasi-utopian tale of life's interconnectedness, the sea, the future of biology, love, and immortality.

"Outgoing Tide" is this author's third short story to date involving sentient land-dwelling beings utilizing science to adapt themselves for life in the sea.

The Greenland shark is presently regarded as the longest-lived vertebrate on Earth, according to studies carried out in 2016 at the University of Copenhagen, which estimate that this particular shark can live to at least 272 years and possibly to the age of 500.

In 2013, however, a 200-year-old shortraker rockfish was caught off the coast of Alaska. One must wonder how long this particular rockfish might have lived if it had not been hooked, and caught, and killed. It has been recognized for some time that certain species of rockfish, such as the shortraker[1] (*S. borealis*) and the rougheye[2] (*S. aleutianus*), appear ageless, exhibiting negligible senescence.

What is the potential lifespan of a shortraker or a rougheye? This is difficult to learn, as in the fish-eat-fish underwater world, most fish do not die of old age. Does the rockfish perhaps hold in its genes the key to agelessness? If man causes the extinction of the rockfish, or other such species, will he lose his chance at discovering biological immortality? What other gifts from nature might man be presently losing in today's ongoing Holocene extinction event, Earth's sixth great extinction event, a crisis caused by the hand of man?

This author would like to end by prompting the reader to:

Imagine love uninhibited by significant differences in age. Imagine a future of human speciation.

Estu Preta.

Niko Zinovii
Santa Monica, California
4 March 2017

[1] Maximum estimated age of a shortraker rockfish: 200 years
[2] Maximum observed lifespan of a rougheye rockfish: 205 years

Niko Zinovii

Ending Note from the Author

I hope readers enjoyed or appreciated these tales in some way. I wrote the stories employing informed imagination, philosophical thought, and a bit of daydreaming. I consider my writing to be nonstandard, sci-fi.

My personal favorites from this collection are:

"Umbrellas Up the Mountain"
"The Last Frog"
"As Old as Stars"

In that order.

Niko Zinovii
Santa Monica, California
17 March 2017

niko@zinoviiartstudio.com

www.zinoviiartstudio.com